ALIENS VS VOODOO

An Ed Turner, P.I. Novel

Glenn Eric

Beachfront Publishing

ISBN-13: 9781892339966
ISBN-10: 1-892339-96-X

Cover design by: RolffImages

Printed in the United States of America

ALIENS VS VOODOO

All you need in this life is ignorance and
confidence, and then success is sure.

Mark Twain

1

I was idly chewing on a cigarette butt, savoring the rich tangy jolt of punchy flavor—everybody worth their salt knows it's the butt of the cigarette that packs the most punch—when Karen Dalton walked through the door advertising Ed Turner, Private Investigator, and entered the office.

Karen's on the short side. And, coming from me, that's saying something. Of course, being a woman, she disagrees and tells me she's average. Then again, anytime I make the mistake of calling her average in any regard, she throws a tantrum and doesn't speak to me the rest of the day—not that I'm saying that's necessarily a bad thing.

Of course, if you're of Earth, you probably already know this about women. They may not be the weaker sex—Karen's beaten me two out of three at arm wrestling—but they are the... how shall I put this?...dafter sex?

There, I've said it. So go ahead and send your letters and emails to the oval office and, by oval office, I mean the nearest wastebasket. I may not be politically correct but I'm not human, so you'll just have to accept my...idiosyncrasies. More on those later.

For now, let's stick to facts, I'm five-foot five inches, five-foot six when the moon is nearest—that chunky rock of displaced earth has that same tugging effect on me as it does on your seas.

Karen favors tight dreadlocks that spill almost to her slim waist. Those dreadlocks were now toxic-dump leprechaun green. The first day she'd tumbled into my office some months ago asking me to look for her missing brother, those locks had been blue. Next, they'd been purple. What was she going to do when she ran out of unnatural colors? Go natural, gods forbid?

Karen also favors tight jeans—not that I'm complaining—and ridiculous T-shirts, like the buttery yellow one she's wearing now that shouts: Sex & Cats & Rock'n Roll!

One out of three isn't bad. It isn't good either. The saving grace being that the one was Sex. I can't stand cats and they can't stand me. Did I mention Karen's adopted a cat? Against my objections? Or quite possibly, now that I cogitate on the matter, *because of* my many objections? No? Well, let's not go down that road or, should I say, wading into that litter box, right now...

Let's just say that the woman seems to relish getting under my skin. She's a lot like a tick that way. *Do not* tell her I said that. But come on, after we found (and lost) her brother—through no fault of my own—she's pretty much latched onto me like a tick, too. What more proof do you need as to her ticklike tendencies?

Do I mind? Not at all. I don't make friends easily, so having one isn't so bad. Although I seem to have no problem making enemies—such as every secret alien-seeking organization on your planet.

Karen keeps me grounded as does my lack of a proper escape ship but that's another matter, too. Things just keep piling up...like my debts.

And rock'n roll? Music died when Elvis left the planet.

I hurriedly spat the wet wad of cigarette goo to the floor. Not a pretty sight, if I do say so myself.

"Hey!" Karen slammed the office door shut behind her. "You're doing it again, Ed." She planted her hands on her hips and loomed over the desk like she might just topple over on me like a battered stone turret straight out of the Middle Ages.

Damn, she'd caught me. Again.

If only she'd let me tie a bell around her neck, we could avoid all this unpleasantness.

"Huh? What?" I riposted lamely, giving her the old innocent eyes look.

Her frown told me I was failing miserably. "Chewing

cigarette butts again. It isn't healthy. It isn't clean. Besides, it's-it's…" She struggled for words.

"Disgusting?" I offered, reaching for my IHOP coffee mug.

"Yeah, that. Who'd want to kiss you with that horrible tobacco taste?"

"You want to kiss me?" I grinned.

"No, I want to kick your butt!" Karen threw herself down in the visitor's chair. The chair held her weight but just barely. I'd bought it at Walmart when I opened the office, not realizing I'd have to assemble it myself. I did a great job of it, considering I'd never done such a thing in my life, and homo sapiens hands are still something of a novelty to me. How do you survive with only five fingers per? Nonetheless, I had four wood screws and one washer left over after I'd finished the job, too! Got 'em in a drawer here somewhere.

Karen locked her hands around the arms of the chair. Was it my imagination or did I hear the chair give out a choked gurgle of despair?

"Who says you can't do both?" I replied.

Karen opted to ignore my question and asked one of her own. "What if a client came in and saw you gnawing on a cigarette butt like it was a hard candy?"

"I'd ask them if they want one?" I suggested.

Karen hurled her set of keys at me. I dodged to the right and the keys struck the wall behind me at high velocity. The jumble of keys crashed to the ground and landed on top of my wet cigarette butt. Karen's a good shot but very predictable.

The first time she'd tagged me with her keys, I took it right in the center of my chest. Since that time, I've come to expect the move. Like I said, she's predictable. And a consistent shot, as you can judge by the tight grouping of scratches and gouge marks on the wall directly behind my desk where those keys have impacted on more than a dozen occasions.

"Besides," I added, "you worry too much. After all, when's the last time we had a client?"

"Yeah," Karen said, sagging deeper in her seat. "Speaking of clients." Karen glanced at the anachronistic black Bakelite phone resting undisturbed on the corner of my desk.

Yes, I have one of those, a real phone. Not one of those wireless jobs everybody calls a phone nowadays. I call those *infinite distractors* because that's essentially what they are. No, I have a real phone. Plugs into the wall and everything. Don't believe me? Think I'm making it up? Look them up in one of your history books... No, wait, real books don't hardly exist anymore either, do they? So scour the Infernal Net, that's what everybody's doing in the twenty-first century.

To be honest, which I am on rare occasions, it's been a long dry spell, and a very long time since I'd had any real calls on that real phone.

Ah, well, such is life on Earth. And I've been here a very long time, since 1947, if you're keeping a diary and want the deets.

I'd tell you where I'm from, but then I'd have to kill you. Haha. But seriously, I'm of a species whose name translates as something akin to Pazu in your English tongue—and by English, I mean as spoken on this side of the pond.

As for my home planet or even star system? Forget it. If we Pazu told you that, you Earthlings just might show up there one day. And, no offense, but we really don't want you visiting. Not even for a pop-in weekend.

"Sorry, no calls," I confessed. I glanced out the window, where I saw some anonymous accountant with a buzzcut, which looked like a crow had given it to him with a dull pair of hedge clippers, drooling over a computer in the office across the street like he seemed to always be doing. "And no smoke signals."

"This is serious, Ed," she admonished. "How are we going to pay the rent?" She pressed her elbows into her knees. "Maybe we should advertise?"

It had been quite a while since we'd had a client. Months. Our last case involved some famous actor's dimwit son who'd misplaced Iggy, his pet iguana. He'd generously offered us five grand—of daddy's money, no doubt—to find the lizard. I'm happy to report that we did find it three days later. Dead at the top of an orange tree in their Beverly Hills neighbor's backyard. Desiccated. Cause of death? I guessed exposure and malnutrition. Not to mention dimwit son's dimwit negligence. Still, we got the five grand—pocket change to him. Besides, as I pointed out to dimwit son when he'd initially balked at the promised fee, we had found Iggy, after all.

With a tear in his eye, and a dead lizard in his arms, dimwit son told us he planned to bury Iggy poolside in daddy's backyard. Pity, I had a hunch dried lizard might make a great jerky.

As I said, that was months ago. Like Iggy, business had dried up. And what little money Karen had inherited from her brother had disappeared on such frivolities as food, cigarettes, whiskey…and rent. LA is great but it is also greatly expensive.

"You've said that before," I said in reply to Karen's suggestion we advertise. With the landline aka phone on my mind, I lifted the receiver and pressed it to my ear. Yep. Buzz buzz buzz. Dial tone was in working order. Not that anybody knew what a dial tone was any longer.

"And?"

"And I keep reminding you that advertising costs money." I rubbed my thumb and index finger together. "Money we do not have."

"Right."

"You could stand out on the sidewalk with one of those signs people wave around. Couldn't cost much to get one of those made up."

"Not happening." Karen appeared to think. "Maybe we can —"

The outer door erupted with a bang!

Karen and I looked at one another.

"A potential client?" Karen asked.

"Or a bill collector?" I replied. "Quite the quantum conundrum. Do we hide or do we answer the door?"

Karen made the executive decision. She jumped from the chair and pulled the door open quickly. "Mr. Ha!"

Chen Ha.

This was worse than a bill collector. This was the bill collector of all bill collectors. This was my landlord. Chen Ha, a sixty-two year old Asian gent dressed in a natty charcoal-colored pinstriped suit and white dress shirt, owned thirty-plus office buildings in and around LA's Toy District. I'm one of his tenants, have been for several years. The Toy District might be an odd choice of location for a private detective agency but the rent was cheap.

An illegal alien—of the extraterrestrial variety—without a pension, Social Security, a 401k, or even a bank account to my name, can put up with a lot as long as the rent is cheap. Even if it meant putting up with all those knock-off Barbie dolls, and imported mountains of toys being shilled all around me. With all the weird gizmos, gadgets, robots, and toy spaceships cluttering the District, it's also a great place for an alien like me to hide. In plain, if quirky, sight.

Mr. Ha is not a tall man, in fact, it takes two of him standing on top of each other to equal me. Okay, so I exaggerate. But he is short.

I've rarely laid eyes on him. Not because he's short, just because he never comes around. So I had to wonder...why was he coming around now?

"Hello, Miss Pretty Lady." Mr. Ha smiled at Karen. Either he never could remember her name or he simply preferred to use his own appellation for her.

"Good to see you, Mister Ha. Nǐ hǎo." Karen performed a half bow and stepped aside for him to enter. Why hadn't she barred the door instead? Had she no survival instincts at all?

Spotting me behind my desk, Mr. Ha slammed his tiny fist into the flesh of his palm. "I am here for the rent, Mister Turner. My bookkeeper tells me you are now more than three months in arrears." He tugged his purple necktie twice. Hard. Any harder and he'd have choked to death.

I glanced out the window. Was that guy I thought was a drooling accountant, Ha's bookkeeper? Was he spying on me all this time? Should I cover my windows in tinfoil? Could I afford tinfoil?

I climbed to my feet and approached my landlord. "Mister Ha." I extended my hand. "So good to see you. Such a rare and unexpected treat!"

"The rent, Mister Turner." He stared forcefully at me via two dark brown marbles.

I smelled black tea and sandalwood. I also smelled trouble.

"Rent? Sure… Well, I—" I looked desperately at Karen hoping she'd be my salvation.

"I'm afraid we don't have this month's rent, Mister Ha. Ed hasn't had a case in months," Karen confessed and my salvation went down in flames.

"Then I imagine you also do not have last month's rent or the rent from the month before that?"

I attempted a laugh which somehow only seemed to scare poor Mr. Ha half to death. Pazus have a horrible laugh, even in human guise. I'm not quite sure why—but I'm not quite sure why everybody says eating an apple a day keeps the doctor away either. Nonsense! I'd be sick. I'd vomit, if I ate an apple even one day. Hell, I'd rather visit some quack with a medical license than eat an apple! Rotten to the core, that's what they are. Rotten. To. The. Core.

While all this was running through my mind, Mr. Ha was backing up in fright, and frantically waving his hands to ward off evil spirits. This didn't surprise me and I should have, and did, know better. You see, in laughing, our Pazu voices produce an unfortunate sound that comes across to human ears as something less than pleasant, and more like a platypus giving a cat a bubble bath while a trio of high-pitched wailing witches repeatedly run their hard jagged fingernails across a Saharan chalkboard.

"Won't you have a seat, please?" suggested Karen. She laid a calming hand on our landlord's shoulder and urged him to alight in the chair opposite my desk.

"Thank you, Miss Pretty Lady." Mr. Ha settled himself

carefully in the office chair. He crossed his legs and motioned for me to sit, all while fixing me with a leery look.

I sank into my swivel chair and swiveled, bracing for the attack to continue. Karen leaned against the wall, out of Mr. Ha's sight but well within mine. She smiled encouragement at me.

I wasn't feeling it.

"I have an offer for you," Mr. Ha began.

I puzzled. "An offer?"

"Yes. Let's make a deal, as you say."

"You want me to go on a game show?"

"Ed!" Karen admonished. "Would you *please* let Mr. Ha speak? And stop interrupting. Can I get you something to drink, Mr. Ha? A cup of herbal tea, perhaps?"

"No, thank you very much, Miss Pretty Lady. No time now. We have urgent business, Mister Turner and I."

"Oh?" I said showing off my eloquence.

"Yes, Mister Turner." Mr. Ha fiddled with a loose pencil on my desk. Noticing the countless tooth marks from my gnawing —you'd be surprised how well a pencil will do in a pinch when you're craving for a blast of flavor and are out of Camels, or maybe you wouldn't—he hastily dropped it. "It concerns Anna Ping."

That got my radar up. "Anna Ping?" The elderly and tight-fisted, sharp-mouthed Anna Ping ran the shop in the lobby. She sells everything: chewing gum, Hello Kittys with digital clocks in their tummies, office supplies, magazines and, most importantly, candy, cigarettes, and liquor. You name it, she's got it or swears she can get it for you. She also charges an arm and a leg for a pack of smokes. And her prices on alcohol are astronomical. Sometimes, I get the feeling she's taking advantage of me just because I'm not from around here.

Did I owe her money too? Did she complain to Mr. Ha?

"Anna Ping is my sister-in-law. Her young nephew, Fu, is missing. She is worried. We are all worried. When his parents died, Anna raised the boy as her own."

"We are so sorry to hear that, aren't we, Ed," Karen replied.

"Yes, of course." Thank goodness I didn't owe her a nickel. "You say his name is Fu?"

"Yes, his name is Fu Chun." Mr. Ha pronounced the name as Foo.

"How old is this kid?"

"Nineteen."

Practically a baby in Pazu years. An ancient relic in canine years. "How long has he been missing?"

"Two weeks. He left for Tulane University to begin classes."

"Isn't that down in Louisiana?" I asked. I'm pretty good at earthly geography.

"New Orleans to be exact," Karen answered. "I had a girlfriend who went to school there."

"Yes, New Orleans," agreed Mr. Ha. "Young Fu was accepted into Tulane's School of Business program. We were all quite proud of him. Not an easy school to get into."

"No, that's great," Karen agreed.

"Fu arrived at his dorm but never attended any of his scheduled classes."

"Two weeks, huh? That's not so long. College hijinks, maybe? A new girlfriend?" I suggested. Human blood runs hot at nineteen.

"Fu," Mr. Ha said, pulling himself straighter, "is a serious young man. He would not simply disappear without letting Anna know."

"No phones calls? No texts?" Karen asked.

"Nothing."

"Have you checked his social media accounts?" Karen pressed.

"That's a thought," I agreed. Social media, the disease of the twenty-first century. Lots of people get lost there and never get out. Maybe Fu Chun was nothing more than a victim of his own internet addiction.

"I-I am afraid I would not know the answer to that question," Mr. Ha admitted. "I'm not sure if he has social media accounts."

"Are you kidding? Nineteen years old? Let's see." Karen pulled me out of my chair. She sat and began typing. "Hmm, I'm not finding any recent posts by a Fu Chun."

"You see? He has disappeared," Mr. Ha said.

"Yes, I see." I picked up the chewed up pencil Mr. Ha had tossed and rolled the eraser across my teeth. "It sounds to me like you or Ping should contact Tulane University. See if maybe somebody there knows something. Talk to somebody in admissions."

"She's done that, Mister Turner. They have provided no answers," Mr. Ha said. "Nor does anyone in his dorm know anything."

"You could check with the police down in New Orleans. Report him missing. I'll bet they could—"

Mr. Ha wasn't having it. He cut me off and came to his feet. Being so short, it wasn't so imposing as you might think. Still, imposing enough considering he had the power to toss me to the street, or pay a few goons to do so, for failure to pay my rent.

"The police have been no help." Mr. Ha pressed his hands against the desk. "Now…it is your turn, Mr. Turner."

"My turn?"

"Yes, you will go to New Orleans and find Fu. If he is in trouble, you will help him. Get him back in school. Or bring him home. Which of the two remains to be seen. Once we understand what has happened, we will make that decision."

"Mister Ha, I'd like to help you…"

"You *will* help me, Mister Turner."

"Of course, we will. Won't we, Ed?" Over the top of the computer screen, Karen death-rayed me with her eyeballs.

"Of course, I'd *like to*," I began, choosing my words carefully, "but you see, Mister Ha, and Karen, New Orleans isn't really my cup of tea. It's hot, humid, and below sea level. Not to mention, getting to the Big Easy isn't so easy. In case you all haven't noticed, we are in Los Angeles. New Orleans is in, well, New Orleans. Louisiana."

Karen knew I hated flying. I know, I know. Sounds silly

coming from a creature who's blasted a gazillion miles across the galaxy and ended up on this world, but it is what it is and I am what I am.

Deal with it. I do.

Apparently, Mr. Ha had tuned me out because he said, "You will leave tomorrow, Mister Turner, you and Miss Pretty Lady." Karen blushed with pleasure. "Time is of the essence."

I, for one, actually for all Pazu, do not believe in time but I wasn't about to get into a philosophical argument with my landlord, to whom I was in serious arrears, over the matter.

Now was not the time. See what I did there?

I felt myself and my world sinking in cosmic quicksand. "You don't understand. It's going to be expensive. I'd have to charge my going rate, plus expenses. And that can get, well... expensive. Maybe you could hire a local detective? Must be plenty of them wandering the French Quarter looking for errant spouses, right?"

Mr. Ha's face scrunched up in a very good imitation of a ripe persimmon.

"I'll tell you what," I added hastily, "I'll make a few calls and find a detective for you myself. Won't charge you or Ping a dime for my time." I thrust out my hand. "Have we got a deal?" *And would you please leave now?*

Karen bit down on her fingernail. "If we go to New Orleans, there's so much I'll have to get done first. I'm going to have to do my hair, pack, let my clients know I'll be away a few days..." Karen takes some side gigs doing her graphic artist thing. She'd like to be a real artist but real artists don't make any real money.

"Oh! Who's going to watch Jujube?" Karen wanted to know.

That's my black cat nemesis.

"No need to worry about that," I said, swatting her concern away. We were not going anywhere.

Mr. Ha looked down at my extended hand. "I'll make you a better deal, Mister Turner. You will find Anna's nephew and I, in return, will forgive your missed rent, keep your rent at the current level for the next twelve months, pay you four hundred dollars a day, cover all expenses and…" Now he winked at Karen. "Watch Jujube."

Karen punched me in the triceps, leading with those hard, bony knuckles of hers. She could've been one of those bare-fisted boxers back in the day and made a fortune. I wish she had been. Then we wouldn't be in this pickle of the Chen Ha variety.

"Shake the man's hand, Ed," Karen ordered.

I knew when I was beat.

"You have a deal," I said.

We shook.

I trembled.

2

Late August. And here Karen and I stood amidst the chaos swirling around on the curb outside the Louis Armstrong New Orleans International Airport. This was midday—midchaos. Jets roared overhead, cars, shuttle buses and vans swooshed past. My head ached, my eyeballs itched, and my teeth hurt—the residual effects of the six whiskies, seventy grams of melatonin, thirty grams of tryptophan, and three Benadryl I'd ingested in the hours leading up to and during our excruciating four-hour flight —coach class no less, because Mr. Ha was a miserable cheapskate —from Los Angeles to New Orleans.

Why all the foreign substances? When you suffer fear of flying, you do whatcha gotta do. I'd recover. I always had so far. Besides, every substance on this planet is foreign to me. I'm an alien, remember? Or did you forget, already?

I saw nothing on the flight but the flight attendant when she popped up on several occasions, and kept my eyes squeezed shut as much as possible throughout our endless journey, belted into my aisle seat. Whose dumb idea was it to add windows to airplanes? I'd had no windows on my now wrecked flying saucer. Didn't need them. The ship saw everything it needed to see to navigate the cosmos and, if I wanted to see what it saw, I had only to check the monitors. Which I didn't.

Then again, quite possibly, I wouldn't have crashed and been stranded on your Earth had I taken a peek every now and then. Such is life.

Such is the life of a castaway…

I should clarify that we Pazu never once called our spacecraft *flying saucers*—I just get a chuckle every time I call it one! You humans do have a way with words. If I'd ever seen an actual flying saucer, I'd be wondering what somebody had put in my teacup.

When we finally, mercifully touched down in New Orleans, Karen nudged me awake and forced me to my feet. She grabbed our overhead bags, then gently guided me off the jetliner, and out the terminal door…and the sun slammed me with its fist, beating my flesh down into the concrete like I was nothing more than room-temperature Jello.

Sweltering.

Oh. The. Joy.

"This isn't the Big Easy. It's the Big Sweatbox," I complained, tugging uncomfortably at the cotton shirt clinging to my chest like a two-dimensional parasite. Five minutes standing outdoors and I was soaked through with my own warm sweat. Basting like an ill-fated turkey. My hair had given up and lay flat atop my skull.

"Stop complaining, Ed," encouraged Karen, checking her phone, trying to determine how far away our requested ride was. "Think of this as a vacation."

"From what?" I yawned and stretched my arms overhead, which is the closest I'd ever come to exercise. "Life? Comfort?"

"Okay, then think of it as a paycheck. A vacation from life on the street or sleeping in the car."

"Right." The car she alluded to was a Tesla, but an early model, a two-seat Roadster. The vehicle had once belonged to Karen's brother Ken. Being dead, or at the very least, no longer connected to this plane of existence, he had no use for a car, electric or not. The sardine can on wheels was definitely not something I'd want to sleep in.

"Besides, you could have worn shorts. What about those board shorts I bought you?"

"Those baggy blue ones with the white hibiscus flowers on them? Not on your life. I mean, thank you. But no."

Karen tsk-tsked me. She loves to do that and I'm always happy to give her the opportunity.

"Suit yourself," she said.

"You know I don't do shorts." Karen does do shorts and she does them well. Like now. She looked hot—and I mean that in an All-American male sort of way, which I wasn't but you get the drift. Witness the tight-fitted green pair she wore now with a complimentary scoop-neck top.

"I think you'd look cute in shorts, Ed."

I tried very hard not to roll my eyes…and failed. Karen was in one of her not-letting-go moods. She's a woman of many moods. When I tell her that, she tells me she's simply *multifaceted.*

"Those board shorts would be perfect for you."

"Board shorts are for surfing, I do not surf. Unless you count channel surfing." I could make the US Olympic team in channel surfing, if I do say so myself.

Our KarRyde driver picked us up in a reasonably clean white Toyota Highlander.

"Welcome, Amil Moreas is here to assist you." Our driver beamed and half bowed. A waft of some strong cologne—bearing molecules of cinnamon, cloves, cumin, nutmeg (more appropriate for cooking than slathering over one's skin)—spilled out. His long arms hung loose at his sides. Tall and the definition of gangly, our ebony-skinned driver rocked a short-sleeve buttery-yellow shirt with the tails out and dangling practically to his knees. Faded blue jeans carried down to a pair of wide feet held in sturdy open-toe leather sandals. He had large green eyes and a toadish face—and I say this with nothing but respect and reverence to toads everywhere; wonderful creatures toads; somebody or something has got to eat all those slugs, worms, and flies.

Slugs are strictly good on toast, flies give me hives. And worms? The only place a worm belongs is at the bottom of a mezcal bottle. Yes, I know those aren't really worms. They're the larvae of the agave redworm moth that favors making its domicile in the wondrous and life-enhancing agave plant. Some say the ugly little beasties are hallucinogenic. Some are wrong. I once swallowed a handful I'd saved up just for the occasion and ingested them all in one giant gulp. All I got for my trouble was bloated.

"Thanks," Karen and I said in unison. Amil promptly scooped up our backpacks. He dropped them in the rear of the Toyota, and carried us directly into the city. The only sound came from the jazz playing over the stereo. I shut my eyes—it was better than watching Amil do what he called "driving."

Soon enough, Amil was guiding us into the French Quarter, as requested. "Here we are." His hands played percussion on the steering wheel. "Amazing, isn't it?"

"So they say," I said.

"I can't wait to explore some," Karen said, pressing her nose to the window. "I hope we have some free time."

"It may not be free," I said, patting Karen's hand, "but that's okay. We've got Ha's credit card."

Amil deposited us outside the entrance to the historic Bourbon Orleans Hotel, located at the corner of Orleans Street and Bourbon Street. Does it get any better than that?

Apparently, Amil agreed with me because he said, "Nice hotel. One of the finest in all the city. You will enjoy your stay."

Was that an order?

"I hope so," Karen said, opening her door and scooting to the sidewalk.

Amil hopped out, popped open the tailgate, and adroitly handed us our bags. He bid us a good day and sped off to terrorize some other unsuspecting passengers. Karen shot him a twenty-percent tip on her KarRyde phone app—courtesy of Mr. Ha—and the liveried doorman, dressed totally inappropriately for the climate in a dark wool suit with shiny brass buttons and black silk bowtie, ushered us inside.

To paradise.

"Ahh…feel how cool it is." I threw my arms out.

"I still can't believe you picked this place, Ed." Karen dropped her backpack to the ground and stared at the impressive lobby. Antique furniture and art filled the grand space and history seemed to live in the air lit up by magnificent crystal chandeliers. "This place is gorgeous...and expensive, I'll bet."

"Yeah, that's what expense accounts are for. All this is courtesy of Mister Ha's credit card, remember?" I'd scoured the Infernal Net in search of the perfect hotel and made the reservation myself.

"Oh, I remember. Let's just hope he forgets or, at the very least, doesn't look too closely at his credit card statement."

"Have I ever told you that you worry too much?"

"Frequently. Have I told you that you ought to worry every now and then?"

"More times than I can count." Actually, I was keeping a secret list. "You know, Karen, your Mark Twain once said something to the effect that he spent his life worrying about a lot of things—"

"Smart guy," Karen said.

"Uh-uh, you didn't let me finish."

"Sorry. Go ahead."

"Thank you. He spent his life worrying about a lot of things —"

"You just said—"

I held up a finger. "Wait for it..."

Karen tapped her foot and held her breath.

"Most of which never happened."

Karen frowned. "Cute. But he didn't have to live with you."

"Very funny." I picked up her backpack and handed it to her. Damn thing was heavy! What the hell had she packed? Not that infernal black cat, I hoped. "Besides, this hotel is called the Bourbon Orleans and it is on Bourbon Street. Too good to pass up, wouldn't you say?" I headed for the check-in desk with Karen tagging alongside.

"Impossible for you, that's for sure," Karen agreed. "Probably give you a free bottle of bourbon when you check into your room."

I stopped dead in my tracks and turned in hope. "You think?"

Karen shoved me onward. "No, I do not think. I was joking. Now, let's get checked in. I want to freshen up and then we need to get to work."

"I wish you wouldn't tease me like that," I mumbled. "It's not nice. Not nice at all." I dropped my arms over the highly-polished wood check-in desk. "Checking in. Turner, for two."

Fingers did some clicking across a keyboard. "Ed Turner?"

"That's me. And that's Karen." I jerked a thumb at my companion.

Karen smiled and waved at the clerk. She's a people pleaser. "I love your hotel. It's beautiful."

The clerk, Wendy, as per her bronze pin, had a corpselike white complexion. "If you say so," she said without expression. Jet black hair spilled down either side of her elongated head. She was attractive…in an Addams Family sort of way.

"We are pretty filled up." Wendy wiggled her chin side to side. "Room six-forty-four, sir?" The clerk looked at me expectantly.

What she was expecting, I had no idea.

Was that a question?

Was she waiting for a tip?

"Six-forty-four? Will that be alright, sir?" Wendy asked again.

"Any number will do," I assured the clerk. Except 9,999 and I'd yet to see that appear in any Earthly hotels. Not even the Dubaians had pushed the limits that high yet.

"Sure, why not." Wendy shrugged her bony shoulders and prepped us two keycards. She gave us directions to our room, the restaurant and, most importantly, the 'O' bar, which I'd read up on online. I was looking forward to trying some absinthe. I was also dying to try a drink called the grasshopper which, disappointingly, according to the ingredient list, did not include any actual grasshoppers. That's not to say the bartender couldn't throw some in, if I asked politely. An alien can hope, can't he?

What else can he do when stranded on a strange planet?

I handed one of the keycards to Karen and we gathered

our backpacks and marched to the elevators. Glancing over my shoulder, I caught Wendy alternately shooting looks at us and whispering to the manager as we walked off. "What's that all about, Karen?"

"I have no idea."

Our room was small but charming enough, with burgundy and white walls. The furnishing, everything from the bed to the night tables, to the small writing desk, suited the age. Karen stepped to the window and pushed open a pair of white plantation shutters. "Hey, there's a courtyard down below. And I see a swimming pool!" She sighed. "Filled with people, too."

"Better than hippopotami."

"I knew we should have brought bathing suits."

I moved in for a look and bumped my head. "Damn!"

Karen rubbed my forehead with her thumb. "Yeah, be careful. The walls are sloped."

"Let's get out of here before this room kills me."

"Where are we going?"

"I'm famished. There's a restaurant downstairs."

"Fine. Give me a minute."

After the usual dithering and dallying—to the tune of forty minutes—Karen proclaimed herself ready. She'd changed into a print linen dress and sandals. I clung to the same wrinkled button-down shirt and tan trousers I'd left home in.

"You going out like that?"

"Why mess with perfection?" I asked, spreading my arms wide.

We got a table in the Bourbon House restaurant. Seafood platter for me and the spring harvest flatbread for Karen. She considers herself a vegan. Personally, with all the weird fruit and veggie stuff she eats, I consider her more a Martian.

The frozen bourbon milk punch I ordered to wash all the seafood down was quite tasty. Although it would have been tastier minus the milk.

We charged lunch to our room, which by extension meant we charged it to Mr. Ha's credit card.

"Give a generous tip," I said. "Service was great."

Karen did.

We hit the streets. And the streets hit us back. It was hot and uncomfortable. Like walking around in a steaming pot of green beans or, this being New Orleans, okra, or maybe even some steamed mussels.

"You're the big detective. What's first on our agenda?" Karen asked.

I shielded my eyes. "We go to Tulane. Talk to the roommate. How far is it?"

"The university?" Karen pulled out her phone and mapped it. "Fu's supposed to be at the Uptown campus. That's about five miles from here."

"Too far to walk."

"We could take a streetcar—that would be so much fun— but it might take an hour or so."

"An hour! Too long. The sooner we find Fu Chun, the sooner we can go home," I said. "Call a cab or one of those rideshares."

"Done," Karen said, typing in a request. Within seconds, who should show up at our door but Amil in his Toyota.

Amil beamed. "Hello, Karen and Ed!"

"Hi, Amil. That was fast," Karen remarked.

"I was napping in my car across the street. I drive day and night so I must catch sleep whenever and wherever I can get it. Hop in." He yanked open the passenger side door. Karen slid in and I slid in beside her.

In minutes, Tulane's Uptown campus loomed before us.

"Thanks again," I said, climbing out of the rear seat and leaving Karen to handle the payment.

Following Karen's phone map, we walked across the sprawling green campus. Students bustled about in every direction. Uptown covered 89 acres, over which 110 buildings spread. This was where most of the schools and colleges were located, and a large number of first-year residents lived. Moss-infected oak trees along the sidewalks provided relief from the sun.

"Is this the right way to the Josephine Louise Residence Hall?" Karen called to a geeky kid on a passing skateboard.

He skidded to a halt beside us and dabbed his forehead with the hem of his blue-striped shirt. "JOLO? Straight ahead. Can't miss it."

"Thanks," Karen replied, as the kid pushed off again.

Sure enough, the arched entry to the old brick building soon appeared. We climbed the residence hall steps. There was no one seated at the security desk so we hoofed up to the second floor in search of room 213.

The door stood ajar. Heavy metal music spilled in from the dorm room next door. Maybe the occupants were trying to drive the cockroaches out.

I stuck my head inside 213. "Hello, Daniel? Daniel Hernandez? You here?" Mr. Ha had given us the name of Fu's dormmate.

Karen bumped up behind me and inside we went.

"Nobody's home." I looked around. Not that there was much to see. It looked like a typical dorm room. Smelled like one two. Sour. Basic sturdy beds pressed against each wall. One bed was a mess, the other was nothing more than a thin bare mattress. I guessed that to be Fu's bunk. Two battered desks stood close to a pair of white casement windows looking out onto the courtyard. A white porcelain sink occupied one corner. An old-fashioned mirrored medicine chest hung over the sink. I peeked inside the cabinet.

"Ed! You shouldn't be doing that!" Karen whispered.

"What? Just doing my job." I closed the medicine chest. Nothing but toothpaste, a bottle of ibuprofen, and a jar of acne cream.

"Hey! What are you two doing in here?" A young man stood in the doorway looking rather belligerent. He had wavy dark hair, swept back over a tall forehead, and equally dark eyes.

Karen and I smiled to ease the young man's concerns.

"Daniel Hernandez?" I inquired.

He loosened his stance just a tad. "Yeah... Who wants

to know?" Wearing loose-fitting olive green shorts that fell to his knees, an equally loose-fitting Tulane University Green Wave jersey in shades of olive green and sky blue—all of some polyester or other manmade material, and scruffy blue running shoes, Daniel was built more like a rugby player than a basketballer. A gym rat, no doubt. Standing well over six foot, he possessed a keglike chest and ropy calves, the kind that humans only got from regular hours spent pumping iron.

Daniel's fingers went to his neck and I noticed the heavy silver chain that disappeared down the front of his shirt.

"I'm Ed Turner. This is my assistant—"

"Partner," Karen interrupted.

"Karen Dalton. We're looking for Fu Chun. His family is worried about him."

"And like I already done told his fucking family, Fu isn't here."

"Right." I struggled to remain calm, appear friendly. "Do you have any idea… Can you tell us where he might be?"

Karen stepped nearer and smiled. Like I said, she's a people pleaser. "Daniel, if there's anything, anything at all you can tell us, we would really appreciate it. Please?"

"You got no right to be here." Daniel's sharp unshaven jaw tightened.

"Anything, anything at all?" Karen persisted. "You'd really be helping us out." She smiled at him.

"Well…" Daniel appeared to waver. Was he hesitant to tell us where Fu had gone off to? Why? Was he sticking up for his roommate? If so, for what reason? If Fu Chun had done something stupid, so what? What kid away at university for the first time doesn't?

"Fu isn't in any trouble, no matter what. I assure you," I said.

"Right, just tell us." Karen coaxed. "Tell us and we'll go." She raised her right hand. "I promise."

Daniel Hernandez's eyes wobbled and lost focus. He suddenly glared at us suspiciously.

"Daniel?" Karen began. "Are you okay?"

"ARRHH!" Daniel bellowed. Without warning, he whipped out a switchblade from the slit pocket of his shorts, popped open the four-inch blade, and lunged for Karen.

"No!" Karen screamed and flinched, taking a half step backward.

From several feet away, I watched as the kid's blade took dead aim at her soft abdomen.

"You. Must. Die!" Daniel roared.

I jumped between them. I quickly—and unceremoniously—shoved Karen across the room, out of harm's way. This was no time for niceties.

Daniel slugged me in the face. I winced and savagely wrapped my fingers around his thick neck before he could strike a second time. I consider myself a reasonably harmless alien but I can be brutal if and when the situation calls for it. I hurled him out the door. He went flying off his feet. His feet did not hit the ground again until he came to an abrupt stop against the wall on the far side of the hallway. The switchblade clattered harmlessly to the floor.

It all happened in the blink of an eye, during which time, if you had not blinked, you might have seen me in my true guise. My form reverts to normal, my normal, during times of great stress and/or exertion.

Karen gasped. The poor dear is still getting used to seeing my true self. In fact, I fear that sometimes she forgets that I am not human.

"Are you okay?" I asked Karen. She was breathing heavily. I saw the tiniest of holes in her shirt. It hadn't been there before. I'd cut that close, no pun intended. I didn't know what I'd do without Karen. The woman hadn't been in my life long but already I couldn't imagine life here, or anywhere for that matter, without her in it.

Fingers trembling, Karen lifted up her shirt and looked at her stomach. She discovered a bright red spot. A single drop of her blood rose to the surface. She smeared it with her finger.

"Yeah, yeah, I'm fine. Shaken up, is all." She fell against the bed.

"Good! Stay here!" I raced out into the hall. I wasn't done with Daniel Hernandez yet.

But it seemed Daniel was done with me. Because he was gone.

3

Two inquisitive young heads popped out of the door up the corridor. "What's up?" demanded a scruffy college kid over the noise of the unending heavy-metal soundtrack. A college girl clung to his arm for protection.

I combed my hair into place and tucked my shirttails into my waistband. The tussle had left me in a state of sartorial disrepair. "Hi, there. Did you happen to see which way Daniel went?"

College Kid frowned at me. He ordered his companion to go back inside the room. She gladly agreed after shooting me a dirty look. "Who wants to know?" demanded College Kid. This one had to be over six foot four inches tall. I was feeling smaller by the minute.

"Daniel Rodriguez, Senior," I said, as implausible as that sounded even to my ears. I stuck out my hand, which he ignored. "Junior got mad and stormed out when I confronted him about his drinking. You know anything about that, young man?"

College Kid relaxed. "Daniel doesn't socialize much with the rest of us on the floor."

"What about his roommate?"

"Who?"

"Fu. Fu Chun." I showed him a photograph of the young man in question.

"Why are you carrying around a picture of your son's roommate?"

"His mother and I prefer to keep a close eye on the boy. We like to know who his friends are."

"Seriously?" College Kid screwed up his face. "Too close, if you ask me. If you don't mind me saying, maybe you should give your kid some space, mister."

"Yes, I suppose you could be right." I folded the photo and slipped it back inside my pocket. "So when did you say was the last time you saw Fu Chun?"

College Kid shook his head side to side. "I didn't say. I've never seen him."

"Yes, that seems to be the consensus," I said.

"Huh?" College Kid scratched his pimpled forehead.

"Nothing, thanks anyway."

College Kid turned his back on me and started through his open door.

"Hey, wait!" I jogged up to him. "If you should happen to see Daniel or Fu, would you please give me a call?" I recited Karen's phone number.

He dutifully tapped it into his own phone and couldn't help adding, "*Space*, Mister Rodriguez. Give your kid some space."

I'd have liked to give smartass College Kid some space. Kick his know-it-all ass into orbit. Who did he think he was telling me how to raise my kid…oh, right, I had no kid.

I stomped back inside Fu and Daniel's dorm room. My nerves on end. Without warning, Karen threw her arms around me. She smacked me on the lips.

"What was that for?" I asked, as we broke for some much-needed oxygen.

"For saving my life, stupid." She pulled back her hand.

I flinched, thinking she was going to slap me, but she cupped my cheek and kissed me again. I swear, Earth women are more inscrutable, more alien, than any lifeform I've come across in the entire galaxy.

"What happened to Daniel?" Karen took a step toward the door and peeked out for a look see.

"Disappeared." I stepped back out into the hall, bent and picked up the dropped switchblade. I pushed the blade shut. "Nasty looking thing." I slipped the knife into my trousers. I didn't want to leave it behind for Daniel to pull on somebody else.

"Tell me about it." Karen tugged at the fresh tiny hole in her shirt. "Ruined."

"So buy a new one and charge it to Ha."

"I just might," Karen said. Using her hands, she pushed herself up onto Fu's bed and sat. "What do you suppose Daniel's problem is?"

"Poor diet?"

"Ha-ha."

"What? Everyone knows how lousy college students eat."

"Look who's talking."

Karen's forever complaining about my dietary choices so I chose not to respond.

"Besides," Karen crossed her legs, "joke all you want but Daniel Hernandez was our only lead and now he's disappeared. Should we notify the police? Or campus security?"

"Naw. It might only make trouble for us." And draw official attention to me. Something I tried to avoid.

"But Daniel could be dangerous and—"

"After that little episode? I'm guessing we and Tulane have seen the last of him. And good riddance. You saw the way he looked, the way he was acting." I rubbed my jaw where he'd sucker-punched me. "Maybe he's overdoing the steroids. That could be making him angry...and unstable. Need I remind you that he went mad and tried to bury his knife in your stomach?"

Karen grimaced reflexively but that didn't stop her from saying, "Need I remind you that if we do not solve this case, we probably won't have a home to go home to?"

"Point taken. Now don't just sit on your butt, *partner*, help me search."

"Fine." Karen slid off the bed and landed on her feet. "What are we looking for?"

"Anything. And everything. We'll know when we find it." Or not. I opened the minifridge, not so much looking for anything helpful to our case but I was quite thirsty. A cold brew would have been quite acceptable. Nothing but orange juice and a moldy loaf of white bread. "What the hell?"

"What is it?" Karen was riffling through a chest of drawers. Brave kid.

"What college student worth their salt doesn't keep a cold six-pack of beer in their fridge?"

"Shut up and keep looking," Karen replied, working her way through a stack of T-shirts.

I checked both desks. A neat stack of unused textbooks sat on the far corner of Fu's desk. Nothing more. Textbooks, notebooks, a cold half-filled mug of coffee and an electronic tablet occupied Daniel's desk. I tapped the tablet to life and scrolled around his hard drive. Nothing useful. And his most recent internet searches had all concerned football and basketball.

Karen peeked under Daniel's bunk. "How can it be so dirty under here already?" She sneezed and worked her way across the room on her hands and knees for a look see under Fu's bed. "Hey, what's this?" She pressed herself closer to the floor and stretched her hand under the bed.

"What have you got?"

"A candle." Karen held up a small black glass jar and read the label, "Voodou Authentica." The wax inside was lavender colored and the wick showed signs of use. A three-inch tall gray voodoo doll stitched together with black yarn was affixed to the side of the candle with a gob of wax. She took a whiff. "Smells like licorice."

"Really? Let me see!" I leaned over and took a whiff. Every one of my senses tingled. Black licorice is to me what catnip is to a cat. I refrained from a second hit. I needed to keep my wits about me. "Maybe the guys use it to cover the smell of pot."

Karen shrugged. "Could be but there are directions on the back here."

"Who needs directions? Take a lighter or a match and light it. What's the world coming to? Is there a warning not to stick your finger in the flame, too?"

"Shut up and listen, Ed." Karen ran her fingernail along the label on the back of the candle as she read. "This is a protection candle. The instructions say to light the candle in private—"

"Sure, so your friends don't see how stupid you look."

"Shush, Ed." Karen shish-kabobbed me with her eyes. "Then you take the crystal and wave it around and say this spell..."

"What crystal?"

Karen peered under Fu's bed once more. "I don't see it. I guess it's missing or he stashed it someplace else. Anyway, you wave the crystal over the flame and recite the spell: *I summon thee Spirits. Hear my plea. Protect me from my Enemies. In Flame and Crystal, thee are Bound by the Words I say. Protect me till my Dying Day.*"

I tittered. "Probably bought it at one of those tourist trap voodoo shops. Better yet, a joke shop. What a hoot. Let's keep searching."

"Don't you believe in voodoo, Ed?" Karen climbed to her feet and set the candle on Fu's desk.

"Nope. Nothing more than the power of suggestion. And I suggest you keep looking."

"Where? We've seen everything there is to see."

I swiveled. "Check the bathroom." If she thought it was dirty under the boys' beds, I could only imagine how nasty that toilet would be. Better her than me.

"Fine," Karen replied, sounding anything but fine. Within seconds, I heard her gasping, coughing—and cursing me out.

I tuned her out.

Running out of places to look, I flipped up Fu's unused mattress and took a peek. Bare. I crossed the small space and flipped Daniel's mattress up on its side, letting it lean against the back wall.

"Bingo!"

"What?" Karen emerged from the toilet, wiping her hands on a paper towel.

I waved a bundle of paper money in her face. "Good old US currency."

"Holy cow!"

Karen watched wide-eyed as I thumbed through the bills. "Nine thousand eight hundred and seventy-two dollars." Mostly $100 denomination. I dropped the cash in my pocket.

"Ed, you can't keep it!" Karen reached for my pocket.

I leapt backwards. "Why not? Finders, keepers."

"But it's not yours and it's in Daniel's room." She made a grab for the money again. She's a stubborn woman. "You found it under Daniel's bed, need I remind you?"

"Need I remind you that he tried to stab you to death?" I countered. "Isn't your life worth nine thousand seven hundred and seventy-two dollars?" I held my hand protectively over my pocket. "Besides, you can buy yourself a new shirt with it. That's the least Daniel can do."

"Well..."

I extracted the bundle of green stuff and waved it under Karen's nose. Ah, the smell of money. There's nothing like it to change a person's mind—works far better than an irrefutable argument anytime.

"Fine." Karen snatched a one hundred dollar bill from the bundle. See what I mean?

"But I'm buying a new pair of shoes, too." She snatched a second Ben Franklin from my fist. I put the rest of the bills back in my pocket before she could help herself to any more. A Pazu can buy himself a lot of cigs and whiskey with close to ten Gs cash money. Pounds and pounds of black licorice too—maybe my own licorice factory!

"Where do you suppose Daniel got all this money?" Karen rubbed the two hundreds together. "That's a lot of money for a freshman to have lying around."

"If you ask me, it's a lot of money for any young person to have lying around."

"Do you think that's why he attacked us?" Karen asked. "He thought we were here to steal his cash?"

"No, I don't think so. No," I looked slowly around the empty dorm room, examining every inch of the space. "There's something else going on here."

"Such as?"

"I have no idea."

"Well, this was a bust," Karen remarked as we trudged downstairs.

"I don't know…we did learn one thing."

"What's that?"

"You saw Fu's bed. Unmade and unslept in. We don't know where he is, but we know where he isn't."

"Sleeping in his dorm room."

"Exactly."

4

Disappointment shadowed us as we tumbled down the JOLO Residence Hall steps, once again immersing ourselves in the steamy sphere that was New Orleans.

"Hey! Psst!"

Karen and I swung around. A young woman stood near the entrance, half-hidden by a massive oak scarred with dozens of hearts, which were themselves notched with pairs of initials—symbols of undying love…at least until the school year ended.

The woman waved.

I waved back.

"Come here!" she stage whispered.

"Friend of yours?" asked Karen.

"No, but I have seen her before."

"Oh?"

"She was with the kid who came out in the hall demanding to know what all the commotion was," I explained.

"She's gorgeous."

"Yes, she is," I agreed.

Karen elbowed me.

"Ouch!" I rubbed my ribs. "What? I was agreeing with you!"

Karen rolled her eyes. "Let's go see what she wants before she breaks out in a rash. Wouldn't want to spoil that perfect complexion of hers."

"True." You know what happened next. You probably knew about it before I felt it. Yes, she elbowed me again. How she managed to hit me in exactly the same spot twice in a row, while in motion no less, is beyond me. Lightning may not be able to strike the same place twice, but for Karen it's no problem at all.

"Hello," I began. "Aren't you the young lady I saw briefly upstairs?"

She bobbed her head in the affirmative. "I'm Jenny. Zane said you're looking for Fu. What do you want him for?"

"That's right. I'm Ed. This is Karen. Fu's family haven't heard from him since he arrived here from California to start classes."

"They're worried about him," Karen explained.

"Yes, his family sent us to check on him."

"Zane said you were Daniel's dad, but I don't see it," Jenny said, looking me up and down.

"Smart girl," I replied. "I confess, I am not Daniel's father."

"Mmm. You with the police?" Jenny worried at the hem of her shirt. She was about my height with brilliant blue eyes and striking blonde hair pulled back in a tight ponytail. She possessed the athletic figure of an aerobics instructor as clearly evident in the black leggings running from ankles to waist. She topped these off with an oversized gameday Green Wave shirt.

"I'm a private detective," I answered.

"Oh, that's okay, I guess."

"So, can you tell us where he is?"

"Not exactly." Jenny smelled like peaches and exhibited a peaches-and-cream complexion, but I wasn't going to hold that against her—even though peaches are deadly poisonous to Pazus. "But right after he arrived, he hooked up with a girl."

"Do you have her name?" I asked. "Is she a student here, too?"

"No, I don't think she's a student. Didn't strike me that way, anyway. And I've never noticed her anywhere else around campus, like classes and stuff."

Jenny ran her perfect white teeth over her lower lip and glanced at the upstairs windows. Was she worried that Zane would see her talking to us? If so, why?

"She looked a few years older than Fu. But pretty and you could see that Fu was really smitten."

"Can you describe her for me?" I asked.

Jenny painted a verbal picture of a young woman in her midtwenties, slender, with shoulder-length dark hair and brown eyes. "Dressed kinda like a bohemian, if you know what I mean. Long, flowing skirts, lots of lace. Embroidered shirts. A blue bandana tied across her forehead sometimes."

"And you haven't seen either Fu or this mystery woman since..."

"In, like, forever. Weeks," Jenny told us.

"And you've really no idea where this girl lives?" Karen said. "Where she works? Where we might find her?"

"No, sorry, I—" Jenny snapped her fingers. "Wait a sec—"

"Yes?" Karen pressed.

"I think she might be a driver for one of those car services, like Uber or Lyft, you know?" Jenny's eyes went from Karen to me. "She drove this battered old blue Prius, covered with bumper stickers. I remember seeing this one particular sticker in the front window of her car. It was a sign for one of those rideshare companies...I think..."

"What about Fu's roommate, Daniel? What can you tell us about him? He behaved rather oddly when we tried to talk to him," I told her.

"Rather oddly? Crazy is how he acted! Tried to stab me to death!" interrupted Karen, tugging at her shirt and showing Jenny the tiny hole in her shirt and matching prick in her stomach. "See?"

"Holy shit!" gasped Jenny. Her hands flew to her face and her eyes widened.

"Nothing holy about that punk." Karen shoved down her shirt. "If I find him again, I'll pluck his eyeballs out. I'll rip him limb from limb. I'll-I'll—"

I decided to interrupt before there was nothing left of Daniel Hernandez but vulture scraps. "What's his story?"

"Well... I-I don't know. Never really talked to him much. He *seemed* normal," Jenny added, her eyes fixating on the hole in Karen's shirt where the tip of the knife had punctured through. "Although, now that I think about it... Recently—"

"Jenny!"

Jenny startled and craned her neck. "Shit! Gotta go!"

Zane glared at us out the window above.

Jenny took off in a blur without another word.

"That was weird," Karen said. "Any idea how we might find this woman Fu was hanging around with?"

"Hardly. The world's full of independent drivers these days. Almost as ubiquitous as real estate agents. Maybe the two should join forces. Pitch properties while schlepping folks around town."

"You're losing it, Ed. Focus."

"Right." I cleared my throat. "As for this mystery woman, we don't even have a name. Not even much of a description."

Karen locked her arm in mine as we walked. "Honestly, Ed, do you really think we'll ever find Fu?"

"Too early to say. This is only our first day. Ask me in a week. If we haven't gotten anywhere by then, I'd say our chances of success are slim."

"Yeah, and that means going back to LA with our tails between our legs and having to tell Mister Ha that we've failed."

"I know I'm an alien," I stopped in my tracks, "but, listen carefully: I *do not* have a tail."

We arrived at Broadway Street and watched the cars and trucks whiz by. Some poor sweating sod pedaling a pedicab creaked along with a pair of gray-haired tourists aboard. The big camera with the extreme telephoto lens screwed to it that sat on the elderly woman's chest could have zoomed in on the smallest moons of Jupiter.

"I'll get us a ride," Karen said, shielding her eyes from the sun. "You know, Ed, all these rides, the hotel, the airfare, meals and such… Expenses are starting to add up."

"So?"

"So couldn't you just, you know—" She waved her hands around in the air like she was chasing a speedy housefly.

"No, I do not know."

"Teleport us back to the hotel."

I looked at Karen like she was crazy, which she clearly was. "Teleport us? Back to the hotel?"

"You know." She gave me a gentle shove as if to kickstart my brain. "Isn't that an…" Karen dropped her voice and whispered, "…alien thing? Can't you just use some Pazu super-teleportation power or blink twice and zap us to where we want to go?"

"You watch far too much TV."

"No, I'm serious."

"You are?" I laid a palm on Karen's forehead. "Clearly, you are suffering from heatstroke then."

Karen swatted my hand away. "I'm just saying."

"And I'm just saying *please* call us a ride. I'm tired of melting in the sun, and I'm not some TV Martian or even a TV genie."

"Fine." Karen tapped her phone to life.

"Thank you."

"Hey, speaking of rides, isn't that Amil?"

I looked where Karen pointed. Sure enough, a sleeping Amil slouched over the steering wheel of his Toyota Highlander. "Amil spends more hours sleeping than he does driving."

We approached and I rapped on the half-open driver side window.

"Hello, Karen and Ed." He rubbed his red-rimmed eyes and managed to smile and yawn at the same time.

"Sorry to wake you," apologized Karen.

"No apologies necessary. You need a ride?"

"Back to the hotel," I replied.

"Hop in!" Amil said and off we went.

"Find out anything interesting?" Amil asked, glancing at us via the rearview mirror. On our arrival in town, Karen and I had filled him in on the basics of our reasons for being in New Orleans and our search for a missing person.

"Nothing," Karen replied, shouldering up against me and taking a swig of warm water from the bottle she'd been toting in her backpack purse.

"Nothing?" Amil swerved around a slowing school bus, came within kissing distance of a horse-and-carriage, and surged through a red light.

Karen squealed. She glared at me like it was my fault.

"Nothing," I echoed. "Unless you count a useless lead on a woman in her midtwenties, who dresses like a bohemian, drives a beat-up Prius and may or may not drive for a rideshare company."

"Alex?" Amil jerked the steering wheel and we jumped the curb. "No problem!" he assured us.

Amil swung the Toyota back out into traffic where it belonged—although not according to the delivery van driver he'd suddenly cut in front of with mere inches to spare, and who was now laying on his horn, flashing his headlights, and shaking his fist at us.

"Alex? You know her?" Karen clutched the back of the front passenger seat and held on for dear life.

"Alexandra. I do not *know her* know her. But I do see her around now and again. If you get my drift?"

"I believe I do," I replied. Although I wasn't sure how Amil, nice a guy as he was, saw much of anyone around seeing as how his eyes seemed to be shut most of the time. "Do you happen to know her surname and the name of the company she drives for?"

"Sorry, no. We're all independent drivers, you see."

"Can you think of any way at all that you could help us find her, Amil?" Karen begged. She still hadn't released her death grip on the back of the front seat.

"Nah, sorry. Wish I could. Could be hundreds, thousands of independent drivers running around the city. Why are you looking for her?" Amil swung his head around to ask.

And off we went into oncoming traffic. Karen screamed. Amil slammed on the brakes. I slammed into the back of his seat. He laughed and slid back over into our lane.

Karen pushed herself deeper into her seat, pulled her seatbelt as tight as she could, and clamped her mouth shut.

"We believe she may be a friend of Fu Chun," I was left to answer.

"Fu Chun?" Amil asked, reverting to the rearview mirror once more to make eye contact.

"The kid I was telling you about. The one we're checking up on."

"Ah, yeah-yeah." Amil palm-thumped the steering wheel. "The college dude." He shrugged. "I wouldn't be worrying too much. The young, they go off to college, they need to release their spirits. Set themselves free of the shackles of parents, am I right?"

"Could be," I said.

"Sure, of course I'm right. We were all kids once."

"If you say so." Now was not the time or place to explain how wrong he was. Besides, there's only one person on this planet who knows the truth about me and, right now, she was frozen in a scared-to-death state and refusing to speak.

"Besides," Amil pontificated, "this be the Big Easy." Big white teeth flashed in the mirror. "Easy to get lost in. Not so easy to get found in, if a body does not want to be found." He waved a finger at me.

"Trust me, I'll find him."

"You so sure, Ed? I like that." Amil managed to just barely outrun an approaching streetcar and cut across the tracks. "Confidence. Yes, that's good."

"I like to think I have a talent for such things."

"Like a sixth sense or some of that voodoo shit?" Amil asked as we slowed and entered the French Quarter.

I nodded. After all, he wasn't far off.

Amil double parked outside the Bourbon Orleans and I shoved Karen out of the Toyota. Before he could speed off to cause more mayhem or find another empty parking spot amenable to his taking his next catnap, I whipped out Fu Chun's photograph and showed it to him.

"Who're all these people?" Amil peered at the photo.

The photograph was one taken at a family gathering. Some were younger, some were older, some appeared so ancient they might have been statues dug up from the 4th century BC. One was a dog. A collie, to be precise. All were seated around a dining table—including the dog who was making itself at home on Anna Ping's lap— in a cozy room, smiling nicely and dutifully for the camera. Of the eight persons in the photo, I only knew three. Anna Ping, Chen Ha, and Fu Chun.

"That's Fu to the right of center in the back there." I tapped Fu's head. "If you lay eyes on him, let me know, okay?" I handed the picture over knowing I could get Karen to download the pic from her phone and get more copies made in the hotel's business center as needed.

"You got it." Amil dropped the photo on the passenger seat. "You don't mind me saying, you check the morgue? Lotsa people turn up there."

I watched as Amil sped off. The man had made a good, if ghoulish, point.

5

I found Karen waiting impatiently for me in the hotel lobby. I told her what Amil had suggested about checking the morgue.

"That's revolting," she said, not unexpectedly, between sips of lemon-flavored ice water.

"Revolting or not, it's a good idea. I should have thought of it myself. Let's make it first on our list."

"Should we go now?"

"No, it's getting late and I'm beat. We'll check it all out tomorrow."

"All?"

"Morgues, funeral homes." I paused. "You think they've got any potter's fields around this town?"

Karen sat her glass down and forced herself up from the black leather chair hugging her bottom. "I don't even know what that is."

"A place where they once buried paupers and such. A common grave."

Karen's blank stare said it all.

"It's an expression from the Bible, Book of Matthew. Story goes that a site called Akeldama, in the valley of Hinnom, was once a source of potters' clay. After they'd extracted all the clay, Akeldama was pretty much useless for agriculture or building anything sizeable. Being a resourceful bunch, the locals got the idea to develop the site as a graveyard for those who were not allowed to be buried in an orthodox cemetery and were penniless and/or whose corpses went unclaimed."

"I'll say it again, for someone who's not of this planet, you are a fount of arcane knowledge," Karen said, slowly making her way to the elevator. "And by arcane, I mean I wish you hadn't told me. I'll never look at pottery the same way again."

"You're welcome."

Karen punched the magic brass button that called forth the elevator. I took that for a win. After all, she could have punched my button nose instead.

We spent the rest of our day mostly camped out in Room 644. Karen scoured the internet for a possible rideshare service driver named Alexandra. I knew this was a complete waste of time but it was her time to waste so it made no difference to me.

I'd had a couple of copies of Fu and Family printed up in the business center and showed them to various staff around the hotel. I also shared the pics with the three guys hanging around the valet stand. I got zilch for my effort. We ordered room service and pigged out. I requested a bottle of their best bourbon. Karen made me cancel the order so I settled for a mid-priced bottle instead.

Smoking wasn't allowed in the room—not by the hotel and definitely not by Karen—so I stole up to the roof and inhaled three Camels before returning to our room. It was 11:20 PM when I crept in.

Karen was lying under the blankets, and out like the lights. I quietly stripped off my shirt and trousers, dumped them on the bedside table, and crawled in beside her. She'd left the TV on. The remote control sat on her side of the king-sized bed. I didn't want to startle her awake—she absolutely hates that—so I was forced to watch a home shopping show.

I have no idea what Karen had been shopping for but, half an hour into some show featuring a far too bubbly and sugary and makeup-slathered TV couple, I saw the officially-licensed MLB ballcaps they next began hawking, on sale for the incredibly low price of $39.99 for two—including shipping and handling—I was sold. Baseball is the only true sport worth watching. And, for the record, the Dodgers are the only true team worth rooting for.

I tiptoed to the other side of the room. I helped myself to Ha's credit card, which Karen kept in her wallet. Next, I picked up the room phone and whispered Mr. Ha's credit card number and my office address to the operator who'd apparently been standing by just waiting for me. I specified two Dodger caps. One for me, one for Karen. She'd thank me in the morning.

While I was up, I flicked off the TV and settled down for a good night's rest. Well-earned, I might add. Mr. Ha should sleep well too—he was getting his money's worth, whether he knew it or not. Maybe I'd send him a glowing report. I could send him a ballcap but I didn't know if he was a Dodgers fan.

I was enjoying myself dreaming that I was standing on the pitcher's mound at Dodger Stadium, decked out in an LA Dodgers' uniform— wearing my brand-spanking new Dodgers' ballcap, of course—winding up and preparing to hurtle my first pitch—a low slider—in an improbable Aliens vs Dodgers matchup, when Karen screamed.

The bedside light on her side flared to life. I bolted upright mid-pitch.

Karen screamed and pointed at the ceiling, which was nothing but popcorn so I don't know what her big deal was. I kind of like popcorn.

"Right there! Right there! She was right there!" Karen swung to face me, eyes agog. "Did you see her, Ed? She was right there."

I blinked, looked closely at the ceiling, and then looked even more closely at my bedmate. "She who?"

"She-she… I don't know who, Ed!" Karen slammed her fists into her pillow. "Some nun. She was right there. Hanging."

"Hanging?"

"Yes, she was dressed like some nun from like a couple hundred years ago. She had a thick rope noose around her neck." Karen's hands went to her own neck. She swallowed hard, as if trying to choke down the nightmare.

"You were dreaming, Karen. Relax, go back to sleep."

"I was not dreaming, Ed. I saw her. I really saw her. She was right there. Swinging from a rope." Karen crawled to the edge of the bed and gazed upwards, then towards the open window.

"Seriously, Karen—" I peered intently at the ceiling. No sign of any rope or hook from which a rope might have hung.

"No, Ed. Please, you need to take me seriously. I really saw her. She really talked to me."

I inched closer to Karen. "What did she tell you?"

"She said that she didn't want us here, that New Orleans didn't want us here. She told me we didn't belong here."

I agreed with the hanging nun, but knew better than to say so. I kept my yap shut.

"She warned me that we had to leave before somebody got hurt." Karen grabbed my arm and squeezed. "She told me one of us in this room, this night, before the week was out would be murdered."

"Karen—"

"And then, she tugged at the rope around her neck, ran across the room, noose and all, and leapt to her death out that window." Karen pointed to the open window as evidence.

With a sigh, I slid off the bed and tiptoed to the window. I stuck my head out. Nothing out of the ordinary. An inviting swimming pool illuminated by faery lights, some outdoor furniture. A group of three persons seated at a small round wrought-iron table drinking and talking quietly. And I wished I was there instead of here listening to the crazy woman who'd disturbed my slumber.

"There's nothing," I told Karen, turning back to face her. "Just some guests. No nun, no body."

"Are-are you sure?" Karen crept to the side of the bed and glanced suspiciously towards the window.

"Come see for yourself." I waved her over.

Karen shook her head. "No, thanks." She slid her bare feet to the ground. "I need a drink."

"Bourbon's on the writing desk," I said, shutting the window before any more ghosts got in…or out.

Karen hobbled across the rug. She stopped suddenly. "Hey,

it's damp."

"What's that?" I yawned and wished I had a cigarette.

"The rug." Karen bent to the floor. "Right here." She patted the rug. "The rug is wet."

Frowning, I placed my hand down on the middle of the rug. I took a sniff and caught a slight ammoniac odor... and something else, something I could not identify but found unsettling. "Nothing but water," I assured. "Harmless water."

"This is directly under where she was hanging from the ceiling, Ed." Karen's knees creaked as she pushed herself erect. "Why would it be wet?"

Hmm, an incontinent ghost?

Another comment I kept to myself.

"Don't let your imagination get the best of you," I implored. "There's probably a plumbing leak somewhere between the floors. This hotel is ancient. Can you imagine how old the pipes must be? Don't worry. I'll report it to housekeeping first thing in the morning. In the meantime," I poured her a generous glass of bourbon, "drink this."

"Thanks." Although Karen was trembling head to toe, she managed to gulp down the booze. She crawled into bed. I pulled the covers up around her neck and shoulders and extinguished the lamp. I climbed into bed on my side.

"Good night," I whispered.

Karen patted the back of my hand. Her fingers were icy cold. "Good night, Ed. I'm sorry I—"

She shot up once again. I winced as the lamp roared to life once more. "Ed?"

"What is it?" I sighed.

"The window."

"What about it?"

"Don't you see? The window was open. It was shut when we went to sleep. If there was no nun and I only imagined I saw her hanging in the middle of the room and then jumping out the window to her death..."

"Yes?"

"Who opened the window?"

"Is that all?" I said lightly. "That was me. I opened the window when I got back to the room," I lied. "I wanted a breath of air. I forgot to close it again, that's all. Sorry."

"Oh." Karen's head collapsed against her pillow and she shut off the lamp. Hopefully, for the last time that night.

I let my own head sink into the plush goose-down pillow. I stared thoughtfully through the darkness at the ceiling.

Why was the floor damp?

And who...or what...had opened the window?

6

The morgue proved to be a dead end. Pun intended.

"That was a complete waste of time," moaned Karen.

"What? Would you have preferred we found Fu Chun's cold dead corpse lying in a storage locker inside?"

"Well, no…"

"Waiting to be dumped unceremoniously into the cold hard ground…or perhaps, set afire and turned to ashes?"

"I said no, Ed."

"Then let's consider our time well spent. A success, even."

We rode in the back of a pedicab, pedaled by a chatty young woman with huge thighs and muscular calves, to the nearest police station. The hotel's concierge let us know this stood on Royal Street, but our energetic cyclist had known this anyway and led us straight there.

Karen tipped the driver and we alighted. A big and blocky, anemic-yellow police station stood before us. Towering white columns framed its entrance. A black iron fence with sharp barbs kept the riffraff at bay and dogs from peeing on the shrubbery.

"Look at it," I said. "It looks more like we've arrived at a bank rather than a police station." The building was bland and boxy. Only its signage proved its identity. We started for the open metal gates. Affixed to the fences on either side of the gates, posted signs let passersby know that NOPD T-shirts were conveniently for sale both inside and online.

"Wow, everybody is in the tourist business here." Karen scratched the top of her head. "Even got one of those handy QR codes."

"Take a picture," I told her.

"What for?"

"You're right. What was I thinking? We'll buy the shirts inside like the sign says. No sense going to the bother of ordering online, and paying shipping charges."

"Ed?"

"Yes?"

"Do you think the police would lock you up if I told them you were from another planet?"

"No." I smiled big. And I can smile real big. "But they might think you're from another planet for claiming so, especially with that day-glo green hair of yours, and lock you up."

Karen frowned. "I was afraid of that." She took my hand and in we went.

The structure's architectural design made sense as we read the large plaque screwed to a wall inside. The story it told let visitors, both those freely entering as well as those entering with cuffs locked securely around their wrists, that this imposing edifice was purpose built in 1827 to be the Bank of Louisiana. Severely damaged by fire, it was rebuilt in 1863. According to the National Register of Historic Places placard, the bank continued to operate on Royal Street until it went bankrupt around 1868.

"So, it was a bank, just not a good one," I remarked to Karen.

The former bank next served as the Louisiana State Capitol for about a year. "The Louisiana Legislature opened its session here in January of 1869. A year later, they were out of there. In December 1870, the building hosted the Royal Street Auctioneer's Exchange. Its next incarnations included a concert hall and saloon," Karen read aloud.

"Both a step up, in my opinion."

In 1874, its owners sold the property to the city. After undergoing even more renovations than the wife of a Beverly Hills plastic surgeon, the criminal court and, later, juvenile court operated from the location. In 1921, the city decided to lease the building to the American Legion. The Legion occupied the site until 1972. At that point, city officials leased it to the Greater

New Orleans Tourist & Convention Commission. They managed to hang on until 1984.

Finally, in 1985, the then mayor and then police chief got together and created the NOPD Vieux Carré District, also known as the 8th District, to patrol the French Quarter and area surrounding the newly-opened Convention Center.

"This building has had more lives than a cat," I remarked.

"Yeah, what took them so long to decide it needed to be a police station?" Karen said, as we stood shoulder to shoulder. "If any district needs patrolling, it's this one."

After a bit of explaining and a whole lotta pleading, a Sergeant Lecourt agreed to speak with us. He led us to his office on the second floor. This proved to be a small, windowless space with one chair for guests and/or suspects. The sergeant was clearly not high in the hierarchy, seeing how he lacked even the most basic of perks. Even I have a window.

Karen sat and I leaned against the wall.

"So you two are looking for Fu..." his voice trailed off as his fingers shuffled a sheaf of papers, "Chun?" With that rectangular head, those thick eyebrows, the silvery hair, and square shoulders, he reminded me of a blue robot. Would I find gizmos and gears inside if I sawed open that chest?

"That's correct, Sergeant."

Sergeant Lecourt nodded. His lips moved as he silently read some typed police report. He looked up. "Sorry, there really isn't much here. We received a call or two from Anna Ping, another from Chen Ha. We offered to look into it. An officer went to the dorm. Talked to the roommate—"

"Daniel Hernandez?" I asked.

Sergeant Lecourt checked his report. "Yep. That's the one. Anyway, nobody knew anything." He dropped the report on his desk and slowly swiveled side to side. "Look, Mister Turner, Miz Dalton, Fu Chun isn't the first college student to skip classes, maybe even drop out and disappear for a bit. And I dare say he won't be the last." He rolled up his shirt sleeves, revealing the green tattoo image of a fanged snake with lion's-paw feet on his left forearm. Sweat beaded on his forehead. "It's always so damn hot in here. Sometimes, I think the spirits don't approve of us."

"Spirits?" I asked.

"Story goes this is an old Indian burial ground. Between you and me, I think they'd like to be rid of us."

"You could be right," I replied. "That could explain why the building's changed hands so many times. Bad juju."

"Hmm, bad juju." Sergeant Lecourt made the sign of the cross.

"If we could get back to Fu," Karen popped in. "You say college kids disappear all the time, but Anna Ping and Mister Ha assure me that Fu is not the sort of young man who would disappear like that, without a word to anyone, not his family, not even his roommate."

Sergeant Lecourt sighed. "That's what they all say, I'm afraid." He folded his hands on his desk. "If you want my opinion," which I did not, "Fu will show up when he's good and ready. More likely, when he runs out of money." He snickered.

"But that's just it," Karen said. "We've checked and Fu hasn't used any of his credit cards or even his bank ATM card. Don't you find that suspicious, Sergeant?"

Sergeant Lecourt shrugged. "Maybe he's shacking up with a friend…or a girlfriend?"

"If so, why keep it a big secret? Why worry his family?" countered Karen.

"Boyfriend?" Sergeant Lecourt next suggested. "Fear of family disapproval?"

Karen shot to her feet. "We're wasting our time, Ed."

I got out of her way as she made for the door.

Sergeant Lecourt rose. "Sorry I couldn't be more help."

"Me, too," I said.

"Seems to me you haven't really tried all that hard," Karen snapped.

Sergeant Lecourt's face showed his hurt. "We only have so much manpower. Besides, maybe Fu doesn't want to be found. Not yet, anyway. For the record, I hope you do find him."

"Thanks," Karen managed to say.

"And off the record…"

"Yes?" I asked.

Sergeant Lecourt popped his head out in the corridor. "Off the record," he began, keeping his voice low, "I might suggest you consult Lola Davies."

"Why?"

"She is a manbo."

"What's that?"

"A manbo is a high priestess in the Haitian voodoo religion. Lola Davies is much powerful. The most powerful, perhaps."

"Come on, Sergeant," I said. "You don't really believe all that voodoo stuff, do you?"

"The eyes do not lie. The ears do not deceive. I have seen and heard many things." The sergeant's hand went to an amulet tucked inside his shirt, hanging from a thick gold rope. He rubbed his thumb and forefinger across the blood-red stone. "She has even predicted my death."

"Your death!?" Karen said.

"Yes, I have marked it on my calendar." Sergeant Lecourt pointed to a 36-month calendar tacked behind his desk. "You see?" A date was circled in red ink. According to the date circled, the good sergeant had approximately two years and one month left to live.

"That…I mean, you-you really believe you are going to die on that exact day?" Karen said.

"I fear so," Sergeant Lecourt answered matter-of-factly.

"That's morbid. Crazy," Karen said.

"We shall see. Until then, I treasure each day. After all, there are not so many left."

"Have you thought about seeing someone, Sergeant?" I asked.

"What, like a witch doctor?" he said.

"Or a psychiatrist," I suggested.

Sergeant Lecourt's belly shook with laughter. "I like you, Mister Turner. You aren't afraid to speak your mind."

"What is it that you think this manbo can do to help us, Sergeant?" Karen cut in, sounding more hopeful than skeptical.

"I cannot say. You must ask her yourselves."

Hands on hips, Karen said, "If you really think she might be able to help us find Fu, why haven't you asked her yourself?"

Sergeant Lecourt looked aghast. "No, no. I cannot do that. The police department frowns on such things—my captain, in particular. We must go strictly by the book, as they say. I'm sure you understand, Miz Dalton."

"I suppose," Karen reluctantly agreed.

"Lola sees many things. She may be able to tell you whether Fu Chun is well. She may even have a vision of where you will find him. If you see her—" The telephone on Sergeant Lecourt's desk blared and he turned his back on us. We were left to let ourselves out.

But not before I grabbed two size-small NOPD T-shirts in the lobby giftshop and paid for them using Mr. Ha's credit card.

"What?" I said in response to Karen's silent but deadly glare of disapproval. "It's a business expense."

"Business expense?" She snatched the credit card from my hand.

"Sure, the profits from the sale of these shirts goes straight into the pockets of the police, I'll bet. Kinda like a bribe. And everybody knows any decent PI worth his salt has got to bribe the police every now and then."

"Yeah, I don't think so."

"Hey, I challenge you to name one TV program where they don't."

"Whatever. So, where do we find this Lola Davies?" Karen asked as we spilled out the door.

"Who knows? If she's so clairvoyant, maybe she already knows we're looking for her, and she'll find us. Hey, I'm hungry. And thirsty."

I dragged her into the café next door to the police station. A green-and-white awning hung over the front entrance. Black-and-white tile covered the interior floor along with a coating of well-trodden powdered sugar. Somebody had painted green palm fronds of some sort on the barrel ceiling. I couldn't imagine why or who—maybe a local budding Michelangelo who'd considered the café his Sistine Chapel.

We helped ourselves to an empty table, rows of which lined each side wall. A glass display case and menu board sat right behind our table.

"All I can say is, she better not try to tell me when I'm going to die. I do not want to know." Karen removed her pack and shoved our new T-shirts inside.

"No? Good to know. My lips are sealed."

"WHAT?!"

"Joking." I took a step back out of harm's—i.e. Karen's—way and threw my hands in the air in what I'd learned from watching old Westerns was the universal gesture of surrender. "Joking."

But was I?

After a quick glance at the menu, Karen ordered herself a coffee and a pecan waffle. I went for the muffaletta. "With extra salami and hold the cheese. And I'll have a side of beignets, extra powdered sugar."

"Yes, sir."

"Really, Ed? All that sugar?" Karen shot me her patented look of condemnation.

Colorado makes some people high—that John Denver folksinger fellow, for one. Sugar sometimes makes me high. Then again, sunshine on his shoulders made John Denver high, too. Say what you want about his music—he was no Elvis—but he was one helluva sensitive guy.

"You're right. Make that two orders of beignets," I boldly told the counterman. "And a mimosa, extra everything." The city's enlightened politicians allow 24/7 alcohol sales. Perhaps not all politicians are all bad, after all.

"Black coffee for me," Karen said, ever the party pooper.

We sat and a server soon brought us our order. We dug in. Conversation dragged as we focused on our meal.

"These beignets are amazing, a real revelation. Fried dough

and powdered sugar!" I licked my lips, then my sticky fingers, one by one. "Who knew such a simple food could be so...so magnificent!" I slid back in my chair and sipped the remains of my mimosa. "Maybe we should think about moving here permanently."

"You may get your wish, because, if we don't find Fu, we may be stuck here permanently," Karen replied. She helped herself to my last beignet, plucking it deftly from my plate.

"Hey! I was saving that!"

"Really?" She arched her brow and glared at me in defiance as she rolled my last beignet around in the mountain of powdered sugar I'd been building up on my plate in anticipation of a glorious sugar-overloaded finale.

"Don't be cruel," I implored her.

"Quoting Elvis again?" With a wicked grin, she stuffed the beignet inside her mouth.

I watched in silent indignation while Karen chewed and swallowed. A thick wet line of powdered sugar rode the ridge of her upper lip. Evidence of the crime. "Happy now?"

Karen smacked her lips. "Yep."

"Good. How about getting us a line on this Lola Davies." I tapped the face of her phone resting on the table between us.

"Fine." After a quick internet search, Karen grinned. "That was easy. Lola Davies has a shop on Saint Ann Street."

"A shop?"

"A store selling voodoo-related items. Plus, she accepts consultations."

"Let's go." I stood. The heat was getting to me—it was as hot and humid inside the café as it was outside. Hopefully, Lola Davies believed in air conditioning as much as she believed in voodoo and witchcraft.

"We can't. Not yet. Hours are three PM to midnight." She dropped a cash tip on the table.

Food checked off our to-do list, and time on our hands, we wandered the colorful, if odor-filled streets, pondering our next move, keeping a vigilant eye open for Fu Chun in the hope that the boy would magically appear before us, saving us a lot of work and plenty of shoe leather.

"Let's go inside," I said coming to a sudden stop outside a black building with blacked-out windows.

Karen frowned. "The Museum of Murder? I'd rather die first."

"Ha-ha," I said. "Are you sure?"

"Very."

"We could go back to the hotel and take a nap?"

"I have a better idea. Let's do some sightseeing. We never get to do that."

"Sightseeing's really not my thing."

"Well, it is mine. I know! We'll go check out the Saint Louis Cathedral. It's a real landmark."

One thing I've learned with Karen is when to push back and when to be pushed. This was one of those be pushed times. Down the street to Jackson Square and into the iconic cathedral we went.

I don't remember much—except that time passed much more slowly for me than it did her. Think of it like a walk through a maple syrup-thick atmosphere on a hostile planet.

It was after four o'clock when I finally managed to extricate her from the cathedral after reminding her that Mr. Ha was paying us well for our time. "And that does not include time spent inside musty old cathedrals," I further reminded her.

7

We hoofed it to nearby St. Ann Street. Manbo Lola Davies' establishment, going by the moniker Enchantments, occupied a neat little West Indies-style house with loud-purple horizontal siding and Martian-green trim. A broad, covered front porch held every manner of things for the souvenir-seeking believer, all laid out in hopes of luring the unwary passerby. Handwritten labels described locally-made gris-gris bags, potions, oils, voodoo dolls, and a wide assortment of other uniquely New Orleanian, African and Haitian spiritual arts and crafts.

A rustic wooden sign nailed outside the door let visitors know that Enchantments also offered readings, rituals, spiritual work and consultations—all performed by an experienced team of in-house spiritualists, and, by special request, the Great Manbo herself, Lola Davies.

Inside we went.

Tightly-packed, dusty wooden shelves began a foot off the creaky floor and climbed to the low ceiling. These shelves held a jumble of religious and spiritual items. This included a selection of black cauldrons. Hand-painted purple irises covered the four walls. No surprise. Tarnished tin tiled the ceiling. A comingling of incense filled our nostrils.

I caught hints of frankincense, myrrh, sage, and Tibetan lotus, amongst perhaps a dozen more subtle smells. Quite the contrast to the not-so-subtle smells of Bourbon Street. Think reek of humanity. No offense, I'm just a visitor here. Humans would probably feel the same way about my planet, if you visited, which as you may recall, WE DO NOT WANT. Read the sign: Earthlings Go Home.

Don't get me wrong. I don't mind that Bourbon Street smells, I simply wish it smelled of bourbon. I mean, whatever happened to truth in advertising?

A zaftig, ebony-skinned woman, perhaps in her fifties, in a colorful peasant dress flashed her white teeth our way. "Welcome," she said with big open arms. "Welcome to Enchantments." She slid from behind the sales counter. "Are you seeking something special?"

"Yes, we are," I said, stepping up to her. "More precisely, someone. Would you be Lola Davies?"

She grinned and said playfully, "I would be if I could, honey, but we already got one Lola Davies and I do believe she prefer we keep it that way."

Noting my confusion, she continued. "I am Ursula. Are you seeking a consultation?" She wiped her sweaty hand across her chest. "I am a spiritualist myself. Perhaps you would allow me to serve you?" She gave Karen the once over. "Is this the wife? Or your girlfriend? Maybe you need something for your love life?"

Karen tittered.

I found myself blushing and unable to speak.

"Sorry, Ursula," Karen said, coming to my rescue, "but we were told to speak with Lola Davies herself."

"Oh? May I ask why?"

"It's a personal matter," Karen replied.

"Actually, a missing person matter," I said, finding my voice.

"Right," Karen said. "Sergeant Lecourt…I don't know if you know him—"

"Lester Lecourt?" Ursula asked.

"I suppose so," I replied, although the sergeant had not offered us his first name.

"We spoke with him at the police station earlier. We're looking for help finding this young man, Fu Chun." I pulled the photo of Fu Chun from my pocket and held it out for her inspection.

"Mmm-mmm. I never see him before."

"The sergeant suggested we speak with Lola Davies."

"I see." Ursula looked over her shoulder in the direction of a green-and-purple beaded curtain. "I will speak with Lola. She does not usually accept visitors without an appointment, but if Sergeant Lecourt has sent you..." She chewed her lower lip a moment, leaving us to inhale the scent of the patchouli she seemed to have bathed in that morning. "You will wait here, please?"

We agreed.

I heard muffled voices, maybe shouting. Several minutes later, Ursula returned with an accompanying tinkle of beads announcing her presence. I'd been in the middle of inspecting an "authentic" voodoo ritual kit. The kit came in a cardboard box folded in the shape of a six-inch coffin.

This particular kit was touted to be useful in unhexing the person or beloved pet of your choice. Everything necessary to perform the hex removal was conveniently included: a small glass vial containing unhexing potion, a candle half as big as my little finger, one wooden match, a stick of lavender incense, a miniature cloth gris-gris bag—I still had no idea what a gris-gris actually was, nor why it was kept in a bag like a miniature bowling ball, although I'd seen plenty of them being hawked around the shops as we strolled—a scrap of parchment the size of a yellow sticky note, and the piece-de-resistance, a five-inch voodoo doll wrapped in burlap and tied up around the neck, wrists, waist, shoulders and ankles with hemp twine.

Enclosed instructions advised lighting the candle and incense, pricking your thumb with a needle and using the ensuing blood to write the name of the person or pet who was the object of this evil spirit's malicious voodoo on the parchment paper.

Something I considered easier said than done in oh-so-many ways. After that, directions bid the buyer to recite the mumbo-jumbo written on the lid of the coffin thrice, while dancing naked under the moon, preferably a full moon.

I wondered what my neighbors back home in LA would

think of me giving them the full moon if I was to follow these directions to the letter in the alley behind our building.

Karen had gotten lost between the pages of a book on beneficial witchcraft and backyard gardening.

"Lola Davies agrees to meet with you both," Ursula said solemnly. "You may come." She held back the bead curtain with the back of her beefy arm.

"How much is this?" I inquired, holding up the voodoo kit.

"Twenty-seven dollars, excluding tax."

"Sounds reasonable. I'll take it."

Ursula held out her free hand. "You've made an excellent choice picking that box. Promise me that you will keep it with you at all times."

"Ah, yeah, sure."

She loomed over me, hands planted on the counter. "Promise?"

"I promise," I said.

"Good. Now, give it to me. I'll wrap it for you. And if you need any further instructions on its use, you just let me know before you leave." The box offered up a death rattle as she shook it in her maw. "Such things can be very dangerous if misused."

"So can credit cards," Karen mumbled as she reluctantly pulled out Ha's credit card and slapped it down on the sales counter.

Ursula eyed the card as if she was a mother lioness with three hungry cubs at home to feed and it was a baby hyena that had just miraculously fallen across her path. "Shall I charge Lola's consultation to the same card?"

Karen's brow shot up.

"Absolutely," I said, starting through the beaded doorway.

"H-How much is this consultation?" Karen asked in passing Ursula.

"Five hundred dollars. Of course, a gratuity is customary. Twenty percent, shall we say?"

Karen coughed and agreed to cough up the extra bucks.

"That's six hundred dollars," Karen whispered to me as

Ursula, despite her size, managed to slip past us and lead the way down an unlit narrow purple corridor that offered up the uniquely New Orleans scent of incense and jambalaya.

"Plus the voodoo kit," I reminded Karen whose only reply was a groan of dismay.

Ursula guided us through a matching bead curtain at the opposite end of the corridor and into a neat and bright little kitchen with strands of garlic hanging over the kitchen window. The window looked out over a small garden separating this property from the one next door. A small black spider fussed with a triangular web in the lower left pane. He appeared to be assembling a tiny satellite dish.

A slender redhead with her back to us stood washing a tall pot at the chipped porcelain kitchen sink centered under the window.

"Lola, these are Sergeant Lecourt's friends," announced Ursula.

Calling us the sergeant's friends was a bit of a stretch but I didn't correct her because what did it matter?

The woman busy at the sink turned and I could see that Karen was as surprised as I was to discover how young she appeared. I'd been expecting an old woman in a tignon, wizened in appearance, with sharp fingernails, three big black warts on each cheek, and wrinkles on her forehead as deep as the Mariana Trench. Instead, Lola Davies was perhaps in her thirties, with a light complexion, hypnotic brown eyes, and red hair that looked about as authentic as Karen's own.

Then again, maybe she really was centuries' old and it was the power of her manbo magic keeping her looking so young and healthful.

Lola Davies turned. "Hello, folks," she drawled, "I'll be right with you." She snatched a green-and-blue striped towel hanging from a copper ring screwed into the upper cabinet beside the sink. She carefully dried the pot inside and out. She rested the pot on a gas burner atop a pale yellow stove that looked at least twice as old as she did herself. The stove quaked under the weight of the pot. Pale purple paint coated the Shaker cabinets and showed signs of brushstrokes. The wooden hardware was green.

"I'll leave you," Ursula said. "I'd best watch the shop." The linoleum floor sagged and creaked as she departed.

Lola Davies wiped her hands on the front of a flowing pleated yellow skirt and thrust out her hand. Her fingers were cool to the touch.

"Ed Turner," I said. "This is Karen Dalton."

"Ed and Karen. Call me Lola. Please, sit." Lola Davies motioned to a red Formica-topped table with rusting chrome legs. Four matching and red vinyl-covered kitchen chairs spread around the table. Lola rolled down the sleeves of her frilly pink top and slid into the chair against the wall. We settled into either side of her.

A tulip-shaped pale-green glass vase with a pebbled texture rested atop a white-lace doily, sprouting red roses and white baby's breath. Lola Davies gently fingered the nearest stem. "So you are seeking a young man called Fu Chun."

We both nodded.

"May I ask why?"

"His aunt, his entire family, is worried about him. They live in California. Fu came here to start classes at Tulane. He arrived on campus but never attended his first classes. I'm a private detective from Los Angeles. Karen's my assist—partner," I added hastily. "We've been sent to find him."

"Sergeant Lecourt said you might be able to help us?" Karen rubbed her hands together hopefully.

"Do you have anything that belongs to him?" Lola Davies asked.

"I've got this picture." I showed her Fu's photograph.

She smiled. "No, I mean a personal item. Clothing, a fingernail, a strand of hair even?"

"I'm afraid not."

"Maybe back in the dorm?" Karen put in.

"Yeah, maybe," I agreed. "But what are the odds? Anything

we might pick up back there could just as well come from Daniel Hernandez."

"Right," agreed Karen.

"Daniel Hernandez?" asked Lola Davies.

"Fu's roommate at Tulane."

Without a word, Lola Davies slowly shut her eyes. And they stayed shut. Her limp hands rested on the tabletop. Her feet, suspended above the floor, did not move. In fact, she barely seemed to be breathing at all.

Karen and I eyed each other uneasily. And the longer this went on—which by the stovetop clock was a solid five minutes now—the more uneasy we became.

Just when we were thinking that she'd never return to us and that we might as well take our leave, Lola Davies' eyes popped open, like the eyes of a startled toad sensing that its pray had just fallen from the sky, or a hiking boot was about to trounce it into a toad pancake.

She turned those big all-knowing eyes on me.

I held my breath.

Lola Davies leaned closer and I felt her warm breath on my face. "I sense something…different about you, Ed Turner."

That got my attention. It got Karen's attention, too.

"Something odd."

Despite herself, Karen tittered.

Lola Davies grabbed my left hand and held it firmly. "Your name does not suit you. Nor do your clothes."

"That's what I've been telling him," kidded Karen. "See?" she nudged me. "You need a new wardrobe."

"Not even your skin suits you," the manbo said eerily, studying me with those x-ray eyes of hers.

"About Fu," I interrupted. This whole conversation was making me uneasy. For a charlatan, Lola Davies appeared to have hit the nail—or rather, the Ed Turner—on the head. And I didn't like it. Not one bit.

"There are many things of this earth," intoned Lola Davies. "There are many things NOT of this earth."

She'd get no argument from me on that.

"Fu Chun." She released my hand and clutched a green jewel she lifted by its chain from around her neck. She kissed it and stared out the kitchen window as she spoke. "You know, they say the swamps are filled with more than alligators, bears and bobcats. Stories speak of ghosts, spirits and more. Missing links, apemen. Even aliens. The swamps and bayous are near infinite."

"Are you saying you think Fu has gone missing in the swamp?" Karen asked.

"I sense the Nikker has touched you," she said.

"W-what's the Nikker?" Karen said.

Lola Davies rose and pulled the kitchen curtains shut. She lit a small black candle on the table and returned to her chair. "Few know of the Nikker. It is a devil best left unspoken of. Merely mention its name—"

"I understand but what can you tell us about this Nikker fellow?" I asked.

"There are powers beyond mine. Powers beyond what I can fathom…" The manbo shook her head violently side to side. "No! I should not be talking about this. The mere passing of its name across my lips could alert it to our presence. The Nikker is very dangerous. It could kill us all."

"Please," I pressed her, "Fu's family is really worried about him. Tell me what you know. I'll handle this Nikker. I promise."

Lola Davies looked at me long and hard. "Perhaps you can." She smiled wanly. "But it is not so simple, Ed Turner. Throughout mankind's history, across Europe, the Nikker, known by its various names, has been a figure that strikes terror into the hearts of many."

"What is it exactly?" Karen whispered, inching nearer to the manbo.

"Very well. Although I have warned you both." Lola Davies folded her hands in her lap. "The Nikker is an ancient being, a dark shapeshifting water demon. It lurks in water, swamps, bayous, ditches and even wells. Bloodthirsty and ever hungry, the Nikker seeks out and ensnares its victims with a hook in order to draw out their life essence." She raised her right arm and bent her hand to the shape of a hook.

"Where did it come from?" Karen interrupted. "How did it get here?"

"The Nikker arrived here from western Europe. Before that? No one knows. Its first reported appearances are in what is known today as Belgium. Some say it arrived on the ships of René-Robert Cavelier, Sieur de La Salle, when he first explored this region in the late sixteen hundreds. Others say it arrived on a Dutch slave ship. All agree it came searching for a new home as Europe became more and more peopled—or perhaps found its habitat growing more unsatisfactory, more challenging. Who can say?"

"What does this Nikker look like?" I asked.

"Those who have seen it and survived, describe the Nikker as being over eight feet tall with fiery red hair, broad bony shoulders, and a toad-like appearance—some even describe a fat toad living under its tongue— and massive legs and feet. Survivors describe smelling hydrogen sulfide—the distinct odor of decaying organic matter—before they'd even laid eyes on the beast itself." Lola paused, then said, "The Nikker is not of the realm of humanity."

Lola grabbed my wrist. "The Nikker lures its intended victims, preferably adults, by imitating the cries of desperate drowning children. When the human enters the water to save such a nonexistent child, the Nikker quickly snatches its victim with its long metal hook. It drags its victims into the swamp where it swiftly drowns and devours them."

"Like an alligator," Karen suggested.

"Maybe it is just gators," I replied.

"You are free to believe as you wish, Ed Turner."

"So... So the Nikker eats people?" Karen rubbed her arms. "Just talking about it is giving me the heebie-jeebies."

"As I said, the Nikker sucks its victim's blood for nourishment and to extract their essence...their soul. This is necessary for its continued survival, just as eating and drinking are to our own."

"Like a vampire?" That was me.

"Yes, very much so. The Nikker imprisons the souls of his victims in upside-down clay urns."

"And you think this Nikker might have captured Fu Chun? Why?"

"I cannot say if, I cannot say why. I only tell you what I sense," Lola Davies replied, letting go of my wrist.

I noticed a red ring around my wrist, as if my skin had been burned. "And this Nikker, where can I find it?"

Lola Davies produced a small smile. "I don't know that you can. The Nikker is much better at finding what it seeks, than it is in allowing itself to be found."

"But if I could?"

"Atchafalaya…perhaps."

"The swamp?"

"Yes."

"Then that's where we'll go," I said, my chair scraping the floor as I stood. "Easy-peasy."

"The Atchafalaya is greater than two thousand square miles," Lola Davies told us as we headed for the side door leading out of the kitchen.

Shit.

8

"Do you really believe Fu got swallowed up by this Nikker beast?" Karen asked. A brown mutt next door barked at us as we made our way past the narrow side garden between houses.

"No. If anything, it's more likely an alligator swallowed him. In case you have not noticed, Louisiana is lousy with them —everywhere from the swamps, to the tacky tourist shops, to the restaurants serving fried alligator tails. Who knows? Maybe working as luggage handlers out at the airport."

We stopped in the street. I felt like a mysterious weight had been lifted from my shoulders and that I had escaped the unsettling scrutiny of some powerful, hidden x-ray machine. What was it about Lola Davies and Enchantments that so disturbed me?

"So you don't believe this Nikker exists?"

The sun was settling over the west. Had we really been inside that long?

"I didn't say I don't believe it exists. I simply do not believe that it is some creature out of your mythology."

"Okay, wise guy, what do you think it is?"

"Well, I can't be certain. The human brain is not the best witness so I'm not sure how reliable Lola Davies' or anybody else's descriptions are… But if I had to guess based on what she described—"

"Yes?"

"I'd say we're looking for a Fleek."

"A Fleek?" Karen frowned. "Okay, now you're just messing with me."

"No, I kid you not. A Fleek. That's what the creature she

described sounds like."

"Okay," Karen said, tapping her foot furiously against the pavement, "I'll play along. What's a Fleek?"

"A Fleek is from a star system we Pazu call Jag-Jag."

"Jag-Jag, huh?"

"Yes, Jag-Jag."

"And where is this Jag-Jag planet of yours?"

"It's not my planet, it's the Fleeks' planet," I corrected her. "And let's just say it's in a galaxy far, far away. Far from Earth, anyway. It's actually only two galaxies over from my home. Good thing, too. Pazu and Fleek do not get along."

That was an understatement. Pazu and Fleek were constantly trying to kill one another every and any chance they got. What can I say? It's just something in our makeup at the cellular level.

"So what's this Fleek doing on Earth? Is it stranded here, like you?"

I shrugged. "That's always a possibility. After all, more than one car breaks down on the highway, right?"

"I suppose."

"Right. But, in this case, I've a feeling our Fleek, this Nikker, came here of its own intent."

"Why would it do that?"

"Fleek are notoriously solitary and avid adventure seekers —strong character traits responsible for their diaspora. I'm guessing it came here, liked what it found—including an ample and tasty food source—"

"You're talking about people, Ed! That's gross!" She slugged me in the shoulder.

"Sorry but, I mean, I'm not the one eating you all."

"Right, sorry." Karen sighed. "So we've got this Fleek named Nikker and he's eating people and maybe ate Fu." She looked me in the eye. "What the hell are we going to tell Mister Ha, Ed? I can't tell him that! Can you imagine him reading the report? Subject Fu Chun determined to be lured to his death by Nikker, aka a Fleek, now residing in Atchafalaya swamp, formerly of

Belgium."

Karen sank to the street and balanced on her haunches. "Oh, brother…" Her hands covered her eyes. "We are in so much shit… And after all the money we've spent…" She groaned. "Tell me, Ed, are there any other alien…um…species on Earth that I should know about?"

"I really couldn't say, not wholly, at least. I am personally only aware of a handful, perhaps."

"Such as?"

"Well, there's the aquatic-based creature you Earthlings call the Loch Ness Monster—"

"Nessie!?" Karen shot to her feet. She lost her balance and I caught her wrists before she landed on her butt.

"Yes, that's the one. She is a survivalist. She's also quite solitary. Her species are also quite fecund. They'll mate with anything! And, as you can imagine, her home world has become quite crowded, overcrowded. She came to Earth fleeing the crowds. She's quite annoyed by all the gawking human tourists at the lake, but still prefers it to her home world."

"Wow, I never would have thought…"

"And then there's Big Foot—it's quite addicted to eating redwood trees, similar to a koala's fondness for eucalyptus. I know of a small band of Alpo—"

"Alpo?" Karen looked at me archly. "That's dog food, Ed."

"One dog's food is another alien species' name. You call them yeti, or abdominal snowmen—"

"Abdominal snowmen? You mean *abominable* snowmen?"

"Yes, abdominal, abominable. Either way, rather defamatory, don't you agree? Anyway, the Alpo are on an extended Himalayan scientific expedition. Let's see," I tapped my index finger against my teeth, "and then there are the Luz. I believe there's a handful of them running about. Mostly in Great Britain."

"The Luz?"

"Yes, you know them as leprechauns."

"Are they small and green and chase rainbows?" Karen

asked skeptically.

"Yes! You mean you've seen one?"

"No. And I don't intend to."

"Better you don't. They are quite the mischief makers. In fact," I said, raising my finger, "it's their mischief-making that got them in trouble back in their own solar system. Always making jokes, playing tricks. The other species finally ganged up and booted them out of the solar system. Exiled for five hundred years. However, in another couple hundred of your Earth years, they will be allowed to return and, if they behave themselves, stay. I could go on…"

"Ed?"

"Yes, Karen?"

"Please, shut up. I don't think I can stand anymore. My brain won't hold it all."

I smoothed her hair from her face. "Information overload?"

"Yes."

"Sounds like you could use a drink." I knew I could. But then, when couldn't I?

"You know what? For once, you're right. Let's get out of here." Karen fished out her phone and pulled up her KarRyde app. "Damn!"

"What?"

"I just remembered I left my credit card inside the shop."

"And my voodoo box! I'll go fetch them."

"No." Karen stopped me. "You'll get distracted, like you always do, and we'll never get out of here. Or you'll spend more money. I'll go."

She clamped her hands over my shoulders and pushed down hard, as if trying to plant me in the sidewalk. "You wait here for our ride. I'll be right back." She took a step then spun around and waved a finger at me. "Do not move!"

"Fine." Within seconds, I spotted a familiar white Toyota SUV coming up St. Ann Street. Breaking Karen's order not to move, I waved to Amil.

The SUV came to a stop and Amil rolled down the window.

"Hello, Ed! You alone?"

"Karen is inside," I explained, sliding in back. "She'll be right out."

And we waited.

And we waited.

"I can't imagine what's keeping her," I said finally. It wasn't like her. It was like me. I pulled at the door handle. "I'll go check on her."

"Nah, you wait here, Ed. Yer all belted up. I'll go."

"Are you sure?"

"Yeah-Yeah. All part of the job. You give me big tip, yes?" Amil winked at me.

"Of course," I agreed with alacrity. Hell, it wasn't my money. And off Amil went, taking long strides up the cracked walk, the stairs, and into the land of Enchantments.

Two minutes later, Amil came out, waved from the porch and Karen followed. Karen climbed in beside me and Amil took the wheel. "Where to?"

"The Bourbon Orleans."

"Right."

And off we went.

"Took you long enough," I said to Karen.

"Did it?"

"Yes, it did."

"Here's your coffin." Karen handed me my box.

"What took you so long?"

"Nothing. I was only gone a minute."

I raised a brow and lowered my chin. "More like five...ten minutes."

"Nonsense. I could sure use that drink," Karen said, obviously trying to change the subject.

"So, Enchantments, eh?" Amil cut in from the driver's seat. "That place be something, eh? Whatchou got there?"

"This?" I responded, holding my souvenir voodoo dehexing kit. I explained its contents and use.

Amil nodded. "I be impressed. You be careful with that

thing, Ed. Voodoo, that's some powerful shit." He swung the wheel sharply and we screeched sideways through a busy four-lane intersection, missing a packed-to-the-gills tour bus by millimeters. Amil waved to the screaming tourists. "You meet the manbo?"

"Lola Davies? Yes, we had a consultation. A cop suggested it."

Amil slowed as we neared our hotel. "Did he now? No wonder. People say she knows everything. She give you any winning lotto numbers?" he asked with a grin.

"Nothing like that," I said, glancing at Karen who was unusually quiet—not that I was complaining. "But she did give us a potential lead on locating Fu."

"Fu?"

"The missing young man."

"Right, right." Amil tapped the steering wheel as he slammed on the brakes at the side entrance to Bourbon Orleans. "You know they got ghosts here?"

"Doesn't every place in New Orleans?" I replied.

"Yeah, yeah." Amil chuckled. "You seen any yet?"

"Well..." I shot a look at Karen who shifted in her seat.

"You know, some people say it's necessary we get the occasional hurricane just to wipe the streets clean of all the blood that's been spilt here."

"What sort of ghosts?" Karen suddenly blurted, her hands clamped tightly to her thighs.

Amil looked at her in the rearview mirror, scratching the top of his head with one hand and steering with the other. "Might have served as a hospital during the Civil War, so Confederate soldiers, I think. Men, women, children—there's no discrimination when it comes to ghosts. This hotel used to be a convent, I believe, so a nun or two. If you believe the stories."

"A-A nun?" Karen's eyes widened. "Why is it you always pick haunted hotels, Ed?"

"I suppose I do have a history." I knew what she was alluding to, a little overnighter adventure in Stephen King's notorious hotel.

"Sorry, I didn't mean to scare you," Amil said. "Ghosts are mostly harmless. I mean, this ain't no LaLaurie House."

"What's that?" I had to ask and wished I hadn't.

"You mean you never heard of the LaLaurie House? Oh, man, oh, man. The LaLaurie House. It's only about the most haunted place around. Delphine LaLaurie and her third husband, Doctor Leonard LaLaurie, moved into the mansion in 1832. They had a reputation for throwing lavish parties."

"Nothing wrong with that," I said. I imagined booze flowing freely and heaps of Southern barbecue.

"And an even greater reputation for maltreating their slaves. Slaves were a thing then. And I'm talking mutilation, torture, you name it. Real Marquis de Sade stuff. Kept slaves in cold iron cages, others chained to the walls. Doctor LaLaurie performed some sick experiments on his victims, so people say."

"What happened to them?"

"A slave, she be smart, started a fire in the kitchen on purpose, hoping the fire department and police would come running with bells clanging. And come they did. They found LaLauries' own personal chamber of horrors. The locals went wild and a mob gathered to sack and burn the mansion."

"And the LaLauries?"

"Fled to Paris. Now that's a place you do not want to spend the night. The mansion, that is. I hear Paris ain't so bad."

"Sounds like you take this hoodoo-voodoo seriously," I said.

"Living here, can't afford not to," Amil answered. "But y'all got nothing to worry about. Just you watch out for room six forty-four. Stay outta there. They claim that's the most haunted room in this whole hotel."

Karen blanched. "That's our room!"

Karen fled the Toyota.

"Sorry, Ed," Amil told me. "Guess I shouldn't have said nothing."

"Don't worry. Not your fault. I'll calm her down. Me and a transfusion of bourbon."

"Speaking of drinking, if you like, I can recommend you a good bar to get a drink later, if you want?"

"Please."

"You try the Lost In Space Bar. It is up on Bourbon Street. Easy walk."

"Perfect." I slid out the door.

Amil honked his horn.

I turned. "Yeah?"

"Don't be forgetting your coffin." He tilted his head towards the backseat. I noticed the box on the floor. "You might be needing it…"

"Thanks. Almost forgot." I grabbed my souvenir, gave it a comforting shake, and went in search of my partner.

9

I found Karen drinking a glass of absinthe at the hotel bar, shoulders slumped. I hopped up on the stool beside her and gestured for the bartender and asked her to bring me the same.

The drink appeared as if by magic. I took a taste. Yep, magic. "Absinthe makes the heart grow fonder," I joked. Karen didn't say a word. Not even a grunt in reply to my lame joke. "Everything okay?"

"Yes," she said, rather tight lipped. Her glass rattled as she dropped it on the bar. "Why do you ask?"

I'd say my antennae went up but that is such an alien stereotype. I do not have antennae. Still, I was man enough—well, sort of—to know something was up. Besides, Karen rarely drank anything stronger than wine, especially at this time of day.

Wisely, I chose to say, "No reason." An MLB game was playing on the three televisions over the back of the bar. LA Dodgers vs Colorado Rockies. My Dodgers were up to bat. I focused on the game. And the absinthe.

After a spell that included a couple of refills and a couple of no-score innings, I had the courage—and/or perhaps the blood-alcohol level—to broach the metaphorical and metaphysical elephant in the bar.

"Are you worried?"

She turned slowly to face me. "Worried?"

"About what Amil said. About the nun ghost."

"Nun ghost?"

"Nun ghost. The one you saw last night hanging from a noose in our room."

"Excuse me?" Karen clutched her drink.

"Are you saying you don't remember?"

"Really, Ed." She stopped and downed her drink. "I have no idea what you are talking about."

And that was that.

We drank some more, shared a bowl of pretzel knots then retired to room 644. I was expecting an argument from Karen about the room now that she was hip to its infamous history, but she barely said a word at all. In fact, she'd barely said a word the whole time we'd been back from our sleuthing.

"I'm exhausted," she said, throwing herself down on the bed. "I'm going to catch a nap."

I pulled the curtains and the room turned to dusk. I laid down beside her and slept with one eye open. If there was a hanging nun hanging out in room 644, I wanted to meet her.

The nun never appeared.

With Karen snoozing next to me in bed, I turned on the television to catch the rest of the ballgame. I muted the sound. It was the middle of the ninth inning and the Dodgers were down 6 to 7 with 2 outs. I prayed for a hit.

Instead, I got one of those stupid news flashes.

"Shit!"

"Huh-wha…?" Karen moaned and rolled onto her side.

I held my breath and soon she was breathing steadily once more, safely in the womb of whatever plant-based dream she was living.

Some smarmy newsman in a suit and tie, whose demeanor was only outdone by the smarmy newswoman in a magenta dress seated at the metro desk beside him, was speaking to the cameras. At the bottom of the screen, one phrase kept scrolling:

Vicious Murder In The Crescent City. Store Employee Found Slashed To Death on St. Ann St.

I snatched the remote and carefully inched the volume up a couple of notches. Fortunately, we Pazu have superior hearing. Then again, we pretty much have superior everything compared to you humans.

The female news anchor was speaking to the camera now, giving it her best trust-me-you're-gonna-wanna-hear-this look.

I crawled to the end of the bed and paid attention. Here's what I learned. An employee of Enchantments, name held pending notification of family—although they did flash a photograph of Ursula that had all the panache of a driver's license photo, and which I suspected it was—had been discovered inside the shop, her neck slashed.

Shocked and stunned tourists, who themselves were in town vacationing from Traverse City, Michigan, stumbled on the victim's body. Authorities believe the woman, found sprawled on the floor behind the sales counter, had been dead for perhaps several hours before being discovered.

Police were attempting to reach the shop's owner, Lola Davies, a popular and well-known local spiritualist. So far, no witnesses to the murder had come forward, and there'd been no communication with the manbo herself.

Authorities were asking any witnesses to please come forward to assist with the investigation.

Why was Ursula murdered? Had Lola Davies slashed her throat? If so, why?

And finally, would Ursula, whose surname I did not know, become the Crescent City's newest ghostly resident?

After promising more gruesome news at ten, we were returned to the ballgame. We'd lost, six to nine.

Shit.

Karen stirred. "What's going on?"

I hurriedly turned off the television.

"You're awake," I said.

"Wow, very good. You really are the world's greatest detective," Karen replied, screwing her fists into her eye sockets.

"Ha-ha." The woman can be quite the comic when she chooses, and even more often when she isn't trying at all. I paced the hotel room.

"What's wrong?" Karen slid her legs over the side of the bed.

"Tell me," I said, my mind racing with possibilities—none of them good, "when we were at Enchantments…"

"Yeah?"

"That is, when you went back inside to get your credit card…" How the hell was I going to phrase this? *Tell me, my dear, did you grab a sharp weapon and slash Ursula's throat?* Hmm, no she might take that the wrong way. And Karen takes lots of things I say the wrong way—some of my best things, if I do say so myself.

I paused beside the curtains and peeked out. "Did you notice anything…unusual?"

"It's a voodoo magic shop, Ed. The whole store is unusual." She slipped her feet into her sandals and crossed to the bathroom. She filled a glass with tap water and drank.

Glug. Glug. Glug.

"So you didn't notice anything odd?"

Karen shook her head, refilled her glass, and swiftly drank again. "Damn, I don't know why I'm so thirsty."

I had to wonder: did throat slashing make humans thirsty?

"How many times have I got to say? To answer your question," Karen managed to spit out between gulps, "no, I did not notice anything unusual. I ran in, Ursula handed me our stuff."

"She handed you your stuff?"

"Yes, she handed me our stuff." Karen sounded annoyed.

"And?"

"And Amil showed up and we left."

"And how was Ursula?"

"What's all this about, Ed?" Her hand went to my cheek. "You feeling okay?"

"Never better," I replied. "Ursula? Maybe not so much."

I followed Karen out of the bathroom.

"What's that supposed to mean? You're acting really weird, Ed. Even for you. And that's saying something! So if you—"

I decided it would be best, for my sanity at the very least, to cut her off at the knees before her tirade left me with a rocketing headache. If I am going to have a headache, I prefer it be bourbon-induced. I blurted out, "Ursula is dead."

That did the trick. Got her attention and shut her up. Momentarily, at least.

Karen blinked. "Ohmygod! What happened? Heart attack? She was overweight. That was it, wasn't it? I know because I had this aunt once. She was overweight, too. Died when I was three years old. Fell dead over into her turkey with gravy and cranberry sauce, right there at the Thanksgiving table. Splat!" She slapped her hands together. "I don't think I'll ever be able to get that image out of my head."

"No."

"No what?"

"No heart attack. Ursula had her throat slashed."

"Her..." Karen's right hand went to her neck. "Throat... slashed?"

"I'm afraid so." And I wondered if Karen would have been able to get that image out of her head. Actually, maybe that image would shove the image of her aunt plopping over dead in the turkey and cranberries right out of her head. See? There's always a silver lining to things if you look hard enough.

"H-How do you know?"

"I watched a news bulletin." I explained what I'd heard.

"And you say this just happened?"

"Probably not long after we left Enchantments." *If not while you were inside and I was waiting outside.* I kept that sentence to myself. Not everything is for public consumption. And I had a constantly developing list of things that were NOT for Karen's consumption.

"Shit shit shit," Karen said eloquently. Her hands transformed into tight white-knuckled fists as she traced a path across the carpet. She stopped and shot me a troubled look. "What does this mean, Ed? What does it all mean? Do you think this has something to do with Fu? Something to do with us going to Enchantments and asking questions?"

"Your guess is as good as mine," I replied. Well, it wasn't but

I feared she wasn't strong enough at the moment to hear that particular truth. I can be sensitive to people's feelings whilst at the same time being oblivious to them.

Her butt fell on the bed leaving a crater the size of...well, her butt. The rest of her followed. "Have you tried calling Lola Davies? She gave us her card."

I felt in my pocket. Karen was correct. "No, we can try calling now but I have a feeling she won't be picking up."

"Why?" Karen's back stiffened. "You think she's been murdered, too?"

"I really couldn't say." And I really couldn't. "But according to the news report, police are hoping to speak with her but have been unable to locate her." I handed the manbo's business card to Karen.

Karen dialed. "Nothing. Not even voicemail." She held the phone up for me to hear—or rather, not to hear. "What's it mean, Ed?"

"It means she is either unable to answer or unwilling."

"By unable, you mean dead...murdered...throat slashed."

"Correct. Or in hiding," I added.

"Because she's afraid the killer will be after her next!" Karen jumped to her feet and began pacing. "Yeah, maybe she witnessed the whole thing."

"Or murdered Ursula herself," I suggested.

"Why would she do that?"

"Employee-employer relationships can be difficult."

"This isn't funny, Ed. A woman we were just speaking to was brutally murdered not long after. What are we going to do about it?"

"Do about it? Ursula's murder is not our case. No one is paying us to solve it. That's what the police are for. We have a missing young man to find—assuming he hasn't become alligator chow or the Nikker's got him, and his poor soul is trapped inside an empty Coke bottle."

"That's such an insensitive thing to say, even for you." Karen pushed off the bed with an exaggerated sigh. "You know what, Ed? You've missed your calling."

"Oh?"

"Yeah, maybe you should give up being a shitty detective. You'd make a great life coach. You are truly inspiring. And uplifting." Karen reached for my bourbon and cigarettes.

I smiled. I was rubbing off on her. "I do my best."

"That's what frightens me." She lit up, hotel rules be damned.

10

We left the hotel and headed into the heart of the French Quarter around 10 PM. We started down Bourbon St where everybody was already publicly inebriated, stumbling around laughing, hooting, eating, singing at the top of their lungs, and drinking some more. And not one of them walked a straight line. Not even the children, but then human children are weird that way.

All this might seem unusual in most other towns, but I think it's the law here.

"I was thinking about that candle," Karen began, her arm in mine.

"What candle?"

"That candle I found under Fu's bed."

"Oh."

"What was he doing with a protection candle? What do you suppose he wanted protection from?"

"Bad grades?"

"I'm being serious, Ed."

"So am I." I stopped as a passel of college kids or college kid wannabes, all wearing LSU shirts and multiple layers of purple and green beads around their necks, herded past us. Glancing in the open doors of a pub, I saw Ursula looking back at me from a smudgy big screen TV. Was it my imagination or were her sultry brown eyes filled with accusation?

Was there something I could have done, should have done that might have prevented her death? If so, what?

They'd released her full name now as displayed across the screen: Ursula Broussard.

"French *Quarter*?" Karen said, as an obese, red-faced drunk bounced off her, mumbled an apology and teetered on. "I wouldn't give you a nickel for it! Too many people rubbing against each other. Mostly drunk and hurling plastic beads at one another. And that foul odor!" She waved a hand in front of her nose. "Big Easy, my ass. More like the Big Queasy."

"I don't know. It's not so bad. I've been to Venus. Now that's downright sulfurous," I said. "As for all the rubbing up against strangers, like you, I do appreciate my personal space. And personally, I'd rather pet a cat than have some drunk in a beer-sodden T-shirt share his or her sweat with me." I'm a Pazu. I do not sweat, so such events are entirely one sided. "Nevertheless, the city does exude a certain aura that I find charming."

"Exude is right." Karen didn't slug me. Still, she seemed to be coming around, acting more like her old self. Maybe the shock of hearing of Ursula's murder was bringing her out of whatever odd funk she'd fallen into back at Enchantments. But she definitely hadn't returned to her so-called normal state.

I could sense something was still off with her at the psychological level. I am a keen observer of humans. Not being one of you gives me objective clarity that your earthly psychologists could never hope to match.

Hmm, should I change career paths? Maybe Karen was onto something, after all. Ditch the detective career and become a psychologist or a psychiatrist. Crazy idea?

As for Karen, whatever had happened to her had likely occurred inside Enchantments while I'd been waiting outside. What could that have been? Was it something Ursula Broussard or Lola Davies had said or done? Or...had she blacked out and committed an unspeakable crime? A cold-blooded murder?

Who was this woman I shared life and bed with? I stole a glance at Karen. Was I strolling the French Quarter with a psycho slasher?

Should I be sleeping with one eye open?

"Where are we headed?" she asked.

"Huh?"

"I asked where we're heading."

"Oh, right here," I said, pausing at the intersection of two busy streets.

"The Lost In Space Tavern?" Karen said, looking up at the neon signage. "How apropos is that, huh?"

I hadn't thought about that but she was right. "Amil recommended it. And I'm liking it already," I remarked, my ears perking up and my foot threatening to tap out a beat. Could it be that...? Did I hear Elvis inside belting out *Jailhouse Rock*? Did the King yet live? Was he hiding out in the Crescent City?

"See that flying saucer?" I pointed to a three-foot in diameter flying saucer, that looked like a pie tin with legs attached to a pole, atop the building. "That's the Jupiter Two."

"Oh? Is that the ship you came to Earth in? You told me it was destroyed."

"Very funny. For your information and sadly lacking education, that is a near-exact replica of the spacecraft that Professor John Robinson, his wife Maureen, son Will, and two daughters named Judy and Penny, along with Major West, a no-good stowaway named Doctor Zachary Smith, and a friendly robot that looked to have been built out of glass jars, bellows, industrial vacuum cleaner hoses, and various lightbulbs, blasted off into space in. Their destination was an Earth-like planet in Alpha Centauri."

"For real?" Karen sounded skeptical. "In that tiny thing?"

"It's not a full-scale replica. And it was a sixties TV series. In the original unaired pilot, the spacecraft was called the Gemini Twelve. Not sure why the writers changed it."

"Maybe it didn't sound spacey enough?"

"You may be right. But Lost In Space—"

"Never heard of it."

"I tell you," I reminisced for my own pleasure, "I've always held a certain fondness for Robot. Did you know the prop department built an ashtray inside the body so the actor inside portraying it could smoke on the job?"

"Add a bourbon dispenser and that could have been your

dream job."

I couldn't disagree. "When we get home, I'll play the entire series for you. I've got the VHS tapes."

"You would."

"The series is based on the Swiss Family Robinson, of course."

"You mean real people?"

I looked at her to determine if she was joking. Nope, she wasn't. "Although said to be inspired by the novel Robinson Crusoe by Daniel Defoe, Swiss Family Robinson is a novel by Robert Louis Stevenson."

Karen furrowed her brow. "That the guy who ran for president in the old days?"

I gave up. Karen was a self-proclaimed poet, not a pop culture historian—not any sort of historian for that matter. No, her poetry-filled head was in the proverbial clouds and forever and ever t'would be. See? I can rant poetic, too.

I dragged her through a pair of slatted swinging red doors. The smell of cheap beer, burning meat, and thronging humanity clogged the air. The tavern was expansive but low ceilinged. Kitschy—and by kitschy I mean phony as boloney—space-based paraphernalia nailed to the walls. Black-and-white publicity stills of the original cast of Lost In Space held places of honor behind the bar. The walls themselves were painted to represent a purple-black universe and an infinity of stars and nebulae. Planets and suns, large and small, in every color of the jumbo Crayola box, hung suspended from the ceiling on clear fishing line.

Something Pluto-ish bumped me in the nose.

Tightly-packed tables kept movement to a minimum. A long wooden stage, less than a foot above the ground, graced the far wall. Elvis, or rather a Latino Elvis impersonator, graced the stage. A five-piece band including two electric guitars, a keyboardist, bassist, and drummer accompanied him.

Greasy black hair, preposterous black sideburns, and a bejeweled white lamé suit, that held more sequins than the

Milky Way does stars, glittered under the red, blue, green and white stage lights. All very trippy and nostalgic. The only possible misstep were the white patent-leather cowboy boots with pink star-shaped sequins cladding his feet. Did Elvis ever in his illustrious career wear cowboy boots?

That would require some fact checking.

Despite the Elvis disguise and absurd wardrobe, I recognized this imposter.

And he was no Elvis.

"Hey, isn't that—" Karen stared, then froze, at the ersatz Elvis as he swiveled his hips and thrust his exaggerated groin in her direction.

"Yes," I said, pulling her along to catch up to the hostess guiding us to a small round table to the side of the stage. "Daniel Hernandez. Who'd have thunk it?"

Karen nodded numbly and went quiet as she sat, eyes glued to the stage.

A packed and boisterous crowd, some standing and others attached to barstools, half-occluded the U-shaped bar looming behind us. Empty upside down beer bottles hung over the bar. An interior design statement?

A plump white cat with pink eyes sat on the bar, snuggled against the black-and-gold cash register. Was the beast keeping an eye on the till? A tempting plate of fried oysters sat beside the awful creature, within inches of its black nose. Despite its being a cat, I had to admire its self-control. Those oysters wouldn't have lasted two minutes beside my nose.

I ordered us a couple of beers for starters.

We drank. Daniel "Elvis" Hernandez sang.

"Anything to eat?" A young woman exhibiting two of the world's largest and whitest snowy peaks slapped a plastic-coated menu between us.

I scanned the menu. "OMG! Oysters and alligator on a stick! I'll have that!" I pointed to the bountiful platter pictured on the menu.

"You got it, dear. And for you, dear?" Our waitress slid her eyes at Karen. "The same?"

"Eww! Are you kidding? That's disgusting. I'll have...I'll have the—"

"There's grilled cheese and fries on the kiddie menu," I offered the suggestion, seeing her dismay at all the animal-based products available. "Or the fried okra?"

Although I've pointed out to the woman more times than I can count that it makes no sense sticking to a strictly plant-based diet when she herself if animal-based, there was no budging her on this point.

"I can ask chef to make your sandwich with vegan cheddar," offered our server, picking up on the issue at hand.

"Fine." Karen handed the menu to our waitress. "I'll have the grilled cheese, vegan. And the okra. It's not fried in the same oil as the oysters, is it?"

"I'll check," promised the waitress.

"And two more beers."

"You got it, dear."

Having gotten the all-clear on the whole life-and-death okra issue, our waitress placed the order and our food and drinks arrived just about the same time that Daniel "Elvis" Hernandez reached his vocal peak with *All Shook Up*. As he sang, his hips shook, his arms shook, his hands shook. Even his feet shook. If I could peak inside his body, I had a feeling I'd discover his spleen and liver shook, too.

I, for one, was feeling all shook up too. I couldn't tell what Karen was feeling because her face looked decidedly un-Karen-like as she stayed focused on pseudo-Elvis. Daniel smiled broadly to his appreciative, if captive, audience. To an accompanying smattering of applause and a number of drunken whoops and whistles—you'd have to be drunk to applaud this clown—the singer/attempted murderer announced that the band was going on a 20-minute break and promised to be back to break out with a little number called *Blue Suede Shoes*.

I cringed.

Karen swooned.

What the hell was wrong with her?

What the Elvis was wrong with her for that matter?

"He's coming over!" Karen giggled like a teenaged school girl.

Daniel walked, no, sauntered, straight to our table. His rhinestone-buttoned shirt gaped seductively open to the navel. Sweat glistened off his skin. He threw a cowboy-booted foot onto the empty chair to Karen's left. This put his crotch at Karen's eye level. And she leveled those eyes on its intended target.

"Hey, good to see you again."

"You, too," Karen teetered.

"You, too?" I fought down the urge to tackle the punk.

"Mind if I join you?" Daniel asked. He sat without waiting for an answer.

"I'd mind if you didn't." Karen scooted closer. "You look thirsty." She handed him her beer. "Want some?"

"Oh, I want some, alright," he said way too suggestively for my taste—but apparently not for Karen's.

The punk leaned across the table and helped himself to one of my oysters. Popped it into his stupid fake-Elvis maw. Smacked his lips with pleasure.

WTF!?

I protectively pulled my plate closer. If there's one thing I've learned in all my years stranded on this hostile planet, it is the art of self-preservation. "Get your own," I grumbled.

"Ed!" Karen slapped my hand. "Be nice!"

Be nice? I'd like to give this imposter a nice kick in his fake-Elvis ass!

Aloud I said, "Fine." Like I said, it's called the art of self-preservation.

"Enjoying the show?"

Even though I wasn't sure whether he was talking about me watching his Elvis impersonation or Karen drooling over his pelvis, I chose to answer for the two of us. "You, sir, are no Elvis."

"I hear you, man," Daniel said with a smile. "There's only one King, am I right?" He extended his fist for bumping and to avoid Karen's ire, I grudgingly completed the silly fist bump. "Still the people want a show and that's what I give 'em." He reached between my arms and snatched another oyster from my plate.

Damn kid was fast!

"What's with the Elvis get up anyway? I thought you were going to school full-time?"

"I am. It's a side hustle. Helps pay my tuition. My folks can't foot the entire bill and I didn't get any scholarship money. Besides, I get a kick out of performing."

"I think you sounded terrific," Karen said, offering Daniel a bite of her grilled cheese sandwich. She turned to me and mouthed *And you stole the poor boy's money!*

I shrugged it off.

Daniel leaned in and snapped off a chunk of the offered sandwich. "Thanks." He chewed and licked his fingers. Who knew licking fingers could look so obscene? "So, you guys are still hanging around town. Still looking for Fu?"

"Yes," I said. "Tell us where he is and as soon as we see him and can let his relatives know that he's well, we'll be out of here."

Daniel seemed to consider my offer. His thoughts—such as he was capable of—were interrupted when the bass player teetered over to our table, bent and whispered something in his ear. Daniel guffawed and slapped the black-clad bassist with stringy dishwater-colored hair on the shoulder. The bass player nodded to us, then shouldered his way to the bar.

"I heard Fu's gone back to Los Angeles," Daniel said.

"Los Angeles?" I echoed.

"Sure, that's where he's from, right?"

"Yes, but our client hasn't said anything about it to us. Are you sure? Where did you hear this?"

"Hmm, not sure. Some chick, I think. Yeah, that was it. Mentioned it at a party last night."

"What's her name? Was it Alexandra?" Our mystery woman and only real lead, courtesy of college-girl Jenny.

"Don't remember her name. I can't even hardly remember

what she looks like. Blonde? Brunette?" He shook his head. In hopes of breaking loose a memory? "Too bad. Wish I could help you more. Guess I drank a little too much. Loud music banging. Shitload of people coming and going. Free beer flowing. You know? The brain gets a little…fuzzy."

Not for the first time, I caught him glancing towards the bar. Was he nervous about something? Was the tavern's owner keeping an eye on him? Giving him the stink eye for lingering too long with the customers when he should be back up on stage shaking his booty?

"Sure, sure," I said. "Fuzzy." He couldn't have helped us any less. Except by dropping dead. I studied his fake sideburns and wondered how much glue, time, and effort it required to paste them on prior to each performance. "How about explaining why you attacked us? Tried to knife Karen?"

"Ed!" Karen scolded.

"What? I'm just trying to do my job. And find out why this kid tried to stick you like a pig."

"Are you comparing me to a pig?" Karen fumed.

"No! No!" I waved both hands in the air. "Not at all."

"I don't know what you're talking about, mister. I don't remember anything about trying to stick anybody with a knife, let alone this beautiful lady." He plucked her hand from the table and planted a kiss on the back of it.

Karen beamed moonbeams.

"You pulled a knife on us," I pressed.

"I don't think so," parried Daniel.

"You don't think so!? I know so!" I countered.

"No." Daniel shook his head vigorously side to side. His sideburns swept the air. "That doesn't sound like me."

"Let it go, Ed," cut in Karen.

"Let it go?"

"Yeah, just let it go," Karen replied.

I sucked my beer. I counted to one million. Then I counted to one million again—backwards…in Roman numerals. When had Karen become so daft? When exactly had we slipped into this Daffy Duck world? And how did we get back to Earth? Damn, never thought I'd be saying those words! Earth is the last place I've ever wanted to be since landing on this ball of cooling magma.

"Okay, letting go." I laid my hands on the table. "Let's stick with the subject here. Stay on focus. We were sent to find Fu. This guy," I jabbed my thumb at pseudo-Elvis, "just might have been the last person to see him." Before he was swallowed whole by the mother of all gators or the Nikker.

"Look, Mister Turner. I don't know why you're making such a big deal out of Fu's disappearance. I mean, I get that his family is worried about him. My folks would worry if I just up and disappeared. But you take my word for it, when Fu wants to be found, he'll be found. Until then, cut the kid some slack. Tell his family to cut him some slack." Daniel slicked back a greasy lock that had dared separate from the herd. "Hell, maybe that's why he's dropped off the radar. You ever think of that? Maybe his family is too controlling. Fu might just need some space."

I counted to 10 million slowly. Daniel was doing wonders for my math skills. I seethed. I was about to blast this doofus into outer space to join the Family Robinson on their never-ending epic journey to Alpha Centauri. They already had one nogoodnik onboard the Jupiter 2, one more couldn't hurt. "Listen, you—"

The band struck up with a bang of drums and a clashing of discordant chords.

"Oops, that's my cue." Daniel shot a look at the stage and waved to his bandmates. "You sticking around for my second set, sweetheart?" He cupped a love-me-tender hand along the side of Karen's jaw.

"Of course."

"Great. I'll dedicate a song to you." Daniel stood, planted an inappropriate kiss on her nose and swung his hips all the way to the stage.

It was all I could do not to swing a fist at his nose.

"I don't trust him," I said.

"You don't trust anybody."

Karen wasn't wrong. Hiding in plain sight on a planet where half the population would be happy to sell your flesh to the highest bidder and the other half would like to take a scalpel to that flesh and slit it open to see how it worked, makes one more than a trifle aloof and mucho distrustful.

"I'm tired. Why don't we get out of here. The clock's ticking and we've got plenty to do." Mr. Ha had texted Karen twice today asking where things stood. She'd replied with some vague words of encouragement.

"You go ahead," Karen said. "I think I'll wait around."

"Wait around? You hate these kinds of places. For what?"

"For Daniel."

"For him?"

"I want to see the rest of the show."

"See the rest of the show? He tried to kill you! Stab you to death! In fact, he would have, if I hadn't come to the rescue."

"Oh, Ed. You heard Daniel. It was all a misunderstanding. A big misunderstanding." Karen patted my shoulder. "Lighten up, already. You go on back to the hotel. I'll catch up later."

"Fine." I climbed to my feet and shoved back my chair. "But if Daniel jams a knife into your stomach and guts you like a carp, don't come crying to me!"

Hmm, that might have been over the top, but by the astonished and appalled look on Karen's face—not to mention the troubled looks we were now getting from the patrons at the surrounding tables—I could tell that she got my message loud and clear.

I huffed off as only a short, plain-looking, unassuming alien in human-hide could manage. Which is to say, nobody seemed to notice me leaving.

11

As I pushed my way around the bar crowd with every intention of leaving Karen to her fate, I noticed a familiar face. "Amil!"

Our frequent KarRyde driver Amil sat on a barstool, legs dangling.

Meanwhile, fake Elvis crooned about his *Burnin' Love*. As far as I was concerned, he should have been belting out the far more apropos *(You're The) Devil In Disguise* and dedicating the tune to Karen.

"Hiya, Ed. I see you made it!" He turned his head quickly to the right. The middle-aged gentleman, clad in black jeans and black T-shirt seated beside him, abruptly rose from his barstool, and made a beeline for the exit. "Perfect timing." He patted the wooden stool. "Park your butt, my friend."

Despite wanting to get out of this joint and free of fake Elvis's warbling and over-the-top theatrics, I shifted gears and sat. "Don't mind if I do."

"Get you a beer?" Amil raised a hand to catch the barmaid's attention. He wore a loose-fitting yellow-and-brown striped shirt and baggy jeans with leather sandals.

Two beers showed up. We clinked bottles and drank.

"So you took my advice and came."

"Yeah, nice place. Love the theme."

"Oh? You into outer space?" Amil asked.

"You might say that."

"Me, too. You might find this funny but I sometimes dream of flying on wings of magic...exploring the universe. Like a magic spaceman, you know?"

"We all gotta dream," I said. "Nothing wrong with that. You come here regular?"

"I come whenever I can and the mood strikes. Lots of live music and the theme changes daily. Today Elvis. Tomorrow, I think, is traditional New Orleans jazz. Country music, world music, reggae… Then they do a heavy metal day—not my thing." Amil spat. "But the headbangers love it. They even put on a Sunday afternoon filk show."

"Excuse my Khmer but what the fuck is filk?"

Amil chuckled. "Sci-fi lyrics set to folk music."

"Seriously? Like: the answer my friend is blowin' in the exothermal-galactic-accelerator wind?"

"You got it."

"And people come to listen to that stuff?"

"Seems so. The show's been running for five years or more. There's usually a headline act, plus an open mic component. I hear if you don't get here early to sign up for the open mic, you're shit out of luck."

"Just my luck we get Elvis tonight. Speaking of which, has he been singing here at Lost In Space long?"

"About a month maybe. Why do you ask this question?"

I explained how Karen and I had talked with him back at Tulane. How he was Fu's roommate. I left out the bit about him trying to poke a big hole in Karen's soft belly with a switchblade. That was between me and Daniel—and I wasn't done with the boy yet.

"The world can be a very small place," replied Amil. To this profound statement, we each hoisted our bottles and dumped some beer down our throats.

"Some show, huh?" Amil said, swinging his eyes towards the stage. "Say what you will, the crowd loves him. He's got something special."

"If you say so. Karen likes him. I prefer the original."

"Original, yeah. Nothing but nothing beats an original. Some things, they be only one, and they be the best."

"Amen to that," I said although I really had no idea what

we were talking about. I think the music was beginning to get to me—that, Ursula's sudden and unexpected murder, and Karen's oddball behavior.

"I don't suppose you know anything about him?" I asked.

"Daniel Elvis? No, sorry, although he has mentioned that he attends school and is from…New Jersey, I think?"

"Hmm. I don't suppose you've laid eyes on this Alexandra woman we're looking for?"

"Sorry, no."

"I didn't think so. There's a hundred bucks in it for you, if you spot her."

"Much appreciated. Thanks!" Amil said.

"No problem." This case was going nowhere fast. I decided there and then to hang around outside and tail fake Elvis when he left. See where it led me. "Tell me, do our beer bottles join those when we finish?" I jabbed my empty bottle towards the dusty dozens hanging empty and upside down above us.

"Nah, that's the tavern owner's concept of a bottle tree."

"Bottle tree?"

"You hang empty bottles upside down to catch evil spirits."

"Does it work?"

Amil smiled a big toothy smile. "You see any evil spirits round here, Ed?"

"Does fake Elvis count?"

Amil laughed heartily. Judging by the three empty bottles on the bar in front of him, he had a jump on me in the drinking game.

"What is that thing exactly?" I pointed to a well-worn brown satchel attached to his belt with a leather thong. "One of those gris-gris bags I see all around town?" I pronounced it *griss-griss*.

"This?" Amil palmed the bag. "Yes. This is my gris-gris bag." He said it again for my benefit. "*Gree-gree.*"

"*Gree-gree*, right. I thought it strange, a grown man like you carrying around your marble collection."

"Do not joke, Ed. Very, very special this." He brought the

leather sack to his lips and kissed it reverentially. "It is what you call a talisman, similar to a lucky rabbit's foot. Only far more powerful. Gris-gris means to cast a spell. You tell somebody that does you wrong that you will cast a gris-gris on them—an evil spell." He lowered the sack to his hip. "Very potent. Maybe you should get a spirit guide to make one for you, Ed."

"Maybe I will."

"It must be crafted and blessed personally for you by a true spiritualist. Do not fall for one of those Chinese knockoffs in the tourist shops. Speaking of spiritualists," Amil's eyes flew to the TV directly behind the bar, "did you hear what happened? Such a one was murdered today."

A cold invisible hand danced up my spinal column as Ursula Broussard glared at me from inside the TV. "I know. Karen and I were at Enchantments earlier today."

"Yes, of course. I did not think about this." Amil's mouth hung open. Sweat oozed from his hairline. "I gave you a lift." He rubbed his gris-gris bag. "Who could predict such a terrible thing would happen?"

"Say, Amil, you went inside the shop. Did you see Ursula when you went in? Did she appear…normal?"

He shook his head in the negative. "No. I did not see her at all. I only saw Karen. Isn't that her seated all alone at that table?"

"Yeah."

"Should we join her or ask her to join us?"

"I think she wants some space."

So, if Amil hadn't seen Ursula when he stepped inside Enchantments to fetch Karen, what did it mean? Ursula had been in the storeroom? In the toilet? Lying dead and out-of-sight behind the sales counter where Karen had unceremoniously dumped her fresh corpse after stabbing her to death?

According to the closed captioning scrolling across the bottom of the TV screen, the police still had no leads as to the identity of the murderer.

"Lola Davies is a powerful manbo. She will find this killer," Amil said.

"So far, the police can't even locate her," I replied.

"This is strange. You have no idea where she might be?"

"Not a clue. When we left Enchantments, everybody was alive and all was well. Hell, she could be in the middle of the Atchafalaya swamp for all I know."

"The Atchafalaya?" Amil went still.

"Yeah. But I'm joking. It's just someplace she mentioned in passing."

"Did she now?"

"I'm thinking of checking it out tomorrow."

"Seriously? Why would you do this? You want to see our famous alligators maybe?"

"No, nothing like that. To tell the truth, I'm not sure why I want to go. No specific reason. It's just something about what Lola Davies said… It's got me curious and I can't let go. Call it a hunch, I guess. I'm a PI. We're required to get the occasional hunch now and then. It's printed in the PI handbook. Still…" I frowned as I glanced towards the stage. Karen was on her feet now and swaying to the music. "It could be an utter waste of time."

"Yes. You must consider this."

"Then again, we don't have any better leads at the moment."

"You have a rental car lined up?"

"Well, no."

"Amil will be your driver."

"You will?"

"Sure. Why not? I know the way and I know something of this swamp."

"I checked the map. It's pretty far away."

Amil grinned. "And you're a pretty good tipper."

He had me there.

Amil raised his bottle in salute. "Here's to good fortune and a successful adventure. Bless us, Mama Z!"

"Mama Z?"

"Mama Z." He pointed to the white cat. It hadn't so much as

shifted a whisker since I'd first laid eyes on the fetid felid. "Sixth generation resident house cat. It is tradition, and considered good luck, to ask for her blessing before undertaking any new journey."

"Fine." As much as I loathed cats, I drank. "Bless us, Mama Z."

12

I checked my wristwatch—a lovely bit of plastic skillfully-crafted to look like a box of Kraft Macaroni & Cheese Dinner —I'd found it inside a cereal box eons ago. It was approaching half-past two in the morning as Karen exited the Lost In Space Tavern. I was tired. I needed a boost and I could have used a couple sticks of black licorice.

I also needed to pee. And I was pissed to discover Daniel strolling with her. I jumped behind a Doric column and stuck my head out for a furtive peek. Despite the late hour, a small rowdy crowd roamed the street. Looking for what? Alcohol? Music? Drugs? Love in all the wrong places?

Karen and Daniel headed off and I followed at a discreet distance. Of note, they were not walking in the direction of the Bourbon Orleans.

Where the devil was he taking her? Daniel had traded his Elvis getup for denims and a navy tee. Weirdly, he was still wearing the cowboy boots with the pink sequins. With each and every step, he clomped loudly, like one of those horses forced to haul tourists up and down the streets all the live-long day and night.

They turned the corner. The Saint Louis Cathedral loomed darkly ahead. They skirted around it and continued on. The streets grew quieter and emptier. Now the pair seemed to be moving towards the Mississippi River. Soon, they entered a small public parking lot.

With an accompanying beep! a compact car's headlights and dome lights blinked on. Daniel suddenly looked in my direction. I held my breath and froze. He didn't seem to notice me. He opened his car door. Where was he going? Was she going with him? Should I stop her?

If I did, would she slug me?

Was it worth the pain?

As I stood debating all my lousy options, rough hands yanked me into a dark and dank narrow alleyway between two moldering red-brick buildings that stank of day-old tuna. Two homeless men huddled on the ground against the wall, watching.

I stiffened and prepared to strike a blow to my attacker.

"Ed! It's me!"

I paused mid-blow. I blinked. Although it was dark, I have superior eyesight. Better than a human's. Better than a cat's, that's for damn sure. "Sara? Sara Chronis?"

Sensing trouble, the two homeless men disappeared, leaving their worldly possessions, gathered in three lumpy black trash bags, behind.

Sara's got flame-red hair and brilliant green eyes. She's very pretty and very fit, as every CIA operative should be. She's under thirty— I'm guessing because even I have enough sense to know not to ask that question. She's also quite the chef. Her chocolate torte is to die for. To die for, get resurrected, and die again for. It's that good.

"Yes, sorry. Didn't mean to scare you." She smiled warmly.

"No problem. I was planning on changing my underwear anyway." That elicited a laugh that she quickly smothered.

"Same old Ed." Sara was clad in dark clothes and dark sneakers.

We'd met some time ago under very different circumstances. Circumstances involving my search for Karen's brother, Ken.

I still wasn't sure how much or how little Sara knew about me. I wasn't sure I wanted to know. "What are you doing here? On vacation?" I heard the sound of a car starting up and driving off. One look told me it was Karen and Daniel, disappearing into the night.

Shit. Sara had found me, but I'd lost them.

"No, I'm on assignment. I'm working undercover," Sara explained. "After my involvement in the Ken Dalton case, I got a promotion. At least, that's what my boss calls it."

"How nice for you," I said but my thoughts were elsewhere. Noting my frustration, she said, "What's wrong?"

"That was Karen who just drove off with a young man I've been keeping an eye on."

"Oh, sorry about that. I didn't mean to spoil anything."

"Forget it," I said. "She can take care of herself." I hoped. She had come to my rescue a time or two. She wasn't completely helpless. "What's got you wandering the streets of New Orleans in the middle of the night? CIA taking up ghost hunting?"

"Actually, you're not far off. Come on," she locked arms with me. "I'll buy you a coffee."

"At this hour?"

"Sure, Café du Monde is still open. In fact— One sec." Sara pulled a twenty-dollar bill from her pocket and set it securely amongst the trash bags. "I feel bad scaring the guys off like that."

"Kind of you."

"So are we going?" Sara asked.

"Are you paying for the beignets too?"

"All you can eat." She smiled and I allowed myself to be dragged along, quite willingly.

Amid the sweet smell of fried dough, powdered sugar, and New Orleans-style coffee—infused with chicory root—Sara told me her story and I told her mine. At least as much as we were each willing to share and able to share.

The chicory root/coffee bean blend was a custom born of necessity by coffee brewers and afficionados during the blockade of the city's port during the War of the States. With coffee in short supply, adding chicory root to the mix was a clever way of making up for the scarcity of beans.

For a root, it wasn't bad but it tasted twice as good when I let a beignet float in the cup for a flavor boost.

I explained that a client had hired Karen and I to find a

young man named Fu Chun.

"Never heard of him. What's special about him?"

"He's a college kid. He arrived at Tulane to start school and then promptly disappeared."

"Sorry to hear that. Wish I could help. There's a lot of that going on in the world."

"Don't I know it. So what's your reason for prowling the Big Easy in the middle of the night? You don't strike me as a vampire or the Jack-the-Ripper type."

"I can tell you this much," Sara went on. "Have you ever heard of the Alien Resistance Corps?"

My radar went up but I tried not to let my interest show. "Hmm, maybe?" In fact, I'd had more than one run-in with ARC personnel. Some of whom ended up dead. Not my fault. The ARC had been on my tail practically since the day I crash landed here.

"Aren't they a bunch of UFO nuts and conspiracy theorists?" I pushed my beignet around in my tiny cup a minute, then swallowed the sweet soggy dough and coffee in one satisfying greedy gulp.

"Yes, you'd think so. Frankly, I think so too. But my boss sent me here. It took some doing, they are crazy suspicious of outsiders, but I've managed to infiltrate the ARC. They think I'm one of them." She unzipped her charcoal hoodie revealing a black shirt bearing the ARC insignia. "Last month, I was in the Pacific Northwest chasing down rumors of Big Foot, if you can believe it."

I could. "And did you find one?"

"Nope. Not even a fuzzy footprint. And I got ticks. Lucky I didn't catch Lyme disease."

"Maybe the Bigfoot have all left on their fall migration." Which I knew for a fact they did.

"Very funny. Just like you to find a joke in everything."

"Better a joke than a tragedy."

"Yeah, I suppose you're right."

"I still don't understand why you're here."

Sara paused and drank. "The ARC believes there is an

alien hiding somewhere in the area. Apparently, several citizens reported sightings of...something. The ARC takes all reported sightings seriously. And if they do, then so does the Agency. And these sightings have been increasing in frequency. Don't ask me why but no sighting is too silly for them to follow up on. And believe me," she said, pushing a lock of hair from her cheek, "I've heard and read some pretty dumb claims."

"But there is something about this latest claim that has the CIA interested enough to send you here?"

"That's right." She folded her hands in front of her plate. Was she afraid I'd swipe the rest of her beignets? My own plate sat sadly empty but for a fingertip's worth of powdered sugar.

"May I ask what?"

"Just between us?"

"Of course."

Sara took a moment to consider. "Here," she reached into her pocket and pulled out her cellphone. "I'll show you." She pulled up a blurry photo and showed it to me.

"Interesting," I said, maintaining my calm as I took in the image on the small screen.

"Weird, huh?" She quickly tucked her phone away. "I mean, it's probably nothing. Could be a hoax, a dead tree that appears to look like some kind of space creature. Who knows what? These things always turn out to be nothing or to have a perfectly natural explanation... But still, it's my job to check them out."

"Silly or not, do me a favor," I said.

"What's that?"

"Tread carefully."

"I always do."

We finished up and said our goodnights. We promised to try our best to get together again while we were both in town. Sara went one way and I went the other.

The image Sara had shared with me remained in my mind's eye all the way back to the hotel. I've seen a Fleek or two in my life. I've seen planets filled to overflowing with Fleek. The Fleek-Pazu conflict was doomed to last as long as our two species coexisted.

The image on Sara's phone may have been blurry but there was no doubting what that image was.

What it was, was a Fleek.

Fleek are nothing but trouble.

And I had Fu to find. More trouble I did not need.

13

Back in our room at the Bourbon Orleans, with no one but myself for company, I grabbed the TV remote and scooted over to the Turner Classic Movies channel—one of my favorites. *Man of the West* was airing. Hoorah, Gary Cooper time!

A bright spot in what was turning out to be one rat-ass ugly day. And much to my dismay, Karen was not waiting for me in room 644. She was nowhere to be found. I'd dialed her cellphone from the room phone and gotten nothing. Not even voicemail. See? Rat-ass ugly!

Then again, Ursula's day had ended far worse…as had her life.

I settled down in the middle of the bed. *Man Of The West* starred Gary Cooper, Lee J Cobb, and Julie London. A noir classic so intense I could even forgive that they'd shot it in DeLuxe CinemaScope instead of glorious B&W. The Gary Cooper flick was only surpassed by *Vera Cruz*. That film featured Gary and a veritable who's-who of the era's biggest box office Western stars. Whenever I need a real dose of Old West reality, I dive into *Vera Cruz* and don't come up for air until the film ends.

Morning came.

Karen did not.

My chin sagged, my red eyes drooped and I was still in a pretty pissy and troubled mood. If anything, worse.

I'd spent the night bingeing on TCM films. I rang up a couple hundred dollars' worth of room service. Everything from a chocolate layer cake, one peanut butter-and-bacon sandwich, a bottle of the hotel's best bourbon, a big pot of jambalaya with smoky andouille sausage and juicy chicken thighs, and a pint of bourbon-pecan ice cream.

Everything but Camel cigarettes. These I was forced to leave the hotel to forage for myself. I picked up a fresh carton at a nearby 24-hour convenience store.

All courtesy of Mr. Ha.

I knew he wouldn't mind. All Mr. Ha wanted for his money was results. Sadly, results were thus far not coming. In fact, now I was in search of a missing Karen Dalton on top of a missing Fu Chun. Twice the work.

Could I dare charge him double my fee now?

I jumped around in a hot shower and changed into fresh clothes. Amil and I had agreed that he would pick me up at 8 AM. A bit on the early side, but we had a long drive ahead of us.

I grabbed a couple jumbo to-go cups of coffee downstairs in the lobby and was already waiting outside the hotel when Amil pulled up in his Toyota.

"Hi, Ed. You don't look so good."

"I don't feel so good." I handed him one of the coffees through the open passenger-side window.

"Thanks. Climb in. Where's Karen?"

"She won't be joining us."

"She feeling okay?"

"I hope so." And I really did. I'd left her a note on hotel stationary explaining that I'd gone off for the day with Amil and that she could contact me through him. We were rarely out of touch this long and I found it unsettling. I hoped I'd hear from her, sooner than later.

"Well, since it's just me and you, you might as well ride shotgun then."

And off we flew.

We left the city behind, sped through the suburbs and onto the great flat swampy world of rural Louisiana. A land filled with mobile homes, mansions, and marinas. And sunbathing alligators everywhere.

Amil had packed us a couple of po'boy sandwiches, filled with fried catfish, alligator sausage and a spicy salsa. Unable to resist the aroma, I tore into mine. It tasted delicious and set my taste buds tingling. The sandwich also had a soporific effect on me. Before long, between the unrelenting heat leaking through the windscreen and the satisfying lump of sandwich, I dozed.

I nodded off and awoke to the Toyota jittering and bouncing over a pockmarked gravel road. I glanced out the side window and saw a huge gator eying me back. I drifted off once more dreaming of alligators, bobcats, and bears.

When I next raised my eyelids, there was nothing but blue sky and white clouds above, and a swampy sea visible for as far as I could see.

Amil killed the engine. "You're awake."

"Yeah." I rubbed my eyes. "Didn't mean to sleep so long."

"Don't worry, you didn't miss nothing."

"No word from Karen?" I'd told him she might be calling his number.

"Not a word."

"Mind if I smoke?"

"You mind sharing?"

I opened the pack and pulled out two Camels. We lit up, rolled down the windows and stared out the vehicle at the great swamp. Nothing but the usual endless water, bushes, trees, birds, and gators. No Nikkers. No Fleek.

What to do now?

We sat at the end of a dead-end dirt road. Two half-rotten picnic tables up to their seats in weeds sat at water's edge. A pair of red-faded-to-pink kayaks, half-buried in the muck, each held one of those double-sided kayaking oars. One of the kayaks had a big dent in its side that looked suspiciously the size and shape of an alligator's snout.

Who put the kayaks there and why they remained there in alligator- and poisonous-snake infested water, I had no idea. Only an idiot would go kayaking in this deadly swamp.

The yellow sun burned a hole in my forehead. I tapped my ashes out the window. What? Ashes to ashes, dust to dust. Nothing polluting about that.

"I'm beginning to wonder why the hell I asked you to bring me here." I scraped my shoe against the ground. "There's nothing here."

Amil spoke up. "If you're interested in having a look around, there's a trail that takes off in that direction." He pointed a long-nailed finger to the left.

"You've been out here before?"

"Had a couple of clients ask me to bring them out this way a time or two. I've got a cousin, she and her granny live out this way, too. They got a house across the way. Can't drive there from here."

"Then, if you don't mind my asking, how the hell do they get to their house? Parachute in?"

"Airboat. That's the best way to get around in the swamp. Though I suppose you could kayak, if you really had a mind to."

"No, thanks." Boats are almost as bad as airplanes. And kayaks? "I'd rather cross the ocean in an inflatable kiddie pool."

"I know what you mean. The Atchafalaya always makes me nervous," Amil confessed. "Bad energy, bad jou-jou."

"Are you talking about voodoo here?"

"No, not voodoo. Something much stronger, much more dangerous and deadly. Don't you feel it, Ed?"

Amil wasn't the only one who felt something...odd. But what that something was I couldn't put my finger on.

There was something off-putting, something unsettling about this swamp. But we hadn't driven all the way out here for nothing and I had no better leads for the moment. And I still had no idea what Karen was up to or even if she was alright.

Shit.

I pushed open my door. "Guess I'll take a look around. You want to come?"

"No, no! I do not like to venture out in the swamp. It is not safe. You must be careful, watch where you step."

Several alligators, big ones, sat tanning themselves nearby, listening in on our conversation.

"You can bet on it. Wait here for me?"

Amil nodded. "I'll be here. I ain't going to leave you stranded. I'm gonna take me a little nap. Wake me when you get back."

I promised I would. Amil settled back in his seat and shut his eyes. I couldn't afford to shut my eyes. I wouldn't mind a pair of alligator shoes but I did not want to become alligator food. Keeping a close eye on the monsters, I tromped up the narrow trail. Might have been nothing more than a deer track.

Deep hot sand made the walking a slog. Mosquitoes buzzed me but didn't bite. Something in my blood chemistry doesn't suit their fancy, I guess.

I wandered for what felt like hours and reached a dead end at water's edge. And never saw a soul—alligator or human. A few snakes, squirrels, and birds, including a couple of vultures who probably thought I'd soon be their dinner, that was it. There was an eerie silence to the place, too.

What I was looking for, I had no idea. Walking around in a swamp was doing nothing to improve that situation. Why had I come? What was it about Lola Davies' words that had compelled me to visit the Atchafalaya? Did I really expect the Nikker to rise up out of the swamp to greet me? Reveal its secrets to me? Cradling the soulless corpse of Fu Chun in his arms?

Disappointed, I turned around and hiked back to the SUV.

The Toyota's doors hung open, including the rear hatch. The dome light glowed.

I saw no sign of Amil.

"Amil?" I peeked inside anyway just in case he was lying down in back somewhere.

"Hello? Amil?"

No Amil.

Shit.

He'd disappeared.

Leaving nothing behind but that ever-present woodsy and spicy scent of his.

I cupped my hands to my mouth and shouted, "Amil! Amil!"

No reply.

I walked slowly around the small clearing, studying the ground. But it was a mess of footprints, animal tracks, and tire tracks and offered up no answers. I noted no obvious signs of a struggle. Yet, there was no sign of the man anywhere. Merely two empty paper coffee cups in the center console, and our two sandwich wrappers lying on the floor half-buried under the brake pedal.

And with Amil gone, I realized his phone was gone too.

More shit.

"You guys see anything?" I asked a pair of fat gators staring blatantly at me through slitted eyes.

No answer.

Was that because they were guilty and had swallowed him up?

Could the Nikker aka Fleek have captured him in my absence? How many people was I going to have to rescue? Their number kept growing!

As I was worrying about that, I noticed that one of the kayaks was missing. Had it come loose and drifted off? Had Amil decided to go rowing around on his own? I doubted it given what I knew about how he felt about even being near the swamp.

Had the gators taken up kayak racing or added molded plastics to their diet?

I figured maybe the best thing I could do was to turn around and drive back to the city. Maybe I'd find Amil there. If not—as much as I hate dealing with them—I'd feel obliged to report him missing to the authorities, and let them mount a search for the poor guy.

More problems. I poked all around but could not find the key to the Toyota inside or out of the vehicle. Pressing my fingers to the ignition switch, I risked detection, and used my unique powers to try to start the SUV. The engine refused my efforts to force it to turn over. Popping the hood and taking a gander inside the engine compartment, I quickly discovered that the starter and battery were gone.

I slammed down the hood with both hands. "What the

hell?"

Then I noticed that it was now nearly dark. A line of brilliant red drew itself across the horizon then winked out of existence. How had that happened? It seemed impossible that I could have been hiking that long.

As night kept falling, the sounds of the swamp kept increasing. Miles from nowhere, I was alone in the swamp. Just me and the ever-hungry, man-eating gators. Not for the first time, I thanked my lucky stars I was no man.

But that begged the eternal question: How do gators feel about raw Pazu meat?

14

I marched to the edge of the murky water. Mist rose and danced. The air smelled like an open sewer. My ears picked up the sounds of primitive drums. I knew that had to be my imagination—an aural hallucination. There was nothing and nobody out there. Drum sounds were an impossibility. Bears, bobcats, and gators lacked the coordination for such musicianship. Plus, I've heard they're tone deaf.

A crescent moon cut the night sky amongst a zillion lesser stars. Somewhere out there was Zyxltl, my home. A home I'd perhaps never see again.

Did anybody up there miss me?

I cupped my hands and shouted once more. "Amil! Karen!" Pause. "Ursula! Lola Davies!" What the hell, couldn't hurt. I'd take any answer I could get. "Fu Chun!?"

Okay, I'd tried.

I stuffed my hands down the pockets of my trousers and contemplated my options. Other than hunkering down and sleeping in the Toyota, there didn't seem to be much I could do.

I froze. As I looked at the myriad stars, a glowing blur sped towards me. Swamp gas? As the blur drew closer, I recognized Karen. Her body was amorphous and elongated. She floated above the swamp maybe ten yards away and twenty feet above the surface of the black water.

She stretched out her arms and appeared to be in agony. "Ed! Ed!" She waved to me. She beckoned.

I inched into the water, felt the warm, gator-piss infused liquid seep through my shoes and socks, and proceed to climb my trousers. Was Karen another hallucination?

"Ed!" she pleaded once again. She shot a fear-filled look over her left shoulder. Her fingers clutched desperately at the air, hoping against hope for something to hold on to, to keep her from being pulled back to whence she'd come.

With a jolt and a scream, her spirit jerked violently and flew backwards. I splashed deeper and stuck out my hands to save her.

But, in a flash, Karen was gone. Only emptiness remained. That and the remnant of her terrified and pleading voice ringing like an accusation in my ears.

I glanced at the Toyota, my sole connection with civilization. Should I stay or should I go?

Idiot that I am, I hopped in the remaining kayak, grabbed the oar, and took off in the direction I'd seen Karen's spirit disappear.

I rowed furiously, water kicking and splashing all around me.

What I had not told Karen, for fear of alarming her, was that Fleek are sort of like evil cockroaches and when you find one you've got to stamp it out of existence.

The trouble is that even when you believe you've stomped one out of existence, it pops back to life. Sort of akin to when the one real Elvis died and 10,000 imposters popped into existence. And there did not seem to be any way of getting rid of all those pests now either—short of tenting the entire planet and running a big hose of deadly chemicals and poisons straight from Jupiter to Earth.

Some might consider that a tad extreme. But if you knew Fleek the way I knew Fleek, you may not find it so unreasonable.

The kayak sucked. Worst human invention ever. When did canoes go out of favor? Hell, I'd prefer straddling a coarse waterlogged log and riding it down the Mississippi River!

Like I said, I hate boats, all watercraft. And they hate me too. For instance, the moment I plunked down in the damn kayak, warm, stinky water streamed inside, soaking my pack of Camels, and wrecking all my cigarettes.

"Damn." I squeezed the pack and watched the smelly swamp water drip out. "How am I going to survive without cigarettes? And in the middle of a damn swamp too!" I yelled at the universe. Of course, I knew yelling would do no good. The universe never listens to anything I say. It's sort of like Karen that way.

I stuffed the ruined cigarettes in my pocket, hoping to salvage them somehow later. Waste not, want not, and all that.

I half-rose and shook my fist at the heavens for what they'd done.

And fell head first off the kayak.

Splash!

Shit shit shit.

The water wasn't deep but it was foul. I swore some more and spat swamp water from my mouth. More leaked from my ears. A pair of alligator eyes glinted in the moonlight. They were moving closer. I hurled myself up on the kayak. The alligator brushed its snout against my thigh. I smashed the end of the oar down between its eyes and it sank beneath the surface to contemplate its next move. Which I hoped would be to Florida. Lotsa slow-moving seniors there. Just saying....

I wiped the putrid, alligator piss contaminated water from my eyes and rowed madly on, further into the heart of the unknown swamp. As much as the Atchafalaya might be a maze capable of holding the Minotaur prisoner during the day, it proved to be nearly impossible to navigate with any precision in the dark. I bumped into submerged trees and alligators and bears and every other manner of obstacle. Twice I grounded the kayak in the shallows and was forced to climb out to extricate myself.

Eternity passed. The Big Bang came and went.

And on and on I rowed. I lost sight of the shore. I lost sight of the moon. I quite possibly lost sight of my senses.

Being stuck on Earth, sometimes I feel like a housefly trapped inside a car, zip-zapping mindlessly, uselessly in all directions...and bouncing off the windows till I got dizzy and disoriented.

Believe me, the hard stuff's a lot easier than the easy stuff.

An otherworldly roar filled the air. I'd never have imagined that the swamp could be louder than LA. And these were natural noises, not the phony sounds of the city. And I smelled a million smells I'd never smelled before. And that's saying something because I've smelled the real real housewives of Beverly Hills— I worked a case once for a very real husband of Beverly Hills whose blonde trophy wife had taken a real trophy Latin lover. Those over-dressed, over-coiffed women carry around more smells than a perfume factory.

The deeper I went in the swamp, the stronger the smell.

I caught a sudden glimpse of Karen between two skeletal trees. The silver-mercury scything moon suddenly reappeared and cut between the trees. Her glowing face radiated fright. She opened her mouth and screamed but no sound emanated from her twisted lips.

"Karen!" I stood suddenly, oar tight in my hands for balance.

And fell in the fucking swamp again. I threw myself back onboard. I looked up. Karen was gone once more.

Was she playing games with me? Or was my mind playing tricks on me?

Either way, I had no choice.

I swore and rowed until my hands bled. I never seemed to get closer to anything or anywhere at all. The kayak constantly slammed into submerged roots that jarred my bones and rattled my teeth. This was worse than a ride across the swamps of the river Acharon onboard Charon's ferry.

And then…there it was. But what IT was, I couldn't say.

15

Well, okay, I could say, if you want to get technical about it —which is something that *technically* I do not like to do.

What it was was a house.

A black house.

An impossibly large black house. A mansion really. Out here in the middle of the Atchafalaya, surrounded by nothing but water and trees and gators. Sitting all by its lonesome in a circle of shallow muddy water cleared of all trees for thirty feet in every direction.

What was this, the Palace of the Gators? Would I find the Alligator Prince inside? Seated at a throne constructed of human bones?

More importantly, would I find Karen inside?

The house, not the Alligator Prince's belly, that is.

I rowed closer and, as I drew nearer, the house loomed all the larger. Built on stilts, the mansion—because that's really how big it was—rose to the moon or so it seemed. It was painted blacker than black.

Three tall roof peaks gave it the look of teeth taking a giant bite out of the sky. I tried to count the number of windows but, each time I did, the number seemed to change.

The long finger of a wooden dock bobbed to my left. Three dingy airboats sat tied up against it. I slid up at the end of the dock, hauled myself onto it, and the kayak up after me.

I was dripping wet, due as much from repeatedly falling in the swamp as from overexertion. I sat on the dock for a moment and studied the enormous house. Why would anybody choose the middle of the fucking swamp for their home?

After a spell, I climbed to my feet. No one had appeared. Not to greet me. Not to eat me.

Both good signs.

Or so I hoped.

I slowly approached the front porch running the width of the house. The closer I got, the more decrepit the house appeared. Built of wood that was cracked and weathered and sagged. What kept it from collapsing? Sheer will power? The eave seemed on the verge of crashing down on my head. I raised my hand and banged on one of two massive twelve-foot doors decorated with grotesque carvings of freaky smiling human skulls. Femurs served as door handles.

I waited and waited. I banged some more. Harder.

I peered in the grimy windows onto the porch but saw little more than dark shadows inside and hints of ancient furniture. No living/breathing occupants. Not even a portrait of such a being on the walls.

"Karen!" I called. "Are you in there?"

Tired of knocking, I pulled both handles and the doors swung outward with a creak like proverbial fingernails on a chalkboard. That is, if anybody remembers chalkboards. I believe they've gone the way of the rotary-dial phone—a device I miss greatly. Back in the day, people actually had to dial the dial, slowly, number by number, if they wanted to reach you, or worse, me. Nowadays, it's far too simple to encroach on one's privacy. And don't get me started on texting! The course of human society seems to be running backwards…what's next, smoke signals?

My skin tingled. Cold air rushed out of the house as if trying to escape whatever dwelt inside. A foul odor came with it. I stepped over the threshold into a grand entry with a tall ceiling holding, of all things, a 30-inch in diameter mirrored disco ball, rotating slower than Venus. And if you know anything about your solar system's individual planetary rotations, that's damn slow.

To my right stood a dark study in which an ornate desk

lumbered at its center. On the left, I noticed a small alcove with a satin-covered bench seat and a brass coatrack holding a lone purple shawl with lace trim.

The front doors closed slowly behind me of their own accord. I heard a click that told me leaving may not be as easy as entering. No matter, I was confident I could deal with my departure when the time came. I may not be able to escape the Earth but I like to believe I'm capable of escaping most locked rooms.

Then...I smelled a smell that every Pazu knows only too well.

Fleek.

I paused, sniffed the air. Yep, there was a Fleek here somewhere. In this house. If not now, recently.

I bristled. My radar went up.

If the Fleek was here now, this wasn't going to end well for at least one of us.

"Karen?" I whispered. Hearing no reply, I lightly tread the worn wide-plank mahogany floor. Crossing through a pair of heavy tied-back navy curtains, I found myself in a large room. Two crystal chandeliers bearing tapered white candles hung from the ceiling. The chandeliers swayed ever so slightly. The candles flickered and danced. Who'd lit them and where had they gone? Was it my Nikker/Fleek nemesis?

I stayed on high alert.

I found myself mesmerized by the movement and had to force myself to stop looking at them. I caught the sound of approaching steps and turned my attention to the right in the direction of a metal-gated grand archway.

An improbable figure appeared from around the corner and pushed open the gate. "Hiya, Turner."

"Daniel?" I relaxed. This was no Fleek. Not even a mythological Nikker. Not even a very real alligator. Just some idiot college kid.

Daniel Rodriguez smiled. "Surprised to see me? Yeah, I'll bet you are." He held a lit candle in his left hand. He ran his right hand through his greasy black hair. He laughed. He shook his finger at me. "I'm mad at you, you know."

"Are you now?" I inched closer. I didn't want to spook him. But I did want to wrap my fingers around his neck and squeeze the living daylights out of him. Especially if he'd harmed Karen in any way. The woman might be annoying as hell but it was my hell and I've become—much to my surprise—kind of very much attached to her.

"Sure, you walked out on my show. What's wrong? You not an Elvis fan?"

It was my turn to smile. "I'm very much an Elvis fan. And if Elvis had been performing, I'd have stayed for the entire show. Sadly, you're nothing but a poor imitation."

Daniel's face darkened. "That's a nasty thing to say." Suddenly, a switchblade appeared in his right hand.

"That again?" I looked at the knife. "Didn't you learn your lesson the first time?"

"This time, I'm prepared. It's your turn to learn a lesson, asshole!" Daniel lunged at me.

I stood my ground. The moment he was within striking distance, I stepped to the side. I grabbed his arm and threw him into the wall. His knife skittered across the floor.

Daniel bellowed and clutched his elbow. "You broke my fuckin' arm!"

"Where's Karen? If you've done anything to harm her, you're arm's not the only thing you're going to have to worry about."

Daniel managed to snicker. "You're dead meat, Turner. Dead. Meat." He sounded deranged.

"Listen, Danny boy. I've been paddling around the swamp for what felt like days, I've digested swamp in the process, I'm hungry and, to top it off, my cigarettes are ruined. See?" I pulled out the soggy pack of Camels and hurled it at him. "Where's Karen?"

"How the hell should I know?" He sat on the floor, cradling his busted arm.

"She left Lost In Space with you."

"Yeah, so? We walked, we talked. She left. Speaking of which…" Daniel scrambled to his feet, moving much more quickly than I'd have imagined—preternaturally for a human—especially with a fresh injury. The pain alone should have slowed him down.

Nonetheless, he ran down the arched hallway and disappeared around the corner. I followed the sound of his racing footsteps. I was determined to get some answers from him.

And came to a dead end.

16

I ran my fingers slowly up and down, and all along the walls, looking for any signs of a hidden passage. Some sick interior decorator had embellished the walls themselves by upholstering the surfaces in bile-green satin. As if that wasn't bad enough, they'd adorned every available inch of space with human thumb bones—proximal and distal phalanxes and metacarpals— all three bones of each thumb carefully stitched together end-over-end with slender silver wire. There must have been hundreds of thumbs running up and down the far wall.

Was this really some sicko's idea of art? Or had somebody or some *thing* deliberately gone to all this trouble to *thumb* his/its proverbial nose at me? If so, that would mean they'd been expecting me... That was an interesting notion.

As for the walls themselves, they appeared solid enough. So where had Daniel gotten to? Had the punk been another figment of my rapidly deteriorating brain?

I didn't think so.

I stopped and sniffed the air fee-fi-fo-fum style. Yep, I still smelled Fleek. Or was that my imagination, too? Maybe I suffered too great an imagination. The solution to that, of course, would be to immerse myself in mindless social media. That would deaden my brain for sure. But I cringed at the very thought of going to such an extreme.

Sometimes the cure is worse than the disease.

I was hearing those distant drums again, too. I chose to think that was the result of all that foul water stuck in my ear canals.

I returned the way I'd come and started once again from

the front door. I turned to my right and entered the study. A tall, wide walnut chair with a torn black leather seat held the skeletal remains of a cat curled up in the fetal position for the night. How cozy.

Musty books stood half-hidden behind thick black candles, crystal skulls, more human and animal bones, a brass telescope, an astrolabe, and all other manner of arcane paraphernalia stuffed the massive dusty black bookshelves.

I came to a halt and gazed out the front windows. Curiously, the window panes were far easier to see out of than into. Elongated will-o'-wisps waltzed across the flat black surface of the swamp. They appeared luminous yellow at the center with a tinge of blue at their edges. According to folklore, will-o'-wisps are ethereal sprites carrying wisps of light to guide their flight. In many Earth cultures, sighting such a creature is considered misfortunate. That's because they're said to harbinger death and other bad news.

This is all malarky, of course. The more likely explanations for such phenomena include marsh gas—perfectly normal, perfectly natural. I mean, hell, I get swamp gas every time I eat Karen's homemade roast beest—her spelling not mine—based on her own personal recipe. Not only does this beest not taste anything remotely like the real stuff, i.e. real meat from a real meat-based critter, but it never fails to give me the worst swamp gas this side of...well, this side of the Atchafalaya Swamp. Not that this was a confession I'd make to Karen, not even on my death bed.

Then there's the feu follet, Louisiana's very own homegrown version of the will-o'-wisp. Some claim these swamp faeries are the spirits of deceased loved ones. Others claim they lure children to their doom and suck their blood. Delectable? I think not. Detestable was the word for that practice. What sort of sick minds come up with such theories? Taken from the French, feu follet means marsh fire or, as some prefer, crazy fire. I'm in the crazy fire camp. Because that's what it was: crazy.

I'd even accept that those will-o'-wisps cavorting outside were the result of a chemiluminescence process. The swamp was nothing but a chemical dump, after all. Why shouldn't it produce some will-o'-wisps for our entertainment?

Now, as to why several of these spritely apparitions appeared to be looking at me and pointing mocking fingers at me, and two others approached the same window I was peering out and were now making hideous grinning faces at me...well, I had no answer for this. Not even a half-assed hypothesis. Which is weird, because half-assed hypotheses are a specialty of mine.

I hurriedly pulled the curtains closed—before these natural phenomena upset me further—and moved closer to the desk. A thick black leather-bound book filled with colorful inked illustrations on yellowed parchment sat open on the desk. The script was written in a language I'd never seen before so I had no idea what any of the words meant.

I flipped to the book's cover. The title was written in English. It read: *Unholy Magick and the Application of Vodou, written by Papa Lafitte.*

Call it a hunch, but I doubted that the manuscript had ever hit the NYT bestseller's list.

I left the study and proceeded slowly through the poorly-lit corridors that wound this way and that. I discovered a kitchen with a wood-burning stove and an actual icebox—remnants of a time long past. How old was this house?

What I did not find was Daniel or any other sign of a living being.

I decided to search upstairs next and proceeded up a steep stairway with tall risers and narrow boards that complained with my every step. The corridor at the top seemed to stretch to infinity to both my left and right. An impossibility, I know, but that didn't make it any less real. I twisted the iron handle of the first door to my right...and stepped into a nightmare.

The room I entered was maybe 40 feet long, 25 feet wide, and another 40 feet high. Rough-hewn wooden rafters thick as my waist strutted across the vaulted ceiling. There wasn't a single window. No one was seeing in or out. Curious.

Deep gray paneling clung to the walls like skin. Large glass jars, shaped like opaque coke bottles but ten times as big, hung upside down from the ceiling, suspended on thick hemp ropes. One after the other, all along the length of each wall. Dozens of them.

Recalling Amil's words, I wondered if these might be spirit bottles. Jumbo-sized. Or did this old house's occupant have an unquenchable thirst for sickly-sweet soda pop?

A glowing globe in the center of the ceiling provided a soft, if unsettling, light. Through the milky glass of the bottles, I discerned movement. The disembodied spirits of the dead?

I walked to the center of the room and turned slowly in a circle, taking it all in. The sudden stench of sulfur assaulted my nostrils. Where had it come from? I sniffed my armpits. I had been slugging around in a warm swamp bath, after all. But I didn't smell any better or worse than usual.

THUMP!

I spun on my heels. A naked 8-foot tall being with fiery red hair, broad bony shoulders, jaundiced skin, and a toad-like appearance loomed over me, having alit from the ceiling. Pointed 4-inch yellow teeth seemed to be sizing me up. The creature hissed and rolled out its wide, warty vermillion tongue like a welcome mat. I caught a glimpse of a bloated fat toad squatting under that awful tongue as if trying to keep out of the rain.

I took a step back, more to escape the godawful smell than out of a sense of caution. The shape-changing Fleek, now wearing the guise of the Nikker of human myth, turned adroitly on its damp webbed feet. Massive legs held it only semi-erect and still it was far taller than me at my best.

"Welcome, Pazu," the Fleek drawled with a pronounced lisp. It rolled its pudgy tongue over its thick lips and composed something probably meant to be a smile but came out as an imitation of a festering, open flesh wound. "I have been waiting for you."

"Sorry I kept you," I said. "I guess your invitation got lost in the mail. Next time, shoot me a text."

Those oversized toady eyes glistened. "Ah, the Pazu. Always with the jokes." The Fleek clenched its fists, opened its hands, clenched them again. The purplish fingers had hooked talons and were as fat as Italian sausages. I knew from experience, and the Pazu history books, that despite its oafish and flabby appearance, Fleek were incredibly powerful.

On the plus side, from my perspective at least, they were also incredibly stupid.

"Oh, look, your shoe's untied," I said, pointing to its feet.

The Fleek's eyes remained glued on me.

Okay, so they're not *that* stupid.

"I suppose I have you to thank for my presence here," I said.

Its grin cut a gash across its toadish face. "I see you're not quite as stupid as you appear."

As you can see, Pazu and Fleek hold similar opinions of each other.

That's because they're too stupid to realize how much smarter and how vastly superior we are to them. In every way.

In a flash, the Fleek threw out its long, crooked arm and punched me in the jaw. I spun in the air and flew across the room, coming to an abrupt and painful—and I admit ungraceful—landing near a cold and barren stacked-stone fireplace that took up a third of the far wall and was tall enough for me to stand upright inside.

I saw stars—none that I recognized.

I crawled to my feet and rubbed my throbbing jaw. I hadn't seen that coming in time… Okay, maybe Fleek do have a trick or two up their proverbial sleeves. Not that they ever wore clothes, to my knowledge.

"This planet isn't big enough for the two of us," said the Fleek.

"With that fat head of yours, is any planet big enough for you?" I replied.

That earned me another swat.

I staggered to my feet and considered my next move. I was tired of being a Fleek punching bag. It was time for some role reversal.

"On your knees, Pazu!"

"I don't think so." My head throbbed and my vision wasn't so good but this Fleek was dead meat—or toad or whatever the hell you want to call Fleek flesh. Hell, at this point, mad as I was, I'd even call it *roast meet à la Karen.*

"I command you make your obeisance. Your soul belongs to Ofeez now!"

"What's that? You say you have fleas?"

Ofeez the Fleek clapped his hands mightily to the accompaniment of a thunderous boom. The bottles hanging from the rafters rattled, shook, and swayed ominously.

I looked up just in time to see one of those suspended bottles falling rapidly from the ceiling. In the blink of any eye—human, not toad—the bottle dropped over me, swallowing me up inside. My world turned milky white. I've said it before and I'll say it again.

Life. Is. A. Bitch.

17

I slammed my fists against the smooth inside surface of my prison. My punches proved useless against the thick glass or whatever exotic material these bottles were composed of. I know, never end a sentence with a preposition... Well, I've got some advice for you, too. Never end your life trapped inside a giant coke bottle.

I glanced downward. Ofeez the Fleek leered up at me. Criminy, how I hate Fleeks. My human guise was doing me little good. In fact, it was holding me back. Figuring I didn't have much to fear out here in the middle of the boonies in terms of detection—I mean, it was highly unlikely that a human would stumble upon me, all bound up as I was sitting inside a giant coke bottle suspended from the rafters of the Prince of the Alligators' love shack/Nikker's lair/Fleek's fortress—I closed my eyes and focused all my energies on becoming me. A Pazu from the planet Zyxltl marooned on Earth.

Certain...faculties of mine I can only utilize in my true form. However, when I do utilize these natural talents, I know I run the risk of detection by those, such as the ARC, the CIA and all the myriad other secretive official and unofficial alien hunters on the planet who'd like nothing more than to trap me in their own glass jars and study me for the next hundred years or so.

But what choice did I have? Risk being detected by my enemies? Or stay trapped in this glass like a toy ship in a bottle?

To take a line from the late-great philosopher-singer—and I'm talking Elvis "The King" Presley, not Bob "the harmonica-playing" Dylan—it was now or never.

Within moments, my body began shifting, rearranging... I could feel myself coming into my own familiar skin... It had been so long, too long. It felt warm and comforting, and I imagined this might be how a butterfly felt being set free of its chrysalis.

What do I look like in my true Pazu form?

Imagine a cross between a Neandertal, a Troglodyte, and a cartoon Martian. Got the picture? Yeah, you're not even close... I can't really begin to describe myself.

My fingers tingled. My entire body tingled. My brain spiraled...

And I woke up in the Coliseum. The fucking Roman Coliseum. And that's in Rome! Italy! Some Americans might know where that is. Most Italians do. Yeah, yeah, don't get all offended. Don't take anything I say personally. That's a slam at the educational system, not your innate human intelligence, such as it is.

And don't even get me started on your politics. How is it that a small portion of people insist on telling the rest of you what to think and how to live? And how is it that the rest of you humans just sit around wanting somebody to tell you what to think and how to live your lives? Beats the heck out of me... baffling.

Then again, remember, I'm from the universe next door. The wrong side of the galactic tracks, you might say. We take what you might call a more...lazy-fair attitude. We leave the whole controlling and manipulating stuff to others...like cats.

So what do you expect from me?

My advice? Just ignore me. That's what Karen does. She calls it her "survival mechanism."

Anyway, while I was busy cogitating, some big oaf in a chariot being pulled by a team of six impossibly large horses, and clutching a wooden shield and wielding a sword, was barreling towards me at top speed. What the hell was he doing here? Didn't he know that chariot races were reserved for the Circus Maximus next door?

Shit shit shit.

That's another annoying thing about Fleek. They have this way of manipulating time and space—distorting it in ways it was never meant to be.

And that can be quite a royal pain in the Pazu ass.

The freaking Fleek had not only caught me off-guard and somehow trapped me, he'd managed to manipulate me to another place…and another time!

Fleek may be stupider than dirt but it seemed they were capable of learning a trick or two. I don't know who said you can't teach an old Fleek a new trick, but when I found him/her/it, I was going to kick his/her/its butt.

So, I considered my situation.

I'd been dropped into a live-action version of the epic cinematic masterpiece *Spartacus*—historical discrepancies and all.

The Fleek had, improbable as it seemed, managed to block my powers…for the moment.

And I was in some weird pseudo-past, about to be trammeled and trampled by a four-abreast team of foaming-at-the-mouth Berber horses. After which, I imagined this pseudo-Spartacus or phoney-Flamma—Flamma was an exceptionally successful practitioner of the gladiatorial arts in ancient Roman times—would try his best to fillet this precious Pazu.

My throat was dry. I'd had nothing to eat or drink—discounting the involuntary quantities of swamp I'd imbibed—since sharing coffee and po'boys with Amil. Worse still, I craved bourbon and I needed a smoke. Sadly, neither has been invented yet.

As for Amil… I wondered what had become of the poor guy. Gator fodder? Would I ever see him or Karen again? Would I ever find Fu Chun and collect my fee?

Would the real Elvis resurrect himself simply so he could kick fake Daniel "Elvis" Hernandez's ass?

Gasps erupted from the crammed seats of the Coliseum. A few laughs, too. Jeers, if I'm honest. Because there I stood in all my Pazu glory looking like an alien who'd just dropped in on them in the middle of their spectacle.

We were playing to all of Rome, so it appeared. Forget SRO, folks were balancing drunkenly atop the columns here. This was a rowdy crowd too, no surprise given that the food and drink ran free and plenty.

Known to the ancient locals as the Flavian Amphitheater, Emperor Vespasian ordered construction of the iconic amphitheater in about 72 CE. Construction wrapped up around 80 CE or so, so I knew I was now parading around sometime after 80 CE. In true Roman pomp, a rhinoceros served as guest of honor at the Coliseum's grand opening celebration. The Coliseum got its name not from its colossal size but rather its proximity to the Colossus of Nero—itself a 98-foot tall bronze statue that Nero had ordered as a monument to himself, of course. And Karen thinks I've got an oversized ego!

The Coliseum stretches over 600 feet, could seat 50,000 or more, and included over 80 entrances—two reserved solely for the emperor and his retinue—for all those Romans to spill in and out of, while inside they watched all that blood getting spilled, both human and other Earthly beasts.

I leapt high in the air as the chariot rumbled over the spot where I'd been standing. The charioteer swore something in Latin, forced his team of horses to a stop and came charging again.

Up in the stands, the Emperor del giorno was shaking both hairy fists and yelling encouragement. And I knew he was not aiming his encouragement at me. A very gaunt, very tall man sat quietly beside him. I had a hunch this was my shape-changing, blood-lusting Fleek, offering his own encouragement, no doubt.

As the sturdy brown Berber horses came galumphing towards me, getting so close that I could feel their foul breath on my cheeks, I twisted rapidly to one side. I snatched the 2-foot long sword from the gladiator's hand and yanked on the blade with all my might. The sharp edges of the blade barely tickled my flesh. Having returned to Pazu form, I was safe from harm. Call it telepathy, call it mind over matter, it's our ability to control objects with electromagnetic impulses.

Now that he'd dismounted, my impulse was to lop this gladiator's head off. Having leapt adroitly from his chariot, he stormed towards me bearing another, longer sword that some dumbass in the stands had flung to him.

The broad-chested gladiator's dark-olive skin glistened. His long, long black hair and unkempt beard fluttered. He had the devil in his eyes. He wore a suit of light armor and bore gold bands wrapped around each bulging biceps.

The crowd chanted his name, fanning his murderous fire: "Flamma! Flamma! Flamma!"

I congratulated myself on getting his name right.

Flamma slammed to a stop in front of me and roared something Latin—but it's all Greek to me. I don't think he was asking me if I'd like the gnocchi or the spaghetti for my entrée. Up close, he smelled of honey, virgin olive oil—though I had a hunch no virgin was safe around this guy—and stale aromatic white wine.

The broad sword swung in an arc towards my head. I raised my shorter sword—well, it was actually his original sword—and countered.

CLANG!

The audience went wild. Everyone came to their feet and shouted. Mostly for his victory and my death.

Why am I always the underdog?

A vibration wormed its way through my fingertips, across my wrists, and up my arms. My teeth rattled.

Somebody yelled, "Die, Pazu!" And there was only one somebody whom that could be. I risked a glance into the stands and saw Ofeez smirking at me.

Taking advantage of my being momentarily distracted, Flamma thwacked me ferociously in the face with his heavy shield.

I spun and landed face down in the dirt. As he aimed his leather-sandaled foot at my head like a footballer, I rolled over and grabbed the hilt of my short sword, which I was surprised to see I still held onto, and jammed it with all my strength upward.

The sword pierced Flamma's exposed stomach. He roared, as much, I suspected, from fear as from pain as from surprise.

Then…to my surprise…Flamma morphed into Karen Dalton!

She clutched her belly, blood spilled forth and she screamed in pain and fear. "Ed! What have you done?!"

Still on my knees, I scrambled and backed up in horror, staring at the sword buried to the hilt in Flamma's—or was that Karen's?—gut!

The bloody hilt stuck out at me like an indictment. "Murderer!" it cried.

I wiped my eyes…

And Karen turned into a giant lion. The angry lion roared at me like something out of an MGM movie. The sword—aka murder weapon—fell uselessly to the ground. There wasn't a speck of blood on it.

Have I mentioned that I hate cats? No matter how big or how puny, I can't bear the furry things. And they weren't helping their case when they were trying to eat me like this one was now doing.

On the subject of cats, I've said it before and I'll say it again: cats aren't human. They aren't of this Earth either. They are aliens, just like me. Why do you think there are so many times when you call and call their names and you just can't find them anywhere? Because they've transported their cat-selves back to their home planet of Elwokimali, where they go regularly to report on homo sapiens activity. Cats have their own agenda, and that's to rule the Earth like they rule so many other planets spread across the Milky Way. To them, the universe is nothing but a giant cat box meant for them to piss and play in.

I squeezed my eyes shut and wrapped my hands around the lion's muscular neck as best I could. I fought my way into its brain. I didn't want to kill the angry dumb beast—besides, hadn't I killed it once already? I wanted to quiet it, to tame it before it could take a chunk out of me. The big feline twitched and, with a snort, settled back on its brawny haunches.

Sounds somewhat of a non sequitur to say it, but the big African cat sat there in the dirt of the Coliseum looking at me with what I can only describe as big puppy dog eyes.

"Good boy," I said, patting it on the nose and rising to my feet. The crowd booed. The anger and disappointment at having been cheated of blood, drove the crowd of more than 50,000 wild. The angry booing echoed in every direction. The force of their emotions was so loud and hard that I could feel it in my bones.

"Tough crowd," I said to the lion. On a certain level, I knew exactly how they felt. They'd given up their normal grind and had come here for the day. They wanted a show. They craved blood. Would even an appearance by Elvis in his prime appease these savage beasts?

"You killed me, Ed. Stabbed me to death," said my seated new friend in a voice that sounded exactly like Karen's. The lion looked down at its chest. "How could you?"

18

"So," demanded Karen the…lion?…person?

Wait, she appeared human again, toxic-dump leprechaun green hair and all—as decidedly not human as that made her look. "What's the plan now, Ed? I'm dying here."

"Well…" I rose on unsteady legs and dusted off my trousers, dismayed to see the relatively-new pair now showed ragged tears at both knees. I know youth, Western youth, in particular, consider holes in the knees of one's pants something worth paying extra for, but I, and perhaps those persons far less fortunate, might not consider this a badge of honor but rather the results of poverty. Plus, Karen had bought me these trousers and, now dying or not, I felt guilty for ruining them. I was beginning to get ticked off.

The roar of the crowd beat against my eardrums.

"Just how do you intend to get us out of this mess?" continued Karen, using both hands to hold her guts in, blood oozing slowly through her fingers.

"Not to worry," I replied. "I have a plan," I lied. A big fat lie.

"And that is?"

I watched uneasily as her intestines squirmed between her fingers like slimy eels. "First, answer a question for me," I said, as a delay tactic.

"What's that?" By the sound of her voice, Karen was getting annoyed. I couldn't blame her. I'd be annoyed too if I was standing in the middle of the Roman Coliseum with my guts spilling out.

Nonetheless, I asked my question. "Are you really Karen?"

Her voice rose in pitch as Karen said, "Of course, I'm Karen!

Who else would I be!?" She looked at me funny. "Are you okay, Ed? Cuz you don't look so good."

"I'm fine...given the circumstances." I refrained from telling her that she wasn't looking so good herself. I've learned the hard way that she gets quite peeved anytime I tell her that.

As I struggled for a string of appropriate, even encouraging —if disingenuous—words to say, Karen collapsed to the ground on her stomach. Her body went still. Her arms stretched out, her legs together—ending up in the shape of a human cross.

In a matter of seconds, flesh turned paler and paler. Skin and hair decomposed and the breeze wafting through the airy Coliseum swept the detritus of her physical being away. All that was left was bones—206 bones, not that I was counting, of all shapes and sizes.

A large, bony hand fell on my shoulder.

I spun around for a look-see. The big dumb Fleek loomed over me. The dolt was more annoying than a blood-thirsty flea on a mutt.

"Off we go," said Ofeez. He bowed to the Emperor high up in the stands, munching on a leg of mutton in one hand, and clutching a mug of wine in his other hand. The Emperor nodded, set down his wine and ran his now free hand along the milky inner thigh of a seductively-clad nubile girl tucked up against him.

"Where to?" I asked, nearly too stunned to think. Was Karen Dalton really gone? Had I failed to save her?

Ofeez toed Karen's ribcage. "We can't leave these bones lying around here forever, can we?"

The Fleek snapped his fingers and two ragged-clothed slaves with bare feet, pulling a wooden cart, ran over. They quickly scooped up Karen's bones and laid them on the bed of the cart. And off they went through the nearest exit.

Having nothing better to do at the moment and not wanting to leave Karen alone in the Fleek's clutches—even if she was now nothing more than a pile of bones—I decided to go along without a fight or even a word of protest.

19

We left the outer defensive walls of Rome behind and soon found ourselves in the fertile and picturesque Italian countryside under a brilliant blue sky. A land of farms and peasant villages. I'd grown numb to the disturbing sound of Karen's bones rattling against the wooden bottom of the cart, and barely took note of its absence when our small party came to a halt.

The slaves pushing the cart carrying Karen's bones led the way into a rustic stone cottage with a narrow door, one window opening, and a simple thatched roof, that was tucked into a hillside surrounded by olive orchards and a small number of orange trees.

We followed.

The interior of the small pitch-roofed cottage held a rough-hewn wooden table and three simple wooden rustic chairs. A gray stone altar hugged the longest wall opposite the door. A monk in a hooded black robe greeted us, his back to the altar, his eyes on us. That is, his eye sockets. Because this monk was deader than dead.

This was the skeleton of a monk that I was looking at. Its yellowed worn teeth revealed a hard life and welcomed me with a lifeless grin. Bent, arthritic fingers poked from the sleeves of its robe. A black cowl with a pointy peak covered its skull. Hobnailed leather sandals kept his foot bones together.

"Consider yourself privileged, Pazu," said Ofeez. "For you are one of the few of the living to see my crypt."

"Your crypt?" I scratched the top of my head.

Ofeez beamed proudly. "The Christians have their crypts...

and I have mine."

"Sure," I quipped, "who doesn't want their own personal crypt?" Anybody in their right mind, that's who. Of course, Fleek are crazy. Everybody in the universe knows that.

And Ofeez appeared to be King of the Crazy.

Was this due to his centuries living on Earth?

Was this to be my fate? To end up as crazy as a Fleek should I stay stranded on Earth for as long as he had?

Not a pleasant thought.

"I must have someplace to store the bones of those whose souls I have taken."

"Like Karen's?" I cast a glance at Karen's bundle of bones atop the two-wheeled cart. The two slaves stood beside it, waiting for orders. Occasionally, they cast uneasy glances at me. Don't forget, at that moment, I looked like me, a Pazu...not you, a Homo sapiens.

"The young woman?"

"Yeah. What's going to happen to her now?" A quick mental inventory assured me that all 206 bones were present. Good, we hadn't lost any in transit. When I put her back together— assuming I could—it would be helpful to have all the pieces.

And I knew I was going to have to try to reassemble and revive her...somehow. Not sure exactly how... It's not like I had access to any state-of-the-art Pazu medical facilities, and even if I had...what were my odds of success? But what's the point of shooting, if you aren't shooting for the moon?

Ofeez studied me. Outside, a pair of wild dogs howled sorrowfully. "What do you care for her or what happens to her soul? She's merely a human, not worthy even of one so lowly as yourself, Pazu." Every time he called me Pazu, it sounded like he was calling me a piece of dog shit.

Ofeez gestured and the scrawnier of the two slaves leapt into action. Grabbing a wooden handle, he raised a wooden hatch on the floor, revealing a steep packed-dirt ramp that led down to the center of the Earth.

I peered inside. Would we find Jules Verne down there

cranking out his latest novel? Like so many in the 19th century, Verne did believe the Earth was hollow, didn't he? And that dinosaurs from the dawn of time mingled with Man's early ancestors as well as a super-advanced civilization of androids determined to keep their presence a secret whilst they studied Earth in all its many facets from geology to flora and fauna? Fauna, that includes you people, too.

It is all true, of course, but you didn't hear it from me.

With the two slaves each grabbing a handle, they guided the cart downward, struggling to hold on to it as gravity tried to force them to let go and for the cart to move faster. Gravity can be a hungry beast at times, demanding to be fed.

Some one-hundred feet or so down, with no light but that from the trapdoor above, the slaves brought the cart to a halt. Ofeez and I halted, too. Without a word, the two slaves busied themselves lighting torches mounted on wooden poles along the walls. Charred stone and soot told me that they'd done this endless times in the past.

With the slaves grabbing the cart once again, we marched on. It was cold and the light was vague. Turning a sharp corner, we came to a second stop.

The slaves lit more smoky torches. And a cavernous chamber revealed itself.

"My cathedral," boasted Ofeez, waving a hand in the chilled air. The room was a good 30 ft high and close to one hundred feet across. I couldn't begin to imagine the manhours and manpower it had taken to create it.

Indeed, compared to the tiny altar in the farmhouse above, this cavern housed an altar worthy of St. Peter's Basilica. Sure, it was a sick, demonic one, but it was a cathedral of the Fleek's own making, of that there was no doubt.

Bones bones bones. Heaps of bones piled everywhere. From floor to ceiling. Covering every wall. Some were nothing more than stacks of femurs and tibias. On the far wall, behind an altar built of a variety of leg and arm bones, he'd ordered his stooges to create a wall of winged devils using human skulls with pelvic bones on each side, like wings, giving them the appearance of flying skulls. They were scarier than those flying monkeys in the Wizard of Oz.

Would they take flight? Dance around the room for the amusement of Ofeez?

A tunnel at the opposite end continued into the darkness.

"Many leagues of catacombs continue onward and downward," Ofeez explained, as if reading my thoughts. "Don't worry, we shall find a perfect spot for you and your Earth woman to rest for Eternity."

"Gee, thanks."

I know things did not seem to be auguring well for me but it's not for nothing that I consider myself the Greatest Pazu Detective on Earth. I mean, I'm no Sam Spade but I'm no garden variety spade either. I am capable of more than digging up a few pesky weeds.

From what I remembered from my reading of your histories, early Christians originally referred to the catacombs as necropolises, cities of the dead. Similar but not quite the same as cemeteries—from the Greek koimētērion and meaning dormitory for the dead, because a cemetery is considered a place to sleep… Until the Resurrection, that is, then it's wakey-wakey time.

The catacombs are chockfull with Christians of all shapes and sizes, running the gamut from patricians to paupers, martyrs to pontiffs to saints. There's a lot of room underground to be chiseled out and used to host the eternally sleeping, if you're so inclined.

Personally, this particular City of the Dead could more aptly be named the City of Dread.

"So," I dithered, stalling for time, "you built this catacomb to house your bone collection?"

"Yes." Ofeez leaned against the altar, stroking a blotchy yellow-brown femur.

"You're the creature that humans call the Nikker."

Anger flashed across the Fleek's face. "Such a horrible name to call me." He softened. "Yet, I suppose it suits. And humans must have their names."

"You're responsible for countless deaths since your arrival on Earth."

"Countless?" Ofeez shrugged. "I could provide an exact number, if I cared to. I like to keep track of my...possessions."

"Souls, you mean. Souls and bones."

"Souls and bones, yes. That is what I collect."

I darkened. "That's sick."

"Sick? I call to them and they come. What could be more natural? They do not suffer."

"Except that they're dead and their souls are trapped forever."

"It is our way."

"It's not my way," I replied. While Ofeez was busy patting himself on the back and admiring his cruel handiwork, I'd taken a good look at my surroundings.

This was the time for action.

I'd already lost Karen, so I had nothing to lose.

With the two slaves waiting obediently, with arms dangling limp beside the cart, I raced to the wall and yanked down one of the flickering torches. The torches, crafted from the stalks of the dried mullein plant, had been used by humans for a thousand years. In some cultures, they were known as witch's or old hag's torches. I dubbed mine the Ofeez-you're-fucking-dead torch.

I tossed the lit torch into the open top of an amphora resting at the side of the altar. By the smell emanating from it, I was fairly sure the clay pot was filled with olive oil. What it was there for, I had no clue. Maybe the Fleek used it in his rituals, maybe he bathed in it. Maybe dipped his feet in the oil and insisted his slaves massage his long fat tootsies. All I knew was that olive oil burned great.

And if I was wrong? Well, I'd cross that Rubicon when I came to it. Et tu, Ed?

I didn't have long to wait. Maybe milliseconds. Maybe

eternity.

WHOOSH!

See?

Flames burst from the amphora. Angry roars burst from Ofeez. Frightened mewls burst from the two near-useless slaves.

Ofeez lunged for me. I lunged for the lit amphora. He met me at the same time I met the amphora and wrapped my arms around it.

I squeezed with all my strength and the clay pot burst, shattering in a million pieces and sending hot burning oil everywhere, mostly on Ofeez and me, because we were at ground zero.

Fortunately for me, but not so much for the big dumb Fleek, I am relatively impervious to flames. Fleeks, on the other hand...well, let's just say that fire is not their friend. It isn't for nothing that they lurk in and near the water and lure their victims to it.

Ofeez relaxed his grip on me and jumped to his feet. He yelled at his slaves to put him out but they just looked at him stupidly while he burned—and fumed, I might add.

Olive oil not only burns well, it's pretty hard to rub off. I mean, it is oily, right?

Meanwhile, the cathedral filled with dense, acrid smoke. Olive oil also burns quite smoky. The slaves fell to the ground in helpless coughing fits. Ofeez's skin blackened and bubbled up. No doubt he'd soon be dead.

Good riddance.

From above, I heard the distant sound of the frightened dogs. Inside, I heard the very nearby sound of a Fleek dying a slow and painful death.

Did I say good riddance? Well, good riddance again.

With the catacomb burning and Ofeez dying, it was, to use an expression popularized in that classic and long-running 1960s TV western Gunsmoke: Time to get out of Dodge.

I grabbed the pushcart still bearing Karen's bones, which itself was burning, and raced for the exit.

20

"The house is on fire! Run! Run! Hurry! Hurry" shouted an unseen distorted woman's voice.

I burst through the floor hatch and spilled out into the stone house that sat above the catacomb, keeping its demented secrets from prying eyes. Smoke followed, filling the small space. The gray smoke that followed me was so thick that I was positive I'd heard the dead skeleton monk coughing and choking in dismay as much as I was.

I flew out the door… And came to a screeching halt. So did the pushcart, of course, having no choice. The bones, all 206 of them, not constrained by my and the cart's stopping, continued on, following a trajectory upward and outward.

Shit!

My jaw dropped.

I was not, as expected, standing outside a small farmhouse located outside Ancient Rome, I was standing in the great macabre chamber of the Atchafalaya Swamp house, the home I'd always think of as the Palace of the Gators! Sure enough, the screeching woman was right, the walls and draperies blazed. Above me, suspended from the rafters, the human-sized milky glass bottles whirled and twirled, and rattled and raged like angry hornets.

"We've got to go! Run! Run!" persisted the unseen woman.

I glanced over my shoulder to see just who was doing all the yelling. Weren't things chaotic enough without some mad woman shouting at me?

"Lola Davies!?" I cried. Although she looked much the worse for wear, her face smeared with tears and smoke, her clothes—the same clothes she'd been clad in the last time I'd seen her—tattered, damp and muddied, I instantly recognized the spirit medium.

What she was doing here and where she'd come from, I'd no idea, nor did I have time to ask. Overhead, a giant inverted bottle burst apart as a result of the intense heat of the flame. Glass shards rained down on us. With a horrible cry, a bluish spirit raced out, flung itself at us, spun 360 degrees, and flew for the exit—all the while taking care to stay clear of the deadly orange flames.

"That voice!" Lola Davies snatched my hand. "Ed? Is that you?" She rubbed her raw eyes.

Oops, I was looking like a Pazu. I shuttered my eyes and quickly corrected the situation, returning to my human disguise. "Yes, it's me."

"Oh!" Lola Davies blinked. "We've got to go!" She pulled me towards the door.

"Not without Karen," I insisted.

"Karen? Karen Dalton?"

"Yes."

"I don't understand. Where is she? Is she here?" Lola Davies' head spun around. "Last I saw her, she was in her hotel room."

I frowned. "Excuse me?"

"In her hotel room…at the Bourbon Orleans."

As if an invitation to the other spirit bottles, two more burst. A heartbeat later, the staccato of bottle after bottle exploding like machine gun fire filled the chamber. Blue spirits streaked between us.

I plucked up the nearest bone, a female ulna. "Then who does this belong to?"

Lola raised her brow. "I really have no idea."

Shit on a stick. Ofeez had really had me going. He should consider himself lucky he was dead…because, if he wasn't, I'd have killed him with my bare hands. Whatever version of hell that big dumb Fleek was stewing in now, I hoped he choked on a chicken bone.

I dropped the unidentified flying ulna to the ground and we hurriedly escaped the black house even as the windows burst and the ceiling continued collapsing around our ears.

"Let me out! Let me out!" The door opposite the front study rattled. "Hey! Whoever's out there! Don't fuckin' leave me here!" Sounds of feet kicking the door from the inside. "Let me out! Please!"

I twisted the skeleton key in the lock. Amil tumbled out, frightened and confused.

"Ed!" He blinked. "And…aren't you Lola Davies?"

The spiritualist nodded and took his hand and mine. By the meager light of the slender moon, we sprinted to the dock. One after the other, we leapt aboard the nearest airboat. The airboat wobbled and bobbled under our weight.

Lola Davies brought the beast to life. The propeller roared and spun, shooting a tornado of air behind it that agitated the black water, whipping it into a frenzy. Good thing she knew how to operate the thing, because I'd had no idea. Amil collapsed on the metal deck.

"Ed, untie the boat!" Lola Davies cried from the wheel.

As I dove for the ropes and struggled to unknot them, I thought I heard a werewolf bay…but I watch a lot, a lot, of old monster movies on TV, so I recognized that might, just might, be my imagination.

I glanced at Amil. He looked a wreck. Then again, he was lucky to be alive. We all were. Did that include Karen? Was she really safe back at the hotel?

Reality can be slippery as a handful of wet kittens. I didn't know what to think or who to believe.

I looked over my shoulder at the house ablaze as it receded in the distance. I hoped Karen was alive and waiting back at the hotel, because I'd left all those bones back inside that burning mansion. Too late to go back for them now.

With uncertainty and doubts clouding my thoughts, I turned my gaze off into the distance ahead of us. Civilization, such as you could call groups of humans living amongst themselves in so-called harmony, was out there somewhere. So long as we survived the gators, we'd be home safe.

I settled down next to Amil and assured him that he was safe and that everything was going to be okay. "How did you get locked in that closet, anyway?"

Amil shrugged and clutched himself for warmth. "No freaking idea. One minute I was sitting in my truck and the next thing I know I'm out at that creepy house with some-some thing hovering over me like I was going to be its supper!" He paused, licked his lower lip before continuing. "Then when that monster —I thought I was hallucinating!—threw my ass in the closet!" He grabbed me. "Thank you, thank you, thank you! I thought I was a dead man!"

I assured him he wasn't and he settled down. Before long, he fell asleep. I stepped carefully over the vibrating deck and sidled up next to Lola Davies. I admired the way she deftly handled the airboat. We barely hit a bump. I had done far worse trying to steer a slow-moving kayak through these treacherous waters filled with hidden roots and logs and teeming with alligators. "You're pretty good with watercraft."

"Thanks." Lola Davies smiled at me. "I grew up in the bayous. They are as familiar to me as the palm of my hand."

"You ride out in this thing?"

"No, I arrived on a pirogue."

"A what?"

"A pirogue—pero. You might think of it as a skiff or even a canoe. Usually pointed at both ends. Flat-bottomed. Perfect for the marshes and swamps that all but consume us here." She patted the helm. "I thought the airboat would better suit our escape. I'll return for my pero later…if it hasn't been destroyed or broken free and drifted off."

"Thanks for showing up when you did. I wasn't sure what I was going to do next." Other than improvise, which I seemed forced to do with disturbing regularity, as Karen frequently reminded me.

What can I say? I'm sort of a fly-by-the-seat-of-my-pants

kind of Pazu. So I make no apologies. Then again, that attitude had gotten me stuck on Earth.

"Some things are meant to be," Lola Davies said rather enigmatically.

"What were you doing there? You know Ursula is dead, murdered, right?"

Lola frowned, lifted one hand from the helm. "Yes, poor Ursula. May her soul find peace." She kissed her fingers and saluted the heavens. There was a long silence, except for the thrum of the airboat and the night-loving insects, before she spoke again. "The spirits told me I might find Ursula's killer in that place." More long silence, accompanied by a troubled expression. "You know, it's funny. I've been to the Atchafalaya dozens of times…I've never seen such a house." She shook her head. "I would not have thought it possible. Not out here."

"Yeah, that makes two of us." I explained what I'd found inside. I did not explain about my visit to Ancient Rome and the Coliseum…nor the Nikker's catacomb.

She might think I was deranged.

"Where were you? I mean, where have you been since Ursula was murdered?" I asked. "You must know the police are looking for you. It's been all over the news."

"Yes, yes, I was aware. This might sound silly, maybe even wrong, but…honestly?"

"Sure, why not?"

"I've been in hiding. When I found Ursula behind the counter…dead…"

"You found her?"

"Yes. I knew instantly that she was dead. There was no saving her. And I felt a presence, a terribly, terribly evil and powerful presence." Lola Davies looked at me for forgiveness. "So I fled." She hung her head.

"Hey, I understand. Nobody wants to die before their time."

"Thank you." She stroked the back of my arm. "I told myself, made a vow, that I would do what I could do avenge Ursula. Trap her killer. I consulted every spirit that I could, made every sacrifice—"

"And that led you to the Atchafalaya?"

"Yes."

"Interesting..." More than interesting. I was impressed. Whether she realized it or not, had magic powers or not, Lola Davies had managed to stumble on the truth.

"You know..." Lola Davies began. The airboat's engine stuttered a moment before continuing on its merry way.

"Yes?"

"For a second there, when I first saw you... You looked very different."

"All that smoke and adrenaline," I said with a grin. "It does stuff to your head."

"Yes, I suppose it does."

"Did you happen to see anyone else inside?" I wondered what had happened to Daniel Hernandez. Had he burnt to a crisp, too? Not that I'd shed a tear over that.

"No, not a soul. The house was burning when I arrived. I tied up and ran inside to see if I could help whoever might be trapped within. That's when I saw...you. Now, it's your turn. What were you doing there, Ed?"

"Long story."

"So give me the short version."

"Okay." I felt I owed her some explanation. She had shown up in the nick of time. And if it wasn't for her, I'd be having to row that damnable kayak back to civilization all on my own right now—all while lugging he-ain't-heavy, he's-my Amil along for the ride. "After what you told me and Karen, I got this tickle in my brain. Call it a hunch, but I had this feeling I should come out to the Atchafalaya and have a poke around."

"And you? Did you see anyone or discover anything that will help you find this young man you are seeking?" asked Lola.

I paused for a deep breath and some deep thinking. "Maybe."

"Maybe?"

"It's too soon to say for certain, but there is one thing I can tell you for certain. And I think you're going to like it."

"Oh, what's that?"

"You're not going to have to worry about the Nikker any longer."

"Oh?" Lola Davies cocked her head, looked at me funny. "Tell me, did the Nikker murder Ursula?"

"I believe so," I said with a nod in the affirmative.

After a moment, Lola Davies said, "Then let Ursula's spirit find peace."

"I'll second that," I said, confident that Ursula wouldn't end up trapped in a giant coke bottle while her bones lie in repose in Ofeez's private catacomb through All Eternity.

"I have some information for you, too," she teased.

"Oh?"

"Yes, I believe I may know where Fu Chun is."

I couldn't help grinning. "That is good news. Where is he? No offense but I'll be happy to get out of Louisiana and back to LA—not that I thought I'd ever be saying I was happy to be getting back to that city of the absurd."

I had visions of a new attraction there—a catacomb of its very own, featuring all the dead celebrities. If folks would go out of their way to look at a bunch of dumb stars planted in a sidewalk, how much might they be willing to pay to go visit the actual bones of their favorite singers, actors and social media addicts?

Lola Davies laughed. "Let me check something first. I'll get back to you later today." Midnight had come and gone. It was indeed a new day.

"Are you sure? Can't you tell me now? I'll sleep better."

"Be patient, Ed. This evening, I promise."

"Well…"

She suddenly cut the engine. The motor went silent and the fan blades stuttered to a stop. Quiet overcame us.

"What's up?" I asked as we coasted to a shadowy shore lined with trees and tall grasses. The airboat drifted slowly forward under its own momentum, hit the sandy slope and stopped.

"My truck's just ahead. I'll give you a ride back to the city."

"Great."

On the open deck, Amil stirred. "Are we there yet?" he mumbled.

We spilled out onto dry land where we discovered, as the spiritualist had promised, an old seafoam green Chevy pickup waiting for us. Lola Davies claimed the steering wheel. Amil and I squeezed into the warm cab beside her.

Lola dropped me off at the hotel. She promised to drop a drowsy Amil—I wondered if the poor guy had been drugged and that was responsible for his torpor—at his pad. She promised she'd be in touch with me later that day.

21

I stopped for a cup of free coffee and a lightly toasted poppy seed bagel in the lobby—I hadn't eaten or had anything to drink for hours, well, centuries, if you counted that stint I'd spent in Ancient Rome. I stuffed the bagel down quickly and rushed to the elevator drinking the last of my coffee. I found Karen up in our hotel room, notorious room 644. The sun was just pushing its way up into the sky. She lay alone on the bed, looking all bright and chipper—not dead at all.

No dead nuns swinging from the ceiling. No ghosts at all, at least not that I could see. Didn't mean they weren't there listening in.

Best of all, no Nikker cum Fleek, because I'd killed him. Put an end to the Nightmare on Nikker Street. Karma might be, as some say, a bitch but immolation? That'll kill you dead.

The bed looked awfully good and not just because Karen was laying in it. I felt like I hadn't slept in a million years.

"Hi, Ed! Where have you been?" Karen asked annoyingly nonchalantly. Because I had, after all, just gone to the ends of the Earth, okay, the Atchafalaya Swamp to rescue her and destroy the Fleek while I was at it.

The bedcovers rose up to Karen's waist. The semi-sheer lacy red peignoir that barely covered her from the belly button up, I admit, did something to dampen my annoyance with her.

"I've been looking everywhere for you," Karen continued. "I've got a lead on Fu."

The TV was on and airing a kid's cooking show, while an electronic notebook sat open in Karen's lap.

"Well?" She snapped her fingers. "What's wrong with you?

Why don't you say something?" Snap! Snap! "Hello, Earth to Ed, come in, Ed!"

I couldn't decide if Karen was a hallucination or figment of my imagination now or if she had been before and the Fleek had tricked me. Or…had Ofeez's death brought her back to life?

I've seen stranger things.

Had Karen been somehow resurrected? There was a lot I did not know about resurrections. Hell, there's a lot I don't know about Fleek. Still, my instincts told me that Ofeez had indeed managed to transport me back to Ancient Rome, which was where he'd created and maintained his personal crypt. Thank goodness, I'd managed to put an end to that. At least something good had come from this trip because, other than that, the trip and the case had been a complete bust so far.

All this thinking was making my head hurt. I grabbed the bourbon bottle off the dresser and poured some into my coffee cup. I poured some bourbon coffee down my throat and instantly felt a little better. I reached for a cigarette and lit up. That lit me up.

As for what was real and what wasn't and what I'd imagined was real? Well, I was going to have to give all that a lot of thought because I had no idea what the truth was.

And the truth is, I can't even swear that I believe there even is one real Truth. And that's no Lie.

What I did know for sure was that I was very glad that Karen was back… Assuming she'd ever been gone at all, that is.

See? It's complicated.

I added another splash of bourbon to my beverage. Drank it down. Smoked a second Camel. Tomorrow, when this was yesterday, I was gonna hate myself. But that was then, or will have been…and this was, is, now.

I sat my empty coffee cup on the dresser, chewed up my two Camel butts for dessert, and approached the bed. Karen turned to me. I took her wrist, felt her pulse. Yep, a beating heart, blood flowing. All perfectly natural. Although I was having a hard time NOT seeing her as a jumble of dry bones.

Karen pulled her hand away. "What are you doing? You're acting funny, even for you and that's saying something. What's wrong?"

I settled beside her. "Nothing. Just checking to see if you're real."

Karen rolled her eyes. "Seriously?"

"Seriously."

She kissed me long and hard. She pulled away. "Well?"

I pulled in a breath before managing to say. "I'd say that's about as real as it gets."

"Told you so." Karen shook her head and folded her notepad shut.

"What can I say? It's been a long night."

"Yeah, speaking of which, where the hell have you been?"

"Me? Looking for you. Where have you been? I haven't seen you since the night before last."

Karen furrowed her brow. "What. Are. You. Saying?"

"What am I saying? I'm saying I haven't laid eyes on you since you left with Daniel Hernandez the other night."

"Daniel Hernandez? Ick! What would I be doing leaving with Daniel Hernandez?" She kicked off the covers, revealing a well-toned pair of long bare legs that she proceeded to flop atop my own rather scrawny legs. Karen does not go to the gym. How does she stay fit? I asked her once and her answer was that she spent a lot of her time running around cleaning up my messes. So you could say she has me to thank for her excellent physical condition.

"Leaving where? Going where?" she pressed.

I took a deep breath. "Leaving Lost In Space. You and Daniel left together after his show."

"His show?"

"His Elvis impersonation show! Are you joking with me now?"

"One of us is joking, Ed, but it is not me." Karen crossed her arms.

"We went to this bar called Lost In Space, you and me.

Daniel was dressed like Elvis and doing his act. I left early. You wanted to stay and you did. Later, you left with Elvis, I mean, Daniel, after the show."

"And you know this because? You said you left."

"I know this because I waited outside the club. And I followed you, both of you."

"Okay, so where did Daniel and I go?"

I shrugged. "You tell me. You got in his car with him and sped off into the night."

"I have no idea what you are talking about. Why would I get in a car with some college punk who tried to stab me to death? Do I look *that* stupid to you?"

No way I was answering *that* question. I know a landmine when I see one.

"Are you telling me you don't remember any of this?"

"Not a single minute." Karen scratched the tip of her nose. "Though, now that you say it, I do remember you and I went to that bar…ordered some beers." She twisted her lips back and forth. "I honestly can't say I remember much after that."

I rested my head on my pillow, eyes staring at the ceiling as I digested Karen's words. What the hell was going on?

"Are you sure? Are you really sure any of that happened, Ed?" She grabbed my hand and held on.

"I saw you myself."

More eyerolling.

"I followed you and Daniel," I repeated.

She shook her head vehemently in the negative the entire time I talked.

"Never. Never. Never," she insisted.

"You two left the club together and got in his car together."

More eyerolling.

"Don't believe me?" I said. "Sara saw you, too."

"Sara? Sara who? That an imaginary friend of yours or some alien from Planet X?"

"Ha-ha. Sara Chronis."

"That beautiful CIA agent!?" Her leg muscled tensed up.

I clamped my mouth shut and kept my answer to a simple nod of the yes variety. Landmines, remember?

"What's she doing here?"

"The Agency has her working undercover. She's infiltrated the ARC. You remember them." Karen and I'd had our very own, very personal experience with that organization and it hadn't ended well. Well, it ended okay for us, not so okay for its agents.

"Oh, yeah. I'll never forget. So you just happened to run into Sara here in New Orleans in the middle of the night?"

"That's right. But let's get back to you and Daniel Hernandez."

Karen leapt to her feet on the bed, balancing precariously. "Get this through your head, Ed." She snatched a pillow, king-sized I might add—and knocked me across the face. "There is no me and Daniel Hernandez!" She collapsed back down on the bed.

Odd, very odd. Karen claimed to remember nothing. Amil also seemed to remember very little of how he'd ended up in the Nikker's house in the middle of the Atchafalaya Swamp. Even Daniel Hernandez, when I confronted him inside that very house, seemed to be having trouble with his memory. What did it all mean?

"I'm thirsty," Karen exclaimed.

"What would you like?"

"How about a glass of water?"

"Fine." I rose and fetched her a glass of water from the bathroom. "Water?" I grumbled. "Why do humans insist on drinking water when there are so many better fluids floating around?"

I handed Karen the glass and she drank it down quickly. "When I came in, you mentioned you might have a lead on Fu Chun."

"Yeah but first tell me where you've been."

"Well..."

She patted the covers. "Sit. Talk."

I did. I spun the entire yarn.

"Wow," Karen managed to say after hearing my tale

of adventure—and misadventure—out in the swamps of the Atchafalaya. "And you, you say I was trapped in a bottle and this Nikker was going to eat my bones?"

"Sort of. I believe your soul was trapped in a spirit bottle and that Ofeez, the Fleek known as the Nikker, meant for your bones to be part of his personal collection for all eternity."

I judiciously left out the bit where I seemed to have driven a sword through her stomach and watched her guts leak out. Some details are not meant to be shared, even with one's closest friends and loved ones.

She kissed me on the lips. "Thanks."

"For?"

"For saving me, stupid!"

My brow went up. "You believe me?"

"Not necessarily but just in case." She kissed me again.

"Okay, I'll take that," I said. "Now, it's your turn. Tell me about this lead you have on Fu."

My lips were sore from all this exuberant kissing but I decided I'd *man*—I use the word loosely—up and work through the pain, so I didn't complain. Hell, she could kiss me again if she had half a mind to.

"I found Alex."

It took me a second to catch on and when I did I sat up straight—something I rarely do. I prefer a good slouch. "You mean Alexandra? Fu's possible girlfriend?"

"Yep." Karen smirked smugly. "Alexandra Streliski."

I was impressed. "How did you manage that?" And was I going to have to make her an official full partner now? Add her name to my office door? Geez, the painter charged me per letter for that.

Karen was still talking, bless her, so I returned to listening mode.

"…and guess what?"

"What?"

"Not only is she a pianist, she's a poet, just like me!"

"You mean she's starving and unemployed too? I guess that

explains why she's working for a handful of ridesharing firms to pay the…"

BOOF!

Karen sucker punched me.

Yep, I was a sucker, alright. "Sorry," I said, rubbing my stomach. "Sometimes my mouth gets ahead of my brain."

"Yes, it does," Karen said sternly. Then more gently, she said, "Sorry, I didn't hurt you, did I?"

"No-no, I'm fine." Damn woman's got a helluva punch and does not know her own strength. "Continue, please." I rested my head on my pillow and shut my eyes—to better focus on her words or to fall blissfully asleep. At that point, I'd have accepted either result. I was just too tired to care. Coffee, cigarettes, bourbon and poppy seeds make quite the sleepy-time cocktail.

Karen pulled her knees up under her on the bed and continued speaking. "To be honest, I didn't find Alexandra."

"You didn't?" I cracked an eyelid and looked at Karen.

"No, she found me."

"She did?" That declaration got me up on my elbows. "And just how did she manage to do that? Amil didn't say anything about getting word to her."

"I don't know. She didn't really say. She rang the hotel and they gave her our room number. She's really nice. We must've talked for an hour this morning."

"And she told you where Fu is?"

"Not exactly."

"Okay, what exactly?"

"She sounded kinda nervous on the phone, like maybe she thought somebody might be listening in, tapping her phone line. So she didn't want to come out and say exactly."

"Where does that leave us?" Because I, for one, was good and ready to bid adieu to the Crescent City and hello to the Entertainment Capital of the World—a town where the civilians were exponentially more entertaining than a gaggle of drunken Hollywood stars.

"We agreed to meet. She gave me her address."

"Her address?" I yawned. "Why doesn't she come here? I just got back to the room. I'm not going anywhere for at least forty-eight hours."

"I told Alexandra she was welcome to but she refused because she said it might not be safe to meet here."

"Weird."

"This whole case is weird."

"You got me there." I yawned again, loosened the top buttons of my shirt, unbuckled my torn and smoke-infused trousers, and stretched my arms overhead. "Fine." I've learned it's better to bang my head against the wall than to argue with Karen. Especially when she's in one of her moods. And she's always in one of her moods. "Wake me when it's time to go."

"Okay."

"Thanks." I shuttered my eyes and lined up a flock of fresh sheep in my mind.

Karen squeezed my thigh and gave it a shake. "Ed?"

"Mmm?"

"Time to go."

22

At Karen's insistence—and while she watched me impatiently—while tapping her foot and making annoying noises with her mouth—I swapped my trousers for a less battle-worn pair and brushed my teeth. She detests the smell of bourbon and cigarettes on my breath, and absolutely hates the taste of them on my lips.

Deciding to give Amil a break, we'd hired a taxi—thanks to the generosity of our client, Chen Ha—and soon found ourselves in New Orleans' Lower Ninth Ward. The Ninth Ward wasn't far away from the French Quarter in terms of miles...but it was worlds away...nine lightyears away...in presence and vibe.

"Did you know that historically this area developed as sugar cane plantations?" I said to Karen from the backseat of the cab. "Later, the ward grew to become an industrial- and shipping-based economy."

Karen gazed out the window. "So what happened? Looks pretty bleak now."

"As that economy declined, so did the Ninth Ward. To make matters worse, what Hurricane Betsy didn't destroy in nineteen sixty-five, Hurricane Katrina took care of in two thousand and five—although by the looks of everything, I'd have believed it if you told me a hurricane had blown through here last week."

"Yeah. Empty buildings and empty eyes." That was the poet in Karen talking.

The taxi slowed to a halt. Alexandra resided in a gray five-story walkup that somehow had survived the storms and the years. Not well, but at least it still stood. The building tilted to one side as if a hurricane had tried to push it over. A tired old Toyota Prius, whose original color was lost to time, sat at the curb. More bumper stickers than I cared to count appeared to be holding the rear bumper unsteadily to the vehicle itself. I guessed this to be Alexandra's vehicle as it matched the description Amil had provided us.

The taxi driver dumped us at the curb and sped off as if fearful something out here would attach itself to him like a life-sucking leech.

"Which floor?" I looked up at the building expecting to see a gargoyle or Quasimodo himself looking back at me.

"Fifth," Karen said.

"Of course. Stupid of me to ask." Before we headed up, I took note of the license plate number of the Prius and took a peak inside the car itself. I discovered it was not locked, so I slid inside and took a poke around, too.

"Ed! What are you doing?" Karen glanced nervously up and down the street.

What was her problem? Not a lot of people about and none seemed interested in us.

"My job. I'm a detective. I'm detecting." I flipped open the glovebox and checked the car's registration. The name and address matched this location.

"I'm detecting a crime in progress," Karen replied. She smiled unconvincingly at a passerby who eyed her back with suspicion and continued on passing by.

"Nothing incriminating in the vehicle and no signs of Fu Chun's having been in it." Then again, what did I expect? Fu to autograph the dashboard? Scratch *Fu was here* into the cheap vinyl dash?

I slammed the door shut.

We hiked to the top of the unnamed building. Karen knocked on 5C. The sounds of loud reggae music rang out.

"Harder," I suggested.

Karen banged her fist against the flimsy pink door. The music stopped.

"Yeah?" came the disembodied voice behind the door.

"Alexandra?" Karen asked.

Nothing.

"It's me, Karen. Karen Dalton. I'm here with Ed."

The door gave a squeak and a pretty face appeared in the crack.

"Alexandra?" Karen repeated.

"Yeah, come on in." Alexandra Streliski pulled open the door and stepped aside to let us pass. She ran a black spider tattooed hand through a thick head of long black hair. Her face was plumpish in a cute way. A pair of black-rimmed glasses hugged her nose. Her eyes were brown. She wore faded denim jeans and a lightweight white sweater with the sleeves rolled up to her elbows to reveal more tattoo art. The one on her left forearm displayed Saint George slaying the dragon. Her right forearm displayed Mickey Mouse and Minnie Mouse smooching.

A tale of two worlds...

She crossed to a coffee table tucked up close to a four-cushion navy sofa and picked up a pack of Camels. I liked her immediately. She turned and held out the pack. "Want one?"

I was in love!

While I happily lit up, Alexandra invited Karen and I to sit at the sofa. She flopped barefoot into a yellow beanbag chair. I counted three silver rings on her toes.

The apartment was small, nothing more than a studio with a living area, tiny kitchen against the far wall, and a double bed on the floor. The biggest item in the room was the matte brown baby grand piano located dead center. I assumed she must be a really good pianist, elsewise her neighbors would have stormed the keep by now and reduced the piano to a heap of firewood.

Olive green curtains hung from wooden rods. Through the dirty glass, I caught a view of the street below and a canal in the distance.

Alexandra Streliski was a real bumper sticker freak. More bumper stickers stuck to the walls, along with an assortment of hoodoo-voodoo items and a golden statue of a meditating Buddha. She'd dedicated a long stretch of wall, with a wooden shelf stretching between the two small windows, to Disney collectible figurines.

The mingled scents of sandalwood, fried okra, scrambled eggs, and pot fought with the smell of burning tobacco.

Alexandra held her lit cigarette delicately in two fingers as she waved her hand in circles, creating a diaphanous cloud around her head. "So…" Puff. Puff. "You're looking for Fu." Her teeth were incredibly white given her affinity for smokes.

"Can you tell us where he is?" I matched her puff for puff. "Please?"

"Karen says you're a detective and that you're looking for him. Rather, his family is looking for him?"

"That's right. They're really worried. It's been weeks since they've heard from him," I replied.

"Mmm," Alexandra muttered. She snuffed out her cigarette in a soot-smeared glass ashtray, and crossed to the piano bench. She sat. Her fingers began working their way idly up and down the keyboard. Tinkle. Tinkle. Tinkle.

Karen cleared her throat. "We only want to be sure he's okay. And to let his family know."

"Yes, it's not like we want to harm him or kidnap him. I mean, it would be great if he'd give his aunt a call, let her know he's alright," I added.

Tinkle. Tinkle. Tinkle. "You know he's into all that voodoo shit, right?"

"He is?" I asked.

"Sure, that and aliens." Alexandra slammed her hands down on the keys. CRASH! "He thinks they are everywhere."

"He-He does?" Karen shot me a look and squeezed her knees together.

"Oh, yeah. Big time. He's even a card-carrying member of this dumb organization…what the hell was that?" Alexandra rose suddenly and crossed to a small paint-splattered bureau. A portrait of Wordsworth stood atop it. England's one-time poet laureate looked out at the world through heavily lidded eyes topped by dark eyebrows and silvery hair—in those areas he had hair at all, that is. Overall, he cast a cadaverous appearance. How many times had his dear wife awoken in the morning and wondered whether or not her dear husband was still amongst the living?

Karen and I watched silently as Alexandra rummaged around in the drawers.

After a couple of minutes, she smiled as she held a black and silver membership card in the air. "Got it! Alien Resistance Corps! The idiot signed up. Ninety-nine dollars down and twenty-two fifty a month for twelve months, he signed up. And what's he get for the money? Some goofy online newsletter, this cheap membership card, and a bumper sticker."

Alexandra pointed to the wall where an *ARC Is Watching The Sky So You Don't Have To* bumper sticker had been affixed. I hadn't noticed it earlier.

"Terry Lawrence!" Alexandra snorted. "Didn't even take the card with him when he left!" She flipped the card in the air and let it fall to the floor. "Paid for with my credit card too!"

"About that," I began. "Why did he call himself Terry Lawrence? Why not stick with Fu?"

"That? Fu came up with that himself. Said he needed an alias because it made him sound cooler. Called himself Terry the Terror. What a doofus! I can't believe I feel for that creep."

Karen decided to speak. "So, if you don't mind my asking, you and Fu were…together?"

"If you mean lovers, yeah." Alexandra tilted her head. "Until he found someone better." She flopped back down on the beanbag.

I leaned toward the open pack of Camels on the coffee table. "Mind if I have another?"

"Want something stronger? I've got some weed," Alexandra replied.

"Do you have any black licorice?" I asked.

"Huh?" Alexandra said.

"Never mind. Not important. A cigarette will do." And it did. "How long's it been since you've seen Fu?"

Alexandra considered the question. "Almost a week."

"Do you know his roommate? Daniel Hernandez?"

"That dickhead?"

Apparently, she knew him well.

"Where is Fu now?" I asked. It was time to get to the heart of the matter. And I really, really wanted to get back to the Bourbon Orleans…back to sleep.

"Probably shacked up with his new old lady friend. And I do mean old."

"Old?" Karen said.

"She must be twice his age." Alexandra stood, walked to her kitchen, rattled open a drawer and removed some rolling papers and a baggie filled with weed.

"Can you tell us her name?" I asked.

"You ever hear of some bigshot high priestess who calls herself Lola Davies?" Alexandra rolled quickly and lit up her joint using the tip of my cigarette. "Thanks."

"No problem," I said.

"What about Lola Davies?" Karen put in.

"What about her?" Alexandra scoffed. "That's his old lady."

That got my attention. No wonder Lola Davies told me she might know where Fu Chun was. He was hiding out with her!

"Well, well, well," I said aloud.

"Yeah," said Karen. "I can't believe it."

"Well, it's the truth." She inhaled deeply, held her breath, then let it out slowly. Words followed. "Tis said, that some have died for love. And here and there a churchyard grave is found—"

Karen straightened, a smile on her face. "In the cold north's unhallowed ground, because the wretched man himself had slain…"

"Excuse me," I butt in. "What am I missing?"

"It's poetry, Ed," replied Karen. "Wordsworth."

"Wonderful." Not. I was being ganged up on by a couple of poets. What could be more humiliating…and emasculating? "Does it have something to do with this case? Because if it doesn't, Wordsworth's words aren't worth anything."

"Ha-ha." Karen rolled her eyes for Alexandra's benefit. Why is it that women always gang up on men?

"Did you know that Lola's…assistant, I guess you might say, was murdered the other night?" I asked.

"Sure. All over the news. Hard to miss." Alexandra's eyes fixed on something only she could see. "Police are looking for the killer but if you ask me, she's right in front of them."

"She?" I had to ask.

"Lola Davies. Who else?" Alexandra snapped.

"Lola Davies? You really think she's capable of murder?" Karen asked.

"That woman is capable of anything."

"What makes you say that?" I asked. "Personal experience?"

"Let's just say I know the type. Plus, I had a friend who worked at Enchantments for six months. Man, the stories she used to tell." Alexandra's voice grew harder with every word. "That woman is a con artist and a bitch. Swindles the tourists and the locals. Calls herself a spiritualist! Ha, if you ask me, she's got no soul.

"She's a sham." Alexandra leaned closer to us. "And her and Ursula hated one another. Used to be lovers once. But that was long ago. Later, they just fought like cats and dogs. They were partners, you know." She fell back into the beanbag, letting it swallow her up.

"No, we did not know," I said.

"I'll bet she was stealing. Holding out on Ursula," suggested Alexandra. "And Ursula was probably pissed, and jealous maybe, that Lola had taken up with Fu."

"Why would Ursula get upset about that, if she and Lola were no longer involved?" I asked.

"The breakup was Lola's idea. At least, that's the way I heard it from my friend," replied Alexandra.

I had to wonder, was Alexandra a woman scorned too or was there truth in what she intimated?

"That would give Lola a motive for the murder, Ed," Karen said. "And she was right there, in the house at the time. She had the perfect opportunity."

"You may be right," I admitted. "According to reports, there was no sign of a break-in." A lot of questions had certainly been raised by Alexandra Streliski. "Has Fu said anything to you about this? Do you think he suspects Lola Davies of murder?"

Alexandra shrugged. "I haven't talk to him since he left. Nor do I want to." She tapped her phone to life and checked the time. "I should be getting to work."

Alexandra stood and we followed her cue.

23

"Do you believe her?" Karen asked me.

Karen and I stood on the cracked and buckling sidewalk outside Alexandra Streliski's building. She'd walked down with us. We watched her decrepit Prius tootle off and disappear around the corner while the unrelenting sun hammered us from on high.

I gave Karen's question some thought. "I suppose. What she said did make sense...of sorts."

"If you say so," Karen crossed her arms. "But what do we really know about her?"

"Interesting that you mention that," I said.

"Why?"

"Because I've been thinking the same thing about Fu Chun."

"What do you mean? We know exactly who he is. He's Anna Ping's nephew."

"What I mean is what do we *really* know about him?"

"Mister Ha told us all about him. He's who we're here looking for!"

"No," I corrected. "Mister Ha told us everything he knew or wanted us to know about Ping's nephew. We've never even spoken with Ping herself. We simply took everything we were told at face value, didn't ask any questions, just got on a plane and started hunting for Fu."

"You make a good point," admitted Karen.

"Thank you." I said. "I've got more. And I'm determined to learn more about Fu. He is the reason we're here. I first thought this was a simple missing person case, now I'm not so sure. I think there is more going on here than meets the eye. And, Fu seems to be at the center of it."

"Eye of the hurricane?" suggested Karen.

"Exactly, and apt. And I want to know why. Once we know that, perhaps we'll find Fu."

"And face the possibility of death as a consequence? Again?"

"Very likely."

"Fine," Karen said with a scowl. "Go ahead, I'm listening."

"Okay," I said and did. "Who is Fu Chun? What are his interests? What's he been involved in? *Who* is he involved with?"

"Like Lola Davies."

"Exactly. If Alexandra wasn't lying to us or misinformed herself. And another thing, why Tulane?" I asked.

"What do you mean?"

"Why did Fu choose to attend Tulane? Why not some other university?"

"Maybe it's the only one he got accepted to," Karen supplied.

"Hmm, possibly. Text Mister Ha. Ask him."

Karen whipped out her phone and shot off a quick text. The reply was quick to come. "Mister Ha says Tulane was Fu's first choice, although he and Ping would have preferred he attend a more local school."

"So maybe Fu wanted to come here expressly because of its nearness to New Orleans and all things voodoo."

"And all things alien, perhaps?"

"Mmm, like the Nikker," I said. "Speaking of which, are you sure you don't remember anything about being trapped in the swamp and—"

Karen's telephone pinged again. "Hold that thought." She checked her message app. "It's Mister Ha again. He wants to know how the case is progressing. He mentions that his credit card charges seem inordinately high." She frowned, her fingers hovering over the tiny virtual keyboard. "What should I tell him? For all our time here, it sounds to me like we have more questions than answers."

I tapped my foot in thought. "Tell him everything is

proceeding smoothly. And that we expect to have results very, very shortly."

"You want me to lie to him?"

"Yes."

"Okay…"

I gripped Karen's hand and she stopped typing. "And tell him we expect to have Fu in hand and that he'll be phoning him personally to assure him he's safe and sound."

"Seriously?"

"Sure. Um, how are you at doing impersonations?"

"Impersonations?"

"Of the young male college student variety."

"Forget it. Not happening." Nonetheless, Karen sent off her message, okay so it was *my* message, and dropped her phone into her bag.

"There is one other thing," I said, frowning up and down the deserted street. "Alexandra drives for a handful of rideshare firms."

"And?"

"And why the hell didn't we hire her to drive us back to town?"

"I blame you."

"Why?"

Karen shrugged. "Why not?"

"Good enough." I snapped my fingers. "Crap."

"Here? Can't you wait till we get inside? Find a restroom?"

"Ha-ha-ha. Aren't we hilarious for someone who was only recently a bag of bones."

Karen shivered and hugged herself. "Will you please stop saying that. Every time you do, it gives me the willies!"

"Last time today," I promised. I made a show of zipping my lips. "Anyway, what I started to say before you interrupted for that lame joke was that I forgot, we both forgot, to ask Alexandra how she knew we were searching for her and where to find us."

"Crap. You're right. How did she know?" Karen scratched her head.

"Get her cell number and ask her," I said. "With her license plate number, you ought to be able to find that." There are all sorts of ways of finding things out on the Infernal Net—most of it crap, too, but such is life. I rattled off the number.

"Can do." Karen began typing. "What was that third letter?"

I repeated it. "But first get us out of here."

Karen switched gears and ordered up a taxi and, while I suggested returning to the hotel for a quick nap, she insisted our driver deposit us outside Enchantments.

24

We discovered the front door of Enchantments firmly locked and not a light on in the place.

"That's odd," Karen glanced from her watch to the sign in the window stating the store hours. "They ought to be open now."

I pressed my hands against my brow and peered through the glass. "I don't see any sign of movement. Let's check around back."

We trudged between the houses and the same dog that had barked at us the first time we'd done so, did so again. Old dogs may learn new tricks, but some dogs never learn a darn thing.

Karen called out, "Good doggie." But that didn't change its attitude towards us interlopers.

At the side of the house, Karen said, "I see a light on inside the kitchen." She rose up on her tiptoes, pressed her fingers into the window ledge for support, and peeked in through the kitchen window.

"Oh!" She dropped to the ground.

"Did she see you?" I whispered.

"I'm not sure." Karen wiped her hands together in an attempt to rid them of the dirt clinging to her fingers. "She's sitting right there at the table but, if she saw me, she didn't react."

"Odd. If I saw someone peeking in my kitchen window, I'd react." Then again, my kitchen window was on the second floor. I'd definitely react. I don't get many levitating visitors, least of all of the human variety.

I tried the side door. It was locked but that didn't stop me.

"Ed! That's breaking and entering!" hissed Karen. "Why don't you just knock?"

"I'd rather catch her by surprise. See how she reacts," I said. I was beginning to suspect there was far more to Lola Davies than met the eye. What was she involved in? What was she hiding? And did that include Fu Chun?

"What if she reacts by blasting you with a shotgun?"

I gave the possibility some thought. "Then I'll duck." I pushed the door open a crack then paused. "In which case, since you'll no doubt be standing right behind me," something she was prone to doing, "you might want to duck, too."

Besides, she'd more likely cast a voodoo spell on me.

"Sounds more like dead goose to me," Karen grumbled, planting her hand on my shoulder as we crept inside Lola's house.

We found ourselves in a tiny mudroom with a pair of women's leather sandals on the floor keeping company or playing footsie with a pair of men's yellow sneakers. Several light jackets and a lavender sweater hung on pegs on the wall. An inverted black umbrellas stood in the corner like it was in time out.

To my right, I spotted a small bedroom with an unmade bed. To the left, I caught sight of a white stove jutting out from the wall, meaning that was the kitchen…and our quarry.

"Wait here," I whispered in Karen's ear. She nodded in agreement.

"Hello, Lola." I burst into the kitchen. The acrid smell of a burning pot whose water had long ago evaporated filled the air.

I'd been expecting a shout, a scream, Lola to fly out of her seat or fall out of it. Much to my amazement, she'd done none of the above. In fact, the spiritualist hadn't reacted at all.

"Ed?" Karen called from the mudroom. "Everything okay?"

"Come on in," I called. Using the side of my thumb, I turned off the flame at the stovetop. I waved my arm. "Karen, you remember Lola."

Karen gasped. "Is-Is she…"

"Yep, dead as a proverbial coffin nail," I said.

"You mean door nail," Karen corrected. "You sure?"

"A dead nail's a dead nail," I said. I crossed to the kitchen table where Lola Davies sat. She was dead alright. Her eyes—once piercing and filled with mystery—were closed. Her mouth hung loosely open. Her face was sallow and cool to the touch. "She's been dead a while," I offered.

"What-What happened to her? Heart attack?" Karen made to touch Lola's arm.

"No. Don't touch anything," I cautioned.

"Right, sorry."

I pointed to the tabletop. "Read for yourself. She's left a note." Lola Davies' left hand held down a single, unlined sheet of paper. An old-fashioned green fountain pen sat near her right hand.

"*Sorry. I never meant to kill her. Forgive me. Lola,*" read Karen. "Shit."

Using the sides of two fingers pressed against the inside wall of the bottle, and being careful not to touch the outside, I stooped and picked up a prescription bottle from where it had fallen and landed against a table leg. We both read the label.

"Sleeping pills? Lola Davies killed herself? Why? Does this mean she really killed Ursula?"

"It would appear that way," I said. I studied the bottle. It had once contained 30 sleeping pills. It now contained zero.

"I can't believe it," Karen said. "What the hell is going on? This was supposed to be a simple missing person case. I didn't think we'd be mixed up with murders and suicides!"

"The case has taken some interesting twists," I concurred.

"We'll have to call the police," Karen said. "Maybe Sergeant Lecourt?"

"Yes." I sat the bottle back on the floor where I'd found it and took a slow look around the quiet kitchen—quiet but for the pounding of Karen's quaking heart. "I wonder where Fu is? Maybe we should search the house and—"

Squeak!

It was a tiny squeak as far as squeaks go, not much more than the sound of a mouse that's been startled by its own reflection but it was enough to set off an alert in my head.

"What was—" began Karen.

I raised a cautioning finger to my lips. I started slowly towards the area from which the squeak had emanated, somewhere near the back bedroom. The thump of quick steps, the sound of a slamming backdoor, quickly followed by the angry yaps of a mutt, told me that whoever had been in the house with us had fled. I ran past Karen and out the side door.

I shot a look up and down the side yard but the only creature I saw was the damn dog. "Which way did they go?"

The dog ignored me. Well, he didn't ignore me, he just kept barking at me. Dogs may be Man's best friend but they were not even so far up the ladder as to be a Pazu's barely tolerated next-door neighbor.

I jogged to the backyard only to hear a vehicle start up in the frontyard. By the time I got to the street, there was no sign of anyone, except for a woman with a young boy and girl in tow. She looked at me funny. I suppose I did look sort of funny myself, disheveled and breathing hard. I smiled and waved to alleviate her anxiety. This caused her to walk faster. She prodded the children in her charge to do the same.

Stepping back inside the house, the first thing I noticed was that the yellow sneakers were gone.

Karen poked her head around the corner. "Who was it? Did they get away?"

"I never caught a look at them. I'm guessing it was a he because there's a pair of men's sneakers missing. It was no spirit from the netherworld, that's for sure. Spirits don't need shoes, and they sure as hell don't make a racket when they run." I pointed to the empty spot on the floor. "Let's check the bedroom."

The bedroom was small and dark. A crack of light pushed its way in through a gap in the blue curtains. An unmade queen-sized bed pressed against the wall to my right. The blanket was knotted at the foot of the bed revealing rumpled yellow cotton sheets. Several pillows leaned against an upholstered tan headboard. An antique dresser and mirror hugged the wall next to it. A hairbrush, a handheld mirror, a teak incense holder, and a brown leather purse sat atop the dresser.

I peeked into the purse. I pulled out a red wallet and checked the driver's license. "Lola's. Not that she'll be needing it any longer. Not where she's going." Was she looking down on us from the spirit world now?

Karen slid open a wooden closet door leading to a space no larger than two feet deep and three feet wide.

"Anything interesting?"

"Her clothes, I suppose. But also a couple of men's T-shirts. And a pair of black jeans, also men's," she replied.

"I'll see your T-shirts and jeans and raise you this Tulane backpack," I quipped, holding up by my finger what I suspected was the property of Fu Chun—a black backpack bearing the green school logo.

"You think it's Fu's?"

"There's a tag here with his name and dorm address on it." I held it up.

"What's inside?" Karen asked, sliding the closet door shut and joining me.

"Let's see." I unzipped the backpack and spilled the contents atop the bed. I wasn't worried about fingerprints any longer because I'd already decided that this backpack was leaving with me. Was that illegal?

Probably. But so is 90 percent of everything you humans do. Fortunately for me and not so much for you, I'm Pazu. Such laws do not apply.

What spilled out onto the bed was a compact, lightweight pair of binoculars, a smelly pair of white ankle-length socks, and a notebook and pencil. I flipped through the lined pages of the notebook.

"Anything interesting?"

"Lots of notes. Observations." I scratched the underside of

my chin. Okay, so that's one thing I have in common with cats, I like my chin scratched. "Our Fu is quite the spy in the making. Snooping around, studying everyone, trying to sniff out who's alien and who's not."

"Weird. I never would have guessed."

"Neither would Anna Ping nor Mister Ha, I dare to venture." I read further, muttering aloud. "Names and dates. Here's something."

"What?"

"He seems to have some suspicions about his roommate, Daniel Hernandez."

"Such as?"

"Such as, he believed Daniel was a servant of a malign spirit."

"Maybe," Karen agreed. "But, personally, I think he's just an asshole."

I returned all Fu's possessions to the backpack and zipped it shut. "Speaking of our young Elvis imitator, I believe we should have another talk with him." I hefted the backpack over my shoulder. "He's tied up in all this. I'm sure of it."

How could he not be? He'd tried to stab Karen to death, then me, out in the Atchafalaya Swamp. If that didn't kill us, his Elvis impersonation would. "The day is young, let's head to Tulane and see if we can find Daniel."

"Okay." Karen glanced up the hall. "But what about…"

"Lola Davies' corpse? We'll phone the police from a payphone, assuming we can find one." I popped my head into the kitchen.

"I've got an app on my phone that lets me make anonymous calls, remember?"

"Right. I'd forgotten." That had come in handy more than once. "Fine, go for it." I laid a hand on her forearm to forestall her. "But not yet. Wait until we're long gone. We do not want to be here when the police show up."

"Fine. What are you doing?" Karen asked me as I approached the body.

"Making sure she's still dead. With powerful manbos like her, you never know." I touched the side of her neck with the back of my hand. "Yep, still amongst the dead. Or undead as the case may be."

"You think Fu knew about Lola? That he might even have been involved in her death somehow? Is that why he ran?"

"I'd like to think not," I said. Would Mr. Ha pay us the agreed upon fee if we found Fu, yet he turned out to be a multiple murderer? "But why else would he run away?"

"Yeah, and what was he doing hiding here in the first place? Why didn't he call an ambulance…or the police."

"All good questions," I replied. "Let's hope Daniel can provide us some answers."

25

We strolled down Saint Louis Street to Antoine's for lunch. The fancy restaurant has been a New Orleans institution since 1840. Original hardwood floors, unique décor, walls filled with photographs of notable visitors and numerous dining rooms to get lost in. It wasn't cheap but the food was first-class.

Thankfully, the good folks at Antoine's ignored their own dress code and turned a blind, if unhappy eye to our dress, which was anything but business casual. More like tourist trash. We got a few disgruntled stares from staff and guests alike, but not the boot. But I expected some of those stares had more to do with Karen's vivid hair color than our style options.

Maybe it was my brand-new NOLA PD T-shirt keeping them at bay? Maybe they thought I was a cop. Heh, maybe they'd comp our lunch.

We were shown to a table in a cozy dining room with tabasco-red walls and handed lunch menus.

"You know Antoine's has hosted countless celebrities over its long and illustrious existence," I said.

"Oh, yeah?" Karen perused her menu. "Like who?"

"Bob Hope, Bing Crosby…"

Karen lowered her menu and pursed her brow. "Who are they?"

"Never mind."

A bemused waiter collected our requests and soon our first courses arrived.

"Worth every penny," I said, gulping down my second serving of Oysters Rockefeller, an Antoine's original.

"I know what you mean. I didn't realize how famished I

was." Karen slid a roasted brussels sprout—the appetizer minus the bacon—through a patch of garlicky oil and popped it in her mouth.

"Brussels sprouts? Yeesh! I'd rather starve."

Next up was my pompano fillet, grilled to perfection, and hosed down with enough butter to choke a cow. It came with jumbo lump crab meat and oniony rice all doused in a rye whiskey sauce. It's normally served with a wine reduction but I can't stand wine—too fruity—and the chef was kind enough to whip me up a whiskey-based sauce.

"I can't remember the last time I ate this well," I remarked, digging into my main course.

Meanwhile, dreary old Karen dug into a gooey mushroom ragout in a burgundy reduction, with fingerling potatoes. *Goo* being the operative syllable. Still, it was Antoine's nod to the vegan crowd, and she was happy with it.

"I don't know how you can eat that stuff," I said, looking at her plate with disgust.

"It's delicious." She extended her fork. "Try a bite."

"No, no!" I waved my hands in the air to fend off her attack.

Karen frowned. "How many times do we have to have this conversation? Eating veggies is good for you. Better for people and the environment, too. And you," she said, pointing her fork at me, "really should make an effort to eat better."

"I do. I eat fine."

"Cigarette butts and black licorice is not fine. You should eat more veggies," Karen schooled me.

"Eat more veggies?" I complained. "How much more humane is that? Some poor laborer has to plant, weed, and pick the horrible things…and all for a peasant's wage."

"Whatever." She scooped up some gooey ragout and ate it up. "It's all that meat you eat that's disgusting."

"So stick to your okra," I said. I took a sip of my rye whiskey cocktail. Karen had ordered herself a mocktail—mocktails are just about the dumbest things on earth! I mean, they contain everything but the most important and essential ingredient, alcohol!

"Do you think Daniel Hernandez will be able to help us?" Karen asked, midway through our meal.

I shrugged. "We can only hope so. Although I suspect he may not be willing to help." I dabbed my chin with my napkin. "He may need some...persuading."

"Right." Karen swirled her drink, a toxic blend of ginger ale, cranberry juice, and Orgeat syrup. I half-expected her to drop dead like Lola Davies had done so recently. I mean, it's the alcohol that's required to kill off all those toxic poisons and keep you alive!

"I still can hardly believe Lola Davies committed suicide," Karen continued.

"Guilt can eat away at a person's conscience."

"Yeah. I guess we'll never know what really happened, I mean, to slash Ursula's throat like that. She didn't strike me as the violent type."

"No, me either. And now, with Lola dead too, her secrets have died with her. Fortunately for us, solving Ursula Broussard's murder and finding her killer was not our case. Finding Fu Chun is what we're being paid for. And I'm positive that was him running out of the house. That reminds me, better call the police."

"Right."

Karen placed an anonymous call to Sgt. Lecourt. Fortunately, he'd given us his direct number. He angrily demanded to know who was calling but she adamantly refused and talked quickly. "He's sending a squad car to the house," she told me after cutting the connection.

"Good. At least that's one case concluded." The case hadn't ended well but at least it was over. "Dessert?"

"I wonder if they have pralines?" Karen said between bites of mushroomy madness. "I've been meaning to try some while we're here. We are in New Orleans, after all."

"Pralines! Finally, something we can both agree on!" I retrieved the menu at the end of the table and scrolled through the dessert list. "Sadly, no pralines."

"Rats."

"Sorry, rats aren't on the menu."

"Ha-ha."

"But now that you've broached the subject of dessert…" I studied the menu some more and then ordered the Baked Alaska for two. It proved to be everything and more with its buttery poundcake outside, rich vanilla ice cream center, and meringue crust, all smothered in hot fudge sauce. Karen nibbled at the fresh-baked dessert, I devoured it. First come, first served and all that. I call it survival of the greediest.

Nearly two hours later, we were ready to hit the road—being stuffed and filled with drink, not so much fit to hit the road—but ready nevertheless.

Our better-dressed waiter handed the bill to Karen. She opened the leather book, glanced at the charges we'd run up and gasped. "Holy shit!"

That earned us some more stares from more patrons and staff.

"Sorry." Karen lowered her voice and pulled out her credit card, okay, Mr. Ha's credit card. The waiter came and swept it away, returning several minutes later with our receipt.

We stepped out into the dying sunlight and pondered our next steps. First and foremost, calling for a ride.

Which is when Karen's phone rang somewhere down in her bag. She grabbed it, looked at the incoming number and frowned. "It's Mister Ha."

I shrugged. "Say hello for me."

"Hello? Mister Ha?" Karen began. "Yeah, uh, Ed says to say hi." Pause. "Right," she said, rolling her eyes at me. Moments of silence followed from Karen, but for an occasional, "Uh, uh-huh, uh…no, yes, yes, sir, right, uh-huh" (again), and finally, "definitely, absolutely, Mister Ha. Yes, I'll tell him."

Karen cut the connection and dropped the phone in her purse. "Dammit."

"Well?"

"He just got a call from the fraud department at his credit card company."

"So why is he calling you? Is he worried we might have a problem?"

"He's not calling me, he's calling you! You just don't happen to have a phone. And he's not worried that we *might* have a problem. He's worried that we *are* the problem!" Karen yelled. "And he wants to know how much progress we are making—"

"I hope you told him things are going swimmingly—"

Karen cut me off. "And he wants to know why our expenses are so damn high!" Karen's voice was high too, attracting odd looks from passersby. And this was New Orleans. It takes a lot to get a look from the locals. They've seen everything.

I guess they'd never seen a toxic-dump leprechaun-green-haired lady yelling at a short alien outside Antoine's before.

"What did you tell him?"

"I didn't tell him anything. He told me!"

"Okay, so calm down and tell me what he told you. And," I said, raising my finger in I-told-you-so fashion, "if you'd only had a proper drink, a proper *alcoholic* drink, with lunch, I dare say you wouldn't be so stressed out now."

Before I knew what was happening, Karen grabbed hold of my finger and bent it perilously backwards.

"Ouch!" I said. Fortunately, I have a strong tolerance to pain. I'd also developed a strong tolerance to Karen.

"*You're* stressing me out!" She sucked in a breath and let it out. Next, she let go of my finger. "He gave us forty-eight hours."

"Forty-eight hours to what?"

"Forty-eight hours to find Fu," Karen explained.

"And if we don't?"

"We go home, Ed. At our own expense. Although, Mister Ha told me to tell you that we won't have a home when we get home. Know what I mean?"

"Oh." I bit my lip. "No office, no home. Kicked out of the building?" Good thing I'd kept that money I'd found stashed under Daniel's mattress as payment for his attack on her. Looked like we might be needing it sooner than later.

"That's what he said."

"Fine," I said, nodding. "It's time to get serious. Kick this case into high gear." I slammed my right fist into the palm of my left hand…and burped, spoiling the dramatic effect I'd been going for.

I'd say Karen rolled her eyes but I'm guessing you already knew that.

26

Karen tapped in a request for a KarRyde driver. We were disappointed when a stranger pulled up in a late-model Accord. We'd grown fond of Amil and missed him. Not that I could blame the guy for laying low after what had happened out at the Atchafalaya Swamp.

Darkness came to greet us as we arrived at Tulane. We crossed the busy campus and made our way straight to Daniel and Fu's dorm room.

The police beat us there. Four uniformed officers and a couple in plain clothes stood at the entrance to the dorm. A pair of EMTs hovered nearby.

Nobody stopped us so in we went.

"Sergeant Lecourt!" Karen halted at the open door to Daniel and Fu's room. "What are you— Oh!"

I peeked around Karen and looked inside the room. Up the hall, a group of students watched the activities.

Daniel lay sprawled atop his bunk. Stone dead. A small hole in his chest with blood circling it.

"Hello, Sergeant," I said. "What's happened?"

"Nasty business. Somebody murdered the boy." He scrubbed his hands across his face. "It's been an awful day."

"Yeah, looks like Elvis really is dead this time," I said.

"What's that?" asked Sgt. Lecourt, looking confused.

"Never mind. Ignore Ed. He thinks he's funny," Karen replied. "When what he is is insensitive."

"What? After what he did to you?" I said.

"He's dead, Ed."

Sgt. Lecourt studied us both and said to Karen, "What did

Daniel do to you?"

"Performed the worst Elvis impersonation you've ever seen or heard," I answered for her. I couldn't have her telling Lecourt that he'd tried to stick her with a knife. That would lead to more complications and questions begging answers.

"I don't understand what—" began Sgt. Lecourt.

An interruption was in order, so I said, "Out of your ward, aren't you?" I happened to know that Tulane sat squarely in the 14th Ward.

"Yes, but the captain suggested I come lend my assistance." He loomed over me. "Because, you see, I have come from Lola Davies' residence."

"Oh?"

"Yes, it seems she's dead of an overdose. And left a note confessing to murdering Ursula Broussard."

"Pity," I said.

"Yes, what a shame," agreed Karen, coloring and looking studiously at her shoes.

"Mmm," Lecourt stroke his chin. "A pity and a shame, yes, that it is. Funny thing is…"

"Yes?" I asked.

"A witness, a young woman and her children, saw a fellow…and, later, a woman, matching the descriptions of you two." He waved an accusatory finger at us. "And Hernandez here was the roommate of the young fellow you told me you were sent here to find. What's your connection in all this? I do wonder."

I cleared my throat. "Really, a man and woman? That describes half the people in New Orleans," I said. "Could've been anyone."

Lecourt stared pointedly at Karen. "Anyone? With lime-green hair?"

Damn, I should have known Karen's choice of hair colors would get us both in trouble someday. Still, how much trouble could we be in? Lola Davies had committed suicide. It wasn't like he could accuse us of being suspects of any kind.

Lecourt folded his arms across his chest. "Mind telling me what the two of you were doing there?"

"Well…" began Karen. She glanced at me.

I took over. "Fine. It's no big deal. You see, we had a lead that the young man we are trying to find—"

"Fu Chun," stated the sergeant.

"Yes, Fu Chun. We heard he might be staying with Lola Davies. So we went to check out the lead."

"And do you mind telling me who gave you this lead? What's this person's name?"

"I can't tell you," I said. "Wish I could but it was an anonymous call," I improvised. I did not want to mention Alexandra Streliski. If the police dragged her in, it could prevent our speaking with her again. And I had a lot of questions for the young woman.

A wicked smile crossed his face and he looked at Karen once more. "Mmm, like the anonymous phone call I received alerting me to go to Enchantments where the police would discover a dead woman. Next time," he said, laying a hand on her shoulder, "you might want to try altering your voice."

Karen attempted a feeble grin.

A change of subject was in order.

"Any idea who killed Daniel Hernandez?" I asked the sergeant.

"No clue. Happened within the hour is our guess." Lecourt glanced down the hall at the gathered students. "Apparently, no one heard anything. There was a loud party going on. Hernandez received a small caliber shot, probably a twenty-two but it went straight to the heart and that was enough to do the job."

"I didn't know he had a heart," I couldn't resist saying.

"Ed!" Karen admonished me.

"Now, what are you two doing here?" Lecourt demanded.

"We came to speak with Daniel. He is, was, Fu's roommate, after all. We were hoping he might have remembered something that would give us a lead on the young man."

"Still no luck?" asked Sgt. Lecourt.

"None good," I replied. I also chose not to tell the sergeant about Fu possibly being present in Lola Davies' home when we'd arrived, figuring it might only complicate the situation. We didn't need the police out looking for him as a potential witness of some sort. That could also spook him and complicate our case. More complications we did not need.

Find Fu, shove him in Mr. Ha's face, collect our fee, and go home—that was my new mantra. And I didn't want anything or anyone preventing that from happening.

"I have to wonder, as do my superiors," Sgt. Lecourt emphasized, "how it is that you two are at Enchantments and two women have now died there since you arrived. And now this." He pointed to Daniel Hernandez's corpse.

"Nothing but an unfortunate coincidence," I said.

Sgt. Lecourt tugged at a chain around his neck and reeled in a silver cross. He stroked it thoughtfully. "Death seems to walk with you two."

The sergeant didn't know the half of it. And that was a good thing.

"Well, since there's nothing for us here, we should be going, Karen." I took her arm.

"Fine," said Sgt. Lecourt. "But I'll expect both of you in my office tomorrow."

"Tomorrow?" I said.

"Ten-thirty. I'm sure we have much to discuss. In fact, the captain will be joining us."

"I'm afraid that's not possible," I said.

"All things are possible, Mister Turner. I suggest you accept my hospitality. I'd hate to have to send a squad car to pick you up."

"No-No. That won't be necessary. Ten-thirty. We'll be there."

"Ed," Karen whispered as I escorted her out of the dorm. "Are we really going to go to police headquarters tomorrow? We're running out of time."

"And options," I added.

We slipped out onto campus.

"So what do we do now?"

"Best case scenario? We find Fu and get him on a plane out of here. Him and us."

"Leave town? What about the sergeant?"

"We'll be out of his jurisdiction."

"Ed, we can't blow him off!"

"No? Fine, then we'll go. But we'll stonewall him. Give him nothing."

Karen came to a stop, bringing me with her. "Stonewall him? And if he decides to lock us up behind four stone walls of his own? Walls with bars."

"Relax, I've been held captive before. It's not so bad," I assured Karen. Big Fat Lie. Actually, it was far, far worse than anything she could imagine. But why spoil her evening? She'd only keep me awake all night with her worrying.

27

The next morning, I discovered a message waiting for us inside our room.

"Hey, what is that?" I said leaning forward and pointing, careful not to spill the coffee cup I'd so carefully filled with a 50-50 blend of coffee to bourbon. Light streamed in through the open window. It was earlier in the morning than I generally like to stir but we had things to do and a missing person to track down.

Glancing towards the door, I'd spotted a slender glass vase standing at attention a few inches inside our door. A fresh yellow daffodil stood in the vase. A folded sheet of hotel stationary sat under the vase. "What is that flower doing here? How'd that get in our room?"

Karen pushed up on her elbows.

"Oof!" I complained as she carelessly planted one of those bony elbows in my stomach.

"Flowers? A note? Is it from the hotel?" Karen asked, taking a look. "Have we been kicked out?"

"And they brought us flowers to celebrate?" I groaned. "Give me a second. I'll check." I crawled out of bed barefoot for the second time that morning. The first time had been to prepare our coffee.

"Who's it from?"

I carried the vase to the table and brought the single sheet of folded paper to the bed. "Hmm, it's written on hotel stationary," I said, unfolding the paper. I scanned the text. "It's from Sara."

"Sara Chronis? What's she want?" Karen called from the

bathroom.

"She wants us to meet her at ten o'clock."

"What for?"

"She doesn't say."

"Tell her forget it," Karen said.

I heard the shower kick on. The woman is a clean freak. Should I warn my partner that a number of guests had reported ghosts suddenly appearing in that shower and getting handsy with bathers? Nah. She'd either discover that for herself or she wouldn't.

"She says she cannot be reached and fears she may be under surveillance and not to try to contact her. We're just supposed to meet her!" I shouted to be heard over the crash of water against flesh.

"Where?"

"The Natchez?"

"You want nachos?"

"Natchez. The Natchez!"

"What?" Karen screeched.

I marched to the shower and cut off the water.

Karen really screeched.

Oops. That's because I'd turned off the hot water. Cold water cascaded the length, breadth, and circumference of her body.

"You idiot!" Karen howled.

I quickly returned the hot water. Too late. Now the only thing hot was Karen—under the collar, that is.

She savagely shut off the water and dripped all over me. I handed her a towel.

"The Natchez," I explained. "It's a steamboat. Goes up and down the Mississippi River."

Karen toweled off. "The answer is still no. We are running out of time *and* we need to be at Lecourt's office at ten-thirty, remember?" She dressed quickly—too quickly for me, I'm a voyeur at heart.

"Plenty of time," I replied.

"How the hell had Sara managed to get in our locked room?" Karen said, studying her reflection in the mirror as she slid clear lip gloss over her pouty lips.

"I don't know. Then again, she is a CIA agent. They have certain…skills."

"Yeah, like breaking and entering," Karen scowled, and ran a brush through her damp green locks.

Scrub-a-dub-dubbed and breakfasted, we wandered down to the river to meet the gently bobbing Natchez, moored at the river's edge. White with red trim and two giant steam-powered wheels aft, at 265 ft long, 46 ft wide, and just shy of 1,384 tons, you couldn't miss her.

"Now what?" Karen demanded, still making it clear that she wasn't happy with the situation.

"According to Sara's note, we're supposed to buy a couple of tickets."

"You want us to get on that thing?" Karen glared at the big boat. "What if it leaves the dock? We'll never get back in time to keep our appointment with the sergeant. It's going to be tight as it is!"

I shrugged. "She says to buy two boat tickets and that she will find us."

Karen swore loudly and, appropriate to the setting, like a foul-mouthed sailor. The ticket taker at the booth reddened— I guess she'd never heard the F-word used so exquisitely—and handed over two tickets. Karen may be a poet at heart but she's sometimes, under the right circumstances, got the mouth of a dockworker and her prose then leans towards the sewer level.

We joined a couple dozen other tourists, young and old, and climbed the gangway. After circling all three decks of the steamboat, we settled for two seats on the upper deck toward the bow. We'd seen no sign of Sara.

"This is ridiculous," Karen said. "What if she isn't even here? We've wasted our time." She plomped herself down on a bench. "May as well enjoy the view."

"That's the spirit."

To Karen's dismay, the boat pulled away from the dock, turned, and started upstream.

"Did you know Mark Twain was a steamboat pilot?" I said.

"I hope he's not behind the wheel today," Karen said, eyes on the receding shore. "I read he had poor eyesight." She turned to me. "Did you know he was a poet?"

"I did not."

"*He'd cuss and sing and howl and pray, And dance and drink and jest, And lie and steal. All one to him. He done his level best,*" quoted Karen. "Sounds almost like he was writing about you, Ed."

I chuckled, let Karen have her joke. Besides, she wasn't wrong really. Then I said, "*When you are old and grey and full of sleep, And nodding by the fire, take down this book, And slowly read, and dream of the soft look, Your eyes had once, and of their shadows deep; How many loved your moments of glad grace, And loved your beauty with love false or true, But one man loved the pilgrim soul in you, And loved the sorrows of your changing face.*"

Karen gasped. "You? Quoting Yeats?" She gaped at me and continued, "*And bending down beside the glowing bars, Murmur, a little sadly, how Love fled And paced upon the mountains overhead And hid his face amid a crowd of stars.*" She took my hand in hers and gave it a squeeze. "I can't believe you know that poem. It's one of my absolute favorites!"

"Hey, you're not the only poet in this outfit."

We heard the sound of two hands clapping and spun our heads around. Sara Chronis stood behind us grinning.

"Hello, Sara," Karen and I said as one.

Looking every bit the tourist, dressed in khaki shorts, leather sandals, and a blue New Orleans JazzFest 2016 T-shirt, Sara returned our greeting and slipped into the seat beside me. Dark Ray-Ban's concealed her eyes and a white ballcap, with NOLA spelled out in big blocky letters, completed her tourist look.

"Ten-fifteen, Ed," Karen said, tapping her watch face. "We're running out of time."

"What's up?" Sara asked. She sucked loudly on a Big Gulp, her lips fastened around a fat red-and-white straw. "What happens at ten-fifteen?"

I explained that a Sgt. Lecourt was hoping to have a word with us regarding our involvement in the deaths of Ursula Broussard, Lola Davies, and now Daniel Hernandez. "He wants us in his office at ten-thirty."

"He *insisted* we be there," Karen emphasized.

"Yeah, I heard a student got shot on campus last night," Sara said, adjusting her cap. "That's rough. You say he's the roommate of the kid you're looking for?"

"That's right."

"I wish I could help but, actually, it's your help I was hoping for."

"Oh?" I said. "How so?"

Softly, she dropped a bombshell. "The ARC is hot on the trail of an alien."

"You don't say," I kept my voice on an even keel. "And you believe this? You said yourself that they're always chasing down the most absurd rumors."

"This time, it seems legit. They claim to have hard evidence, although I haven't seen it yet. They're keeping it close to their chests. The ARC's leaders themselves are flying in today from DC. I know this sounds crazy but I've a hunch they might really be onto something," Sara said quietly.

"And if they are, the CIA wants to be in on it," I stated.

"That's what I'm here for. If there is an alien, it's my job to bring it in...alive, if possible." Sara wiped a fingerprint smudge from her sunglasses with the hem of her T-shirt, then pushed them up her nose. "But these ARC people are... I don't know... They can be a bit extreme, you might say."

"I think as alien hunters, that's a prerequisite." And ARC's members, from my up-close and personal experiences with them, were a particularly unstable bunch. They had no scruples and were not above the use of torture when it suited their aims.

"I'm not joking, Ed. This is serious." She removed her cap,

combed her fingers through her hair and resettled the hat atop her head. "People could get hurt...or worse."

"Sorry."

"I'm afraid they're going to turn into an ugly blood thirsty mob. What if they really are hot on the trail of an..." She paused and made sure no one was within listening distance. They weren't. "An alien. A real alien. Can you imagine the implications? The repercussions?"

I could.

"We might have our first contact with an extraterrestrial. The last thing we want is for them to kill it. We'd lose our first real hopes of communicating with a species from another world."

"And you want my help why?"

"Because," explained Sara, pausing to slurp her slushy beverage, "the Agency is afraid of word getting out. I can't bring in another agent, let alone a dozen! You can be there. ARC's membership won't suspect you. You're so...normal."

Karen groaned.

"I've seen you in action, Ed. There's something unique about you. You can handle yourself. You're good under pressure and you seem to have a knack for handling difficult situations. Also, you're unofficial. You're not handcuffed with the same constraints that I have to work within. That could be a bonus in a situation as delicate and unpredictable as this."

Sara squeezed my hand. Hers was cold to the touch but I didn't mind. Karen, on the other hand, did.

I quickly unhooked myself. "When is this all supposed to take place?"

"Tonight. Midnight."

"Where?"

Sara shook her head in frustration. "That I can't tell you because I don't know. The higher ups are remaining tightlipped about it. All I know for sure is that we are to meet at the ARC offices at eleven-thirty and be ready for action."

I sighed and clung to my knees. Time was short. But Sara

was a friend. "Where is this office?"

"Right here in town. On Derbigny Street. It's really a small house in the Ninth Ward."

"The Ninth Ward?" I said. Alexandra Streliski's neighborhood. Coincidence?

"Rents are cheap."

"Of course. Well, I'm sure I—"

Karen tugged on my arm. And when I say *tugged*, I mean she practically ripped my arm out of its socket. "Ed, could I have a word with you, please?"

"Sure, go ahead."

"In private." Karen smiled a big phony smile at Sara.

"I suppose." I allowed Karen to drag me to the rail. "What's the big deal? What's wrong with you?"

"Nothing's wrong with *me*," Karen said, looking over my shoulder in the direction Sara sat. "It's you I'm worried about. What's wrong with you? You cannot go help Sara capture an alien. Maybe kill an alien."

"She's a friend. She's counting on me."

"That's all well and good, Ed, but what if *you* are the alien that they are hunting?" Karen jabbed me between the ribs. "Think about it! You might be the alien the ARC is hunting. Capturing! Killing! Slicing and dicing!"

I frowned. "You have a point." The ARC was relentless. And it wouldn't be the first time the ARC had had me in their deadly sights.

"Yeah, I do!" Karen gripped me. "Besides, we don't have much time left to find Fu before Mister Ha cuts us off, pulls the plug on us. We'll be left with nothing, no money, no office, no house, no way to get back to Los Angeles."

"Nothing?" Except the 10 grand burning a hole in my pocket. Well, the nightstand back at the hotel where I'd secreted it.

"Nothing!" Karen built a zero with her thumb and forefinger and stuck it in front of my nose. "We've got to focus, Ed. Focus!"

I glanced at Sara and wiggled my fingers at her. "What do I do? How can I say no?" On the other hand, I didn't want to be captured again or killed. And the idea of being sliced and diced didn't sound so good either.

"Let me handle this," I told Karen, giving her a reassuring pat on the arm.

Karen let out a sigh of relief. "Thank god."

We walked back to Sara, cradling her Big Gulp. "Well?" she asked.

"Okay," I said. "I'm in. You can count on me."

Karen screamed. Passengers looked all around, half-expecting that we'd hit an errant iceberg, far from its natural habitat, and were in imminent danger of slowly sinking and quickly drowning.

"Oh, yeah," I said with a glance at my partner. "There's one condition."

"What's that?"

"Karen insists on coming, too."

My partner groaned, then whimpered, then crossed to the nearest railing and vomited up her breakfast.

While my partner was busy wasting a perfectly good breakfast by feeding it to the fish, I took the opportunity to show Sara a picture of our missing boy.

"Terry? Terry Lawrence?" Sara said.

"You know him?"

"Hell, yeah. He's a monster hunter, his term, not mine."

"A monster hunter?"

"Monster hunter, alien hunter...conspiracy wacko. Oh yeah, he's crazy obsessed with all that stuff."

I rubbed my hands together. Now things were getting interesting

"And you're sure this Terry Lawrence is the young man in this picture?" I held the photo aloft.

"Definitely. Not a doubt about it. I wonder why he's using an alias?"

"Me, too," I said, as Karen hobbled over on wobbly knees

and plonked down beside me. She looked a little green, and I'm not talking about her hair color. Her face looked green as a tomatillo.

"What's going on?" Karen asked. She snatched Sara's Big Gulp from the agent's hands and helped herself to a big gulp. She licked her lips and burped.

I explained that Sara recognized Fu as a member of the ARC group she'd infiltrated.

"Shit." Karen offered Sara her drink back.

"You keep it," Sara said.

Karen did.

"This Terry, or Fu, is one crazy dude. Wears a gun and a knife everywhere he goes. And he's trigger happy! I once saw him shoot what he thought was an alien."

"See?" Karen said, elbowing me.

"Did he hit it?" I had to ask.

"He hit something but it was no alien. It was a twelve-foot gator. Nice shot, though, right between the eyes."

"Between the eyes, Ed," Karen repeated.

"Yeah, yeah. He does sound unstable," I said.

"Thinks he sees aliens everywhere and is dying to get his hands on one," Sara told us. "He's the one person I worry about the most."

"I can see why," I replied.

"I can't believe it," Karen said. "I mean, I thought we'd be looking for some meek college student not some maniac alien hunter!"

We all felt a bump as the Natchez returned to the dock and the engine shut off.

Karen glanced at her watch and jumped to her feet. "Sonofabitch."

"What?" I asked.

"We're nearly an hour late for our meeting with Sergeant Lecourt."

"Relax," I said, climbing to me feet. "He probably hasn't even noticed yet."

"Oh, yeah?" Karen stood at the railing, pointing at the shore. "Then what's that?"

I joined her at the side of the steamboat. An NOPD squad car sat in front of the gangway, lights flashing. Two hefty and armed uniformed officers leaned against the hood of their vehicle, looking our way. "Well, look at that. I guess he sent a welcoming party."

28

Hunkering shoulder to shoulder in the back seat of a squad car that reeked of coffee and pungent cologne, Karen whispered in my ear. "See what you've done? Now, we've got the police mad at us. Forget stonewalling. When we get to the station, let's just tell Lecourt whatever he wants to know. Let him handle everything. We're out of our league, Ed. Time to pack it in."

"And go back on my word to Sara?" I bristled.

"Yes!"

I did some head shaking before responding. "Don't you see," I told Karen, matching my whisper to hers. "Now more than ever we need to lend our assistance to Sara tonight. We need to be there when the ARC does whatever it is they are gathering to do. That is our best chance yet to get our hands on Fu Chun. And get ourselves out of this jam we are in."

"And get ourselves killed in the process," came her reply.

"You know what they say, can't bake a cake without breaking a few heads," I said.

"Eggs, Ed, eggs."

"Potato, tomato."

"Whatever." She clutched onto me as the police cruiser bounced in and out of a pothole. "Get real, Ed! We've really stepped in it this time and I don't see any good way out."

"That's where you are making your mistake," I said. A mistake she makes regularly but I wasn't about to point that out here and now—not being in the mood for one of her famous sucker punches.

"How's that?"

"Your being…how can I put this? Realistic."

"What the f—"

"Do not bend to reality," I cut in. "Make reality bend to you."

"Really, I think your mind is bent."

"See," I replied. "It's working already."

"Maybe I should go back to being a graphic artist," Karen said, watching the world go by outside the rear window, her nose pressed to the glass.

"You hated that job."

"Maybe, but I liked being alive. Not to mention having a steady paycheck." She levelled her eyes on me. "One of us needs to be the responsible party in this relationship. Since you're incapable of it, that leaves me."

"Trust me," I said. "I've seen the future. Everything is going to turn out great."

Karen narrowed her eyes at me suspiciously. "Seriously?" she said softly. "You can see the future?"

"Of course," I said with a shrug indicating it was no big deal. Of course, it was another BIG FAT LIE. I'm an alien, not a magician. "We've got this. Everything is lining up perfectly."

"You're sure?"

I could hear it in her voice, see it in her eyes… Karen really, really, really wanted to believe me. Who was I to let her down? It would be unkind of me… So I lied some more.

"Scout's honor." I raised my right hand and held up a bunch of fingers that might have resembled something a scout might do—then again, it might have been something I'd seen Mr. Spock do on Star Trek. Either way, I was pretty sure Karen wouldn't know the difference—she'd never been a Boy Scout and wasn't into science fiction.

We arrived at the 8th District police station. One officer escorted us inside while the other drove off with the squad car— perhaps on a beignet run…perhaps to toss some colorful plastic beads at a young woman down on Bourbon Street in exchange for her flashing her breasts at him—this was New Orleans, all things were possible.

Sgt. Lecourt kept us cooling our heels out in the hall for an hour, then interrogated us for another hour or two. Finally, we were free.

"I felt like I was in high school all over again," Karen groused as we marched outdoors. "Waiting endlessly outside the principal's office, then listening to some dumb lecture."

"Something of a miscreant in school, were you?" The sun and humidity hit me hard. Karen hadn't warned me that walking the streets of New Orleans would be much like visiting Venus. If I'd known, I might have packed an air-conditioned spacesuit.

Karen grinned. "I had my moments." Her phone chose that moment to jingle-jangle. "It's a text from Mister Ha," she said, taking a look.

"What's he say?"

"Just this." She held up the phone. *24 HOURS*

"Hmm, succinct, isn't he?"

"Yeah, but he's made his point. What do we do now, Mister Detective? By the way, you never told me—why did you become a detective?"

"I had to do something. At the same time, without any real skills, at least none that apply on this planet, and no real ID, I came to the conclusion that being a private investigator, operating at the edges of the law might be something I'd be best suited for."

"I guess that makes sense. Although the pay sucks."

"True. It's not like I'm getting rich doing this. As for what we should do next? Let's think… What would Sam Spade do?"

"Drink and smoke, if I remember my Dashiell Hammett correctly," wisecracked Karen.

"True. Always a good option."

We did have some time to kill and no good leads to follow up until our meeting up with Sara Chronis and the ARC mob later that night. Karen and I had stayed true to our plan and given Sgt. Lecourt little information, none that he wasn't already aware of. All in all, a successful, if time-wasting, exercise for us.

Sgt. Lecourt wasn't happy. He'd considered Lola Davies a friend and had revered her for her talents. To now view her as a murderer was quite disheartening for him. But he seemed resigned to accepting this.

As for the murder of Daniel Hernandez, he admitted to us that the police were clueless as to who had committed that crime and why. The police considered it most likely that he'd been murdered by a fellow student and that drugs and/or jealousy over a girl might have been the reasons for that crime.

Those were not bad theories but I doubted either was right. They just didn't ring true. Not that I had any theories that were particularly better.

Daniel Hernandez had been tied up in our case from the beginning. Now he was dead—leaving us with one more dead end and plenty of unanswered questions. Who had killed him and why remained a big question in my mind. Lola Davies was dead. Ofeez was dead. Neither could have shot Daniel Hernandez to death. And as much as I might have felt the urge to shoot him dead for attempting to stab Karen, not to mention that godawful Elvis impersonation he persisted in cursing the world with, I didn't shoot him.

So who did?

Fu Chun?

The possibility seemed likely. More than likely. Far too likely. But why kill Daniel Hernandez? Did Fu hate Elvis impersonators as much as I did?

Did he suspect his ex-roommate had been an alien and, thus, he needed to rid the world of it?

And what would it mean for our potential payday should we find Fu but in the process find out that he was a crazed killer? Would Mr. Ha reward us or punish us?

In answer to Karen's question about what we should do next, I replied, "I'm still a little hungry. Let's catch a bite then go out to the Ninth Ward and see if Alexandra Streliski is home."

"Okay but why? I mean, I know we have to be out in the Ninth later anyway, but what do you want to talk to her about?

She wasn't exactly helpful the first time."

"No but maybe that's because we weren't asking the right questions. And I have so many questions I want to ask her. First and foremost: how did she know about us and where to find us in the first place? She called you at the hotel, remember?"

"Huh." Karen scratched her head. "Yeah, I'd forgotten about that."

"I also want to ask Alexandra if she knows where Fu is now. With Lola dead, he might have returned to her apartment, looking for someplace to hide and someone to hide him. Maybe, just maybe, we'll find him sooner than later."

"I like it."

"Great. You pick the place to eat. We'll walk until you find a restaurant with a menu that looks good to you." Karen is a much pickier eater than I. "And let's not worry about prices, it may not matter much longer."

"Yeah, don't remind me." Karen took my hand and turned up the sidewalk. "Ed!" she shrieked and slammed to a halt, releasing my hand.

"What?"

"Your hands!"

I lowered my eyes and raised my hands. "YIKES!" My hands looked and felt like two big bright-red balloons. "What the hell! It's just like that Pink Floyd song!" I gazed in horror at my two big red balloons as I gesticulated madly. I half expected my hands to disengage from my wrists and float up to the sun.

"Pink who? What the hell are you talking about?"

"Pink Floyd!" What the hell were my hands doing?!

"Who's he?"

"The band, Pink Floyd! They've got a song about—"

Karen looked at me blankly.

"Seriously? You don't know Pink Floyd? Hope and Crosby, I suppose I can understand you not being familiar with those guys, but the band Pink Floyd isn't that old." I shook my head with amazement. "Sometimes, I wonder which of the two of us is really from this planet and which isn't, because sometimes it sure as hell isn't obvious!"

Karen shrugged. "Sorry, never heard of them."

"Dark side of the moon? Brick in the wall? Mean anything to you?"

Karen stared at me as if I had a brick for a brain. I threw my hands in the air defeated. "Yikes! My hands!" I'd almost forgotten there were more important worries at the moment than my partner's lack of contemporary music history knowledge. I would leave Karen comfortably dumb.

"Forget Pink Floyd!" screamed Karen. A small crowd had gathered. Even a couple of cops watched from the steps of the police station. "What about your hands? What's wrong with them?"

"I don't know. Come on." I walked quickly and turned the corner, out of sight of the police. I didn't need them butting in, asking questions. I paused in the alcove of a shuttered office. I thought quickly. What could I possibly have been exposed to? "It must have been something I ate," I concluded.

Sgt. Lecourt had offered us some food and drink. Lunchtime leftovers from home, packed for him by his doting wife, he explained. Karen had settled for a chunk of cornbread.

"Oh, oh." Karen pressed her hands to her face. "Peaches."

"Peaches?" My heart stilled. My mind raced.

"Yeah, peaches. I thought it smelled sorta fruity. Th-There might have been peaches in the sauce of that braised chicken Sergeant Lecourt offered you." She stared at my hands. I couldn't blame her. They looked hideous, bloated and red.

"Peaches! What was he thinking? Was Lecourt trying to poison me? Kill me?"

"I'm afraid so. I mean, not that he was trying to kill you. He just didn't know about your...uh...allergy?"

"Shit." I shook my balloon hands. A new crowd was gathering. I was becoming as popular as that clown who blows up those animal-shaped balloons at the carnival.

"We've got to get you to the hospital. The emergency room!"

"Emergency room? Hospital? Are you crazy? We can't do that!"

"Why not?"

"Because they might want to do tests, x-rays, god knows what!"

"So?" Karen grabbed one of my bratwurst fingers and gently squeezed. "Does it hurt?"

"Only when I look at them!"

"Are you afraid of doctors?"

"No, I am not afraid of doctors. But I am afraid of what they might find. You should be, too." My insides were decidedly not human and my vital signs would shock a physician. Hell, they'd shock a zoo veterinarian—and they've seen the insides of platypuses!

"Oh, shit." Karen released my finger. "Right. So what are we going to do? You can't stay like this. And you can't walk around looking like that. People are staring. The ARC membership will definitely think you're some sort of alien if you show up with those freak hands of yours."

"I know that." I made a snap decision. I couldn't snap my fingers but it was a snap decision nonetheless, just minus the theatrics. "We'll go back to the hotel. Wait for the swelling to go down."

"Are you sure?"

"That the swelling will go down?"

Karen nodded.

"No."

"And if it doesn't?" She looked with worry at my giant red five-fingered balloons.

I thought about that. "Well, the timing could be right seeing as how the detective business might soon be coming to its end…"

"And?"

"Join the circus?" I suggested. I stuffed my balloons as best I could under the front of my shirt to hide them from public view and we fleet-footed it to the Bourbon Orleans.

29

Back in our room, Karen and I tried everything shy of grabbing a sewing needle from the complimentary repair kit under the sink, and trying to pop my big red balloon hands. Among other things we did try, Karen applied a hot compress using a couple of hand towels. When that failed to work its magic, she valiantly tried a cold compress. Failure #2.

I suggested bourbon. Karen scoffed at the idea but called room service and ordered a bottle anyway. Good thing she acceded to my wishes. No way in hell I could dial with my big red sausage fingers.

I swigged bourbon and more bourbon.

I soaked up a lot of bourbon. Karen ordered bottle #2. I even soaked my hands in a bathroom sink full of bourbon and hand soap.

No effect.

We were striking out.

"Shit shit shit," I said, eying my hands as I reclined on the bed.

Karen fell onto the mattress beside me. "Cheer up, Ed." She gently held my wrist. "I think the swelling's starting to go down."

"You think?"

"Sure," she said, although she didn't sound all that convincing to me. "And look on the bright side."

"What's that?"

"It was only your hands. Imagine if it had been your feet!" Karen smothered her giggles. "Imagine trying to walk like that!" She failed to smother the next round of laughs. "Or your head!

Imagine yourself with a big red balloon head!"

"You, Karen Dalton, are a cruel one." I folded my arms crossly over my belly. "If Elvis was alive today, hell, if Daniel Hernandez was alive today, I'd pay him twenty bucks to sing *Don't Be Cruel* personally to you!"

Karen made a not-so-genuine show of remorse. "Sorry." She sat up on her knees. "Anything else I can do for you?"

"Sex?" I raised my brow in hope.

Karen locked her hands against her hips. "Sex? Now?"

"I've heard it can be a universal cure-all."

Karen frowned. "You have, have you? And just who is it that says that?"

"Who? Are you seriously asking that question? All the most advanced species, that's who." I pressed the back of my head into my pillow, grateful that it was not the giant red balloon my partner had suggested it might have become. "Of course," I said, shuttering my eyelids and doing my best to look and sound self-pitying, "what was I thinking? I mean, you *are* an Earthling. Hardly one of the most advanced—"

"You are pathetic."

"But—"

"Shut up, dummy!" Karen said with a touch of humor. She tugged at my trousers and she got no argument from me. Karen did things to me that no Pazu has ever done to another Pazu. I did my best to keep up, but with big red circus balloons for hands, my options and skills were limited.

Nonetheless, we muddled through.

When we were done, and the damp sheets wrapped themselves around our lower extremities, we held each other close and shared a drink.

"What time is it?" Karen asked, her words riding the crest of a yawn.

I untangled myself, turned on my side and eyed the clock on the nightstand. "Nine o'clock. Shit." I rubbed my face. "Nine o'clock!"

"I guess we dozed off." Karen patted my leg, a tight twist

of green blanket snaking around her bare belly like a cuddly python.

"Right. No harm done. Still plenty of time." I slid my feet off the bed and to the floor, rubbed my hands across my face once more. My tongue felt and tasted like an old shag carpeting left out in the dumpster for about a month—don't ask.

"Hey!" Karen exclaimed.

"What?" I tugged my trousers up off the ground. How the hell had they gotten themselves under the nightstand?

"Your hands, Ed. Your hands!"

I looked at the implements in question. "Normal." Well, each appeared about the correct size, just a little pink was all, like cotton candy. "How about that!"

We sorted ourselves out and hailed a cab. I gave the cabbie directions to Alexandra Streliski's apartment. He dropped us off at the curb and zoomed hurriedly away.

Under the halo of a lamppost, we watched him speed around the corner with an accompanying tire squeal.

"What is it about this place that makes everybody do that?" I asked.

"Are you kidding? This place is creepy. Beyond creepy. With a capital K," Karen replied. "I get the heebie-jeebies every time I lay eyes on the place. And it's much worse in the dark!"

The building indeed stood in shadows. An aura of mystery, emptiness and neglect hung in the air, seemed to swallow the entire street. Looking up and down the street, everything was colored in shades of gray and black with an occasional light burning in a window. Few lights illuminated the windows of Streliski's tilted building. From the sidewalk, I couldn't be sure which windows belonged to her.

"I understand what you mean...I guess. But I believe you spell creepy with a C, capital or not, your choice," I corrected.

"That was a joke, Ed." She ran her knuckles into my shoulder. Not too hard but hard enough to get my attention. "How many times do I have to tell you? I can be funny when I want to."

"Hmm, I guess this was just one of those times where you did not want to," I made the mistake of saying. So, so many times my mouth gets ahead of my brain. I blame it on the influence of my adopted human makeup. I'm much smarter than that normally, really, I am.

Karen pinched me.

"Ouch!" Then she kissed me. She's a complicated person, my poet partner.

"I don't see Alexandra's Prius anywhere. Now what?"

I rubbed my chin between thumb and forefinger. Not that I really needed to but it was just so-soooo nice to have normal—well, Earth normal—fingers once again that I could barely keep my hands off myself. Karen had yelled at me in the backseat of the cab because the cabbie kept looking at me nervously via the rearview mirror as I unconsciously rubbed my hands up and down my body. What could I do? It felt so good!

"Better still," I said in response to her remark. "New plan."

"And that is?"

"Breaking and entering."

"And if someone calls the police on us?" Karen trudged resignedly up the stairs with me. She knew better than to argue with me when my mind was made up.

"I don't see that happening. Not many folks about, plus I'm very good at what I do. I rarely get caught."

"Rarely?" Karen whispered to the stairwell. She was breathing hard. "Oh, that's a confidence builder."

We arrived at the fifth floor landing. Nobody was around. We'd passed no one on our way up the stairs, either coming or going. All we caught were the occasional voices of people talking coming from unseen radios and televisions. Everyone tucked in for the night.

I pressed an ear to Alexandra Streliski's door, held my breath and listened. "I don't hear anything."

"That doesn't mean she isn't home."

"Her car's gone, remember?"

"And maybe her car broke down and is in the shop, or she

loaned it to a friend."

I pointed to the ground. "There's no light coming from under her door." And there had to be a half-inch gap between door and floor.

"Still… I don't like this. We don't know what we'll find on the other side. She might be waiting for us on the other side of the door pointing a gun filled with bullets."

"Why must you always assume the worst?"

"I like to be prepared. And the unknown scares me." Karen squeezed her hands together. "What if Alexandra's got a roommate? What if they're home?"

"For that matter, what if Fu Chun is snoozing in the futon inside? Shouldn't we find out? Opening this door could be the answer to all our problems."

"Or the biggest mistake of our lives," Karen had to say.

"A small price to pay," I replied. "And there's only one way to find out." I reached for the door knob.

Karen stopped me, placing her hand over mine. "Seriously, Ed, what if she's home?"

"Fine. I'll knock." Anything to speed things along.

"Thank you."

I rapped my knuckles—yes, I could see my knuckles once more—on the door.

And the door to the unit behind us shot open. We spun around. A very large man filled the doorway. Well, either a very large man or a very small gorilla.

30

"Who the hell are you?" the big stranger demanded. His deep voice filled the hallway.

Okay, we'd learned one thing. The big hairy goon was capable of human speech—English, too. So possibly he was human. But god he was hairy!

And big! Did I mention he was big?

This guy was as wide as my refrigerator. He had massive arms, not super muscular, but thick, the girth of a pair of plucked frozen turkeys.

A ribbed white T-shirt did its best to hold itself together against his massive chest. Curly black hair sprouted from his flesh in all directions. Black hair everywhere! Black hair sprouting like kudzu from his upper chest, arms and belly. A head filled with curly black hair running down his skull and covering most of his face.

Dark brown eyes and a bulbous nose provided something of a contrast. Frayed, loose-fitting blue jeans fought valiantly against gravity but the signs of a losing battle were evident— his pants hanging low on his wide hips. He was barefoot and I noticed that his toes had more hair on them then I had on my entire torso!

"Well—" I began.

Karen retreated behind me.

"You here to take a look at the apartment across the way?" he demanded. He wore the smell of beer like an invisible cloak.

There was still a remote possibility that I was being confronted by a talking gorilla. A talking gorilla with a New Orleans accent…and a penchant for an evening brewski.

"The apartment? Yes, the apartment! Yes, that's right. Here to see the apartment," I said.

"That was fast." He turned his eyes on Karen. "You two together?"

"Y-Yes," she said, not moving from what she hoped was the protective zone of my much smaller corpus.

"So, what are you bothering me for? Go in, already." The fat cigar shoved up in the corner of his mouth jiggle-jaggled as he growled. "Youse can knock if you got any questions."

He shut his apartment door in our faces.

"You heard the man," I said, gesturing at the door to my left.

Karen turned the handle to Alexandra Streliski's place and in we went.

Darkness greeted us.

Karen fumbled for a light switch. "Got it." The bare bulb overhead popped into existence.

I stepped past Karen. "Hello?" I took two more steps. "Anybody home? Alexandra?"

"Wow." Karen did a slow turn. "Empty."

"Pretty much, yeah." The piano, the mattress in the corner, a broken three-legged stool, and a whole lot of dust. That was pretty much it. Even the portrait of Wordsworth was gone, as was the bureau he had been hanging above. A bent nail jutted from the plaster, proof that it had once hung there and we hadn't imagined it.

The curtains were pulled tight. A half-dead fern sat in a small blue pot atop the brown piano. And that was the most alive thing in the apartment. An upside-down yellow plastic lid off a margarine container served as a cheap plant saucer.

"Alexandra?" repeated Karen, sticking close to me. "I guess she isn't here."

"There's no place to hide, that's for sure. Unless she's in the bathroom."

Karen veered to the bathroom in the far corner of the room and peeked inside. "Empty!"

I checked the fridge. "Empty, too." All her possessions save for the piano and bits of worthless miscellany had gone. Not a stitch of clothes and not a bite to eat remained.

"I wonder where she went?" Karen said.

"More importantly, why did she leave? Why did she feel compelled to suddenly abandon her apartment?"

"Yeah."

I riffled through the kitchen drawers. Nothing but a few rubber bands, paperclips and expired grocery coupons. "Time to have a chat with the gorilla next door."

"I suppose but that guy scares me," Karen said.

"Nothing to be scared of. I'm sure he's nothing but a big pussycat," I replied. Of course, I hate pussycats every bit as much as they hate me.

We closed Alexandra's door and knocked on the gorilla-man's door. The ground shook, presaging his approach. The door was flung wide.

"Yeah? Whadya think?"

"The apartment? It's empty," I said.

"Course it's empty. I mean, you got that piano. But you can keep it. I ain't hauling it out. Was a bitch getting it in in the first place. So it stays." He shoved his mitts into the pockets of his jeans. It was all his pants could do to remain up. "Either of you play?"

"Only with each other," I replied for the both of us. "We're exclusive."

"Huh?" He blinked.

"He means the piano, Ed. Right?" Karen said.

"Oh, the piano. No, neither of us play."

"Thank god for that," the guy muttered. "Day and night, night and day…middle of the night…fuck, that woman liked to play her—"

"She must have been quite good," I said.

"She was no Jerry Lee Lewis," he answered. "Played all this weird shit…hardly music at all, why—"

"So Alexandra Streliski moved out?" Karen interrupted his rant to ask.

That caught him by surprise. "You knew her?"

"Only casually," I explained.

"Ah," he scratched his beard. "I thought you'd seen the flyer. Guess she told you about the place?"

"Right," I said, because it seemed like the right thing to say, not because it was.

"You're the manager?" Karen asked.

"I own the building. Freddy Rabbitt," the gorilla-man answered, pulling himself taller and…somehow, even broader. I half-expected him to pound his chest with his fists and growl.

Rabbit? Had this guy ever looked at himself in a mirror? He could be the genetic result of T. Rex breeding with a lowland gorilla, maybe with a little genetic material from one of those ridiculous giant bunnies in that *Night of the Lepus* horror flick. Despite its all-star cast, Janet Leigh, Rory Calhoun and Stuart Whitman, the film had flopped bigger than a rabbit's floppy ears. No surprise. A bunny is still just a bunny, even if it is trying to devour you.

The movie really was awful. I mean, I've watched it on six or seven occasions and it's just as bad each time. Even the star power of DeForest Kelly, the original Star Trek's Dr. Leonard "Bones" McCoy, couldn't save it from being called a movie so bad that it made *Attack of the Killer Tomatoes* look like an Oscar contender.

"So?" He looked down at us. "You interested?"

"Y-Yes," I said, the world coming back into focus. "Although I am rather surprised that Alexandra left. I mean, her lease wasn't up, was it?"

"Like the flyer says, I rent month-to-month. Course, it's the middle of the month now but she wanted to leave, so leave she did. She's impulsive. Lost half a month's rent. Her problem, not mine. Not that she complained about me keeping her money. She had a coupla guys help her move with their truck."

"Did you know them? Had you seen them around before?" I asked.

"Nope. Never seen 'em before, not so's I remember."

"Hmm. Did she mention where she was going?" I asked him.

"Why she was in such a hurry?" added Karen.

"Nope." When Freddy Rabbitt rubbed his mitts together, it was like watching a pair of randy marmosets mate. "She did seem upset. Angry. Scared. I can tell you that."

"Did she say why she was so upset?" Karen asked.

"She just kept saying she didn't care about the money she was going to lose. Just kept saying 'I don't care. I don't care. He's a monster. He's a monster.'"

"Who was a monster?" I asked.

"I don't know. She was rambling. Only kept saying 'He's a monster. He's a monster.' That's all I could get out of her."

"Do you think she meant Fu?" I asked.

"You mean Foosball? You know that kid, too? Hell, he's no monster. He's a little goofy, yeah, hell yeah, but no monster."

"Foosball?"

"That was my nickname for him."

"Have you seen him lately?"

This caused him to turn down his lips and think a moment. "Na, not too lately. Those two broke up."

"So he hadn't helped her move?"

"Nope."

A roar came from the direction of the TV somewhere in the bowels of his apartment and he turned his thick neck for a look at the screen. "Look, are you interested in renting the place or not?"

"Sorry, we didn't mean to keep you," I said. "We'll mull it over and let you know tomorrow. Would that be alright?"

The gorilla-man slammed the door in our faces.

"I'll take that for a yes," I told the door.

31

Karen's phone buzzed in her purse as we clomped down the poorly-lit stairwell somewhere in the limbo between the fourth and third floors.

"Now what?" she grumbled, pausing to balance on a warped wooden tread so she could extract her phone. "I hope it's not Mister Ha again…continuing his damn countdown."

"If it is our employer, simply tell him our assignment is ninety-percent complete."

"So, lie again?

"Yes, lie again. Lie again and again and again. Sooner or later, it could become true."

Karen looked at her phone. "Oh!"

"Who is it?"

"Sara Chronis. She's at ARC headquarters. They've moved up the time for the mission. She says to hurry."

"Does she say if Fu Chun is amongst them?"

"No, she doesn't mention him."

"Ask."

Karen typed. Sara replied with a thumbs-up.

"Let's hurry." I grabbed Karen's hand and we resumed our descent. Out at the street, all was quiet. "Not a mouse is stirring, maybe a monster or two, but the mice are all glued to their respective boob tubes—watching something cheesy, no doubt," I noted.

"Ha-ha."

"How far to the house on Derbigny Street?"

Karen consulted her map app. "Quarter mile."

"Fine, quicker to walk than to wait for a ride."

Karen sighed. "I'm tired, my feet are sore and my legs ache. Couldn't you just, you know, zap us there?"

"What? Like teleportation?"

"Yes, exactly!"

"Snap my fingers and instantly transport us across physical space?"

Karen looked at me eagerly.

"You're not going to let go of this silly notion, are you?" I asked with a frown.

"Nope. I know you're keeping secrets from me."

"Fine. I give up. I don't know why I didn't think of that myself." I wrapped my left hand over her forearm and raised my right hand. "Like this?"

Karen nodded.

"Ready?"

"Yes-Yes!"

SNAP!

I released Karen and started walking towards Derbigny Street.

"Hey! What happened?" Karen shouted. I heard the sound of her running steps as she hurried to catch up with me. "You were supposed to teleport us!"

"My subatomic molecular rearranger must be on the fritz," I said.

"Your... Oh, you lied to me."

"To say I lied is rather harsh. Let's agree that I was pulling your leg."

"Oh, yeah? Do it again and I'm going to pull your teeth out!"

We kissed. Hey, it's what we do. Don't judge.

A sliver of moon followed us.

"Remain vigilant," I said, approaching the small nondescript house some minutes later, careful to keep a monstrous live oak in front of me. "Let's keep our voices down."

"Shouldn't we go in?"

"Not yet. I want to make sure this isn't a trap. The ARC can be quite devious. I do not want to be captured by them again. You remember what happened last time.”

“Yeah, I saved your butt.”

“Yes, but not before I’d practically had my private parts fried!” I reminded her.

Karen giggled. She has a weird sense of humor bordering on the macabre, especially when it comes to my private parts.

“I can’t see anything. All the curtains are shut.” Karen stated the obvious.

“We’ll go around back but let’s be quiet about it,” I reminded her.

The house had a small footprint and was a simple one-story rectangle with a low sloping roof. Black iron bars protected the front windows. A half-collapsed 4-foot chain-link fence did little to protect the backyard from intruders.

A sliding door leading to the patchy lawn was uncovered. We heard voices and saw a dozen or so persons standing and moving around inside. If you didn’t know better, the scene appeared more like a black-dress-required neighborhood get-together and not the alien lynching party that it was intended to be.

“There’s Sara,” I said. The undercover agent stood next to a squat white porcelain kitchen table.

“Hey, I think that’s Fu!” Karen whispered urgently, her fingernails digging into my shoulder.

“I believe you’re right. Although he does seem to be embracing his Terry the Terror alter ego at the moment.” Dressed in black from head to toe, including a black beanie, a handgun sat on one hip and a bowie knife on the opposite—like he was attending an adults-only costume party, deadly weapons optional.

“What should we do?”

“We could go in and grab him. I don’t think the others could put up much of a fight.” They looked more like a bunch of meek tourists than they did an alien-fighting militia.

“Kidnap him?”

“Sure. Tie him up and haul him home.” I was really missing

home. Even though Los Angeles wasn't *home* home, it was my home on Earth. And alien enough in its own way.

"I don't think the airline will like that."

"No, I suppose not."

"Should we go in?"

"Yes. They don't seem to be lying in wait to trap me. Although, maybe you should go first...just in case."

"Ha-ha." Karen shoved me forward.

I rapped on the glass.

A dozen heads turned our way. Three people pointed handguns at us, including Fu Chun. A waiflike woman, dressed in black like everyone else in the bunch, waved a nasty-looking sawed-off shotgun at my nose.

I flashed my teeth and waved. "Hello. Hi, Sara."

"It's okay," Sara said, approaching the door and sliding it open. "This is the couple I was telling you about. Come on in," she said to me and Karen. "You're just in time. I was afraid you weren't going to make it."

"Sorry," I apologized. "We got hung up," I explained, hoping this gang didn't string us up.

We stepped up into the kitchen warmed by the bodies of the fanatics crowding it. A pot of coffee burbled on the counter. A clumsily ripped open bag of pretzels sat beside it, pretzel knots spilling out.

The waif pounced up to greet us, hand extended, shotgun pointed at the linoleum. "Liz Peters. You must be Ed and Karen." She pumped our hands violently. "So glad you could join us. We can use all the help we can get." Liz Peters waved to the others and they smiled back sheepishly. "I hear you guys are the best, real pros!" She smiled big.

"Liz is in charge of the operation," explained Sara.

"Regional director of the Alien Resistance Corp," put in another fellow.

Fu said nothing, while shooting us suspicious looks. Almost like he was ready to shoot us or gut us like a pair of perch at a moment's notice. Would Anna Ping even recognize her nephew buried inside the guise of this crazed Terry the Terror Lawrence?

"Right." Liz Peters brought her shotgun to waist level. "It's go time, people. Grab your gear and your weapons." She pushed through the assembled members and led us through the front of the house, out the door and into a pair of waiting black vans. We joined Sara and Liz in the lead van. Luckily, Fu and another couple accompanied us in the rear.

"Where are we heading?" I asked, seated on the hard metal floor in back of the van because there were only two seats up front.

"The lake," Liz Peters answered, behind the wheel.

"The lake?" Karen asked.

"Pontchartrain," Sara replied. She was riding shotgun, both figuratively and literally because she was clutching Liz Peter's shotgun while the other woman was busy steering.

"That's where the alien's been sighted," Fu said, suddenly breaking his silence. He gazed steadily at me.

"Hmm. Right, the alien."

"Locals call him the Nikker. But I know better."

"The-The Nikker?" Karen shot me with a look.

"We believe this Nikker legend is the result of an alien living on the fringes," Sara began.

"In the swamps and lakes surrounding the city," Fu said. "I've been tracking it."

The couple riding with us agreed with Fu and claimed to have spotted it themselves. "It's big," claimed the man. "Me and Diane have both seen it. Bigger than a person."

"Much bigger," agreed his mate. "And ferocious."

The man nodded. "We'd seen it rip a gator to shreds. With its bare hands!"

Karen shivered. Rummaging in her bag, she pulled out a stick of spearmint gum. She wadded up the empty wrapper and tossed it on the bare metal floor. Popping the raw stick in her mouth, she started chewing madly and nervously.

Sometimes I fear the poor dear isn't cut out for the

GLENN ERIC

detective biz.

32

"Getting close, now," Liz Peters said in hushed tones. The van slowed.

I peered out the narrow side-panel window. We'd come to a quiet location far from the bustling world. The van groaned to a stop. Fu pushed the sliding door open and jumped out. The second van pulled in behind the lead van.

We spilled out the side while Sara and Liz Peters exited the front. I noticed that no overhead lights came on in the van as the doors opened, either they were broken or they had disabled them earlier to keep from drawing unwanted attention during this stealth operation. I was guessing the latter.

I wrapped my fingers around the door handle and started to push the door shut.

"Leave it," Fu instructed. "We might need to move fast. Better to keep the door open."

"Right." I took in our surroundings...and we were surrounded, at least on three sides. Picture dead live oaks sprouting like gray immobile giants from the cracked earth. Tombstones lay scattered about, some tilting, some fallen, all old, terribly old. An ornate crypt stood in the distance. The faintly lit waters of Lake Pontchartrain glittered behind it.

The stars looked down on us as if we were crazy to be there.

And I'm sure we were.

"This is crazy," Karen said, proving my point. "A creepy old cemetery? What would an alien be doing here? Why would an alien be interested in a graveyard filled with decaying corpses?"

"Maybe it feeds on the flesh of the dead," whispered a male voice behind us.

Karen jumped. "Like a zombie? Ed!"

It was Fu speaking. He clamped his hand tightly over her mouth. "Shh!" he cautioned. "We do not want to let the Nikker know we are here. We must catch it by surprise. Okay?"

Karen nodded.

Fu lowered his hand.

I sidled over to Sara who was in a low-voiced conference with Liz Peters. "What's the plan?"

"We are going to surround the crypt on three sides," Liz Peters explained. "We'll capture the alien as it comes up from the lake."

"And if you can't?" I had to know.

"We'll kill it," Liz Peters said.

"Seems a shame," I replied.

"I agree," said Sara. Sure, I knew what she wanted, what the US Government wanted, a live alien. One they could study at their leisure.

Been that, done that.

"A dead alien specimen is better than no specimen at all," insisted Fu Chun aka Terry the Terror.

"Shouldn't we try communicating with it before doing anything drastic?" Karen couldn't resist saying.

Fu Chun snorted. "You can't reason with an alien! You know that. Aliens must be exterminated. That's our mission." He turned to Liz Peters. "Seriously, who are these two?"

"I can vouch for them," cut in Sara. "I've worked with them a couple of times. Trust me, they'll do what needs to be done when it comes to crunch time."

"Absolutely," I assured everyone. "Right, Karen?"

"Of course."

"You'd better be right," Fu Chun said, as if issuing us a warning.

Liz called for everyone to get in position around the deserted crypt.

Fu Chun drew his pistol with his right hand and held his knife at the ready in his left hand. "I'll take point."

Liz Peters put her hand on his shoulder. "Be careful."

"Always," Fu Chun promised. "This is one alien whose time on Earth is about to come to an end." He disappeared in the direction of the lake, weaving his way between fallen headstones as he proceeded.

I kept my eyes on him. I could not afford to lose sight of him again. This was our best chance for capturing him, Nikker be damned.

Karen pulled me aside. "What's going on? Do you have a plan yet?"

"Still playing it by ear," I confessed.

"Yeah? Well, consider yourself lucky if that hothead Fu doesn't shoot—or slice—both your ears off!"

"Why would he do that?"

"Oh, I don't know…a souvenir, maybe, a trophy to show his crazy friends!"

"What's up?" Sara interrupted. "Liz wants us to take cover."

"Sorry."

Karen stuck her tongue out at me but followed along.

"What do you think about all this, Ed?" Sara asked. "Team members have reported numerous sightings of this Nikker or alien or whatever the hell it is. You think it's really out there?"

"Hard to say," I said. "I guess we may be about to find out."

"Yeah, I just hope these people don't all open fire at once and kill it. Worse yet, each other. How the hell am I going to explain a dozen dead civilians to my boss?"

"Let's hope it doesn't come to that," I told her.

Sara dropped off into position behind a tall grave marker and stuck a pair of night-vision binocs to her eyes.

Karen and I moved behind a gray granite plinth for cover.

"I don't like this, Ed."

"Relax," I assured her. "Nothing is going to happen."

"No?"

"No. If these yahoos think the Nikker or any other alien is coming out of that lake like the creature from the black lagoon, they are in for one very big surprise. I didn't have the heart to tell them, or Sara for that matter, but you and I know that they're going to be very disappointed, because the Nikker slash alien they are hunting is dead. Deader than dead."

"Thank heavens for that."

"On the contrary, you can thank *me* for that," I corrected. "Ed Turner, PI, and destroyer of Fleeks."

"Remind me to pin a badge on you later," Karen said.

"I'll do that and you can also—"

A horrible scream interrupted our playtime.

"What was that?" Karen's eyes went wide with fear.

"If my ears don't deceive me, and they rarely do, that was our meal ticket!"

"Huh?"

"Fu," I replied. "Stay here." I heard gunshots. Shouts. More screams. Bouncing flashlight beams darted across the cemetery grounds.

I took off at a run towards the sounds of commotion, hoping the fool woman would listen to me for once and remain safely behind. The last thing I needed was to have to worry about protecting her butt at a dangerous and potentially deadly time like this.

I stopped momentarily, swung back to look at Karen and waved my finger at her like I was wielding the Sword of Damocles. "Do. Not. Move," I commanded.

I mean, it was a cute butt and all, but now was not the time for matters of the gluteal sort. Right now, I had other fish to fry and I feared this was no perch.

33

Ofeez!

The Fleek had his back to me but I'd recognize his sorry butt anywhere. After what we'd gone through together, how could I ever forget?

And why was he here? More importantly, why wasn't he dead? How rude of him.

The alien was on display in Nikker form. Water dripped from his inhuman flesh as he slogged towards the lake, getting further and further from me and closer and closer to his escape, his refuge.

Ofeez carried Fu Chun under his arm like he was nothing but a flimsy ragdoll. The Fleek had caught the unlucky boy in a headlock. Fu Chun gasped for breath and clawed desperately at the Nikker's inhumanly strong arm. Fu's weapons had vanished, probably lost during the one-sided fight.

A woman screamed nearby.

I turned. "What the hell!? Karen!?" I hollered at my partner. "Don't you understand—"

WOOMPH!

Something hard struck me in the back of the head. It could have been a speeding locomotive. It could have been Mount Rushmore. But no, it was Ofeez's big stupid fist.

I went flying, tumbling and tumbling, until I landed on my head and rolled onto my stomach. "Shit!" Pazus aren't built for flying, not without our flying saucers, anyway. "What the hell!?" I hollered at Karen again, wiping dirt from the corners of my eyes and blowing more out my nose. "You distracted me! See what happens?"

"Sorry!" Karen's eyes grew wide. "Ed, watch out!"

I looked up and saw a pair of giant Nikker feet attached to a pair of giant Nikker legs towering over me. Between Ofeez's feet, in the distance, I saw Fu Chun crawling around in circles on his own relatively-puny knees and elbows. He appeared dazed and confused. That made two of us.

All the others had fled. I saw them running towards their vans as fast as their scaredy-cat feet could carry them. Even their leader, Liz Peters had left the field of battle.

Only Sara remained.

I looked up at Ofeez as the Fleek raised its foot as if he meant to stomp me to death. I rolled to the side.

"Geezusfreekingchrist, Ed!" Karen yelled. "I thought you said you killed it!"

"I did, I did!"

"Yeah, well, I don't think that monster got the memo!"

Ofeez turned his attention to my partner and grinned a hideous grin—teeth like sharp, polished silver spurs. "Hello, Karen Dalton. Nice to meet you again. Or should I say nice to *eat* you again. Your soul, that is."

Ofeez kept spouting but I could barely make out his words over Karen's screams spilling from her ashen face twisted in fear.

Fu Chun, to his credit—and utter stupidity— had reclaimed his bowie knife. He launched himself on the Nikker's back and thrust his knife in deep. Ofeez howled like the king of the werewolves and stiffened. He reached back, plucked Fu from behind and hurled him into the lake.

I pushed Karen behind a large urn and jumped in front of Ofeez. This time, I wasn't worried about ordering her to stay put. Fear would freeze her in place.

I knew I could best defeat Ofeez if I shed my human body, but I didn't dare morph into my Pazu form with Sara present. We were friends but I wasn't sure that she would not try to capture me for the government. How deep did her allegiance lie? I couldn't risk finding out.

The Fleek charged at me. I braced myself for the impact.

"Stop!" Sara aimed a ginormous handgun—with a barrel big enough to hold a golf ball—at Ofeez.

BLAM!

Ofeez staggered. Looked at his chest in surprise. Sure enough, Sara had made a dent in him. But if he'd been human instead of Fleek, that bullet would have punched a golf-ball sized hole straight through him.

In a rage, Ofeez plucked the nearest tombstone from the ground and hurled it at the agent. The heavy spinning stone caught her unawares, striking her in the ribcage. Her gun dropped to the ground and she dropped too.

Sara moaned and Karen raced to her aid.

Turning my attention back to Ofeez, I saw him running rapidly into the lake, splashing up a storm. In a flash, he disappeared beneath the surface.

34

"He's getting away!" Karen cried. She leaned over Sara and helped her to her feet.

I jogged over to join them. "Everybody okay?"

"I'm fine," Karen said first.

"And I'll be fine, too," Sara groaned, clutching her ribs and wincing. "That fucking thing's fast. And strong. Got me good. Speaking of which, what was that thing?" She looked from me to Karen and back again. "It was almost like he knew you."

Rather than answer her question, I raised a more important and pressing concern. "Hear that?"

"What?" Sara asked, leaning against Karen for support.

"Sirens. Police sirens," I replied.

"The neighbors must have reported all the commotion," Karen said.

"Yeah." Sara frowned. "And the gunshots. Shit." She looked around the now deserted cemetery. "We can't stay here."

"Can you move?" I asked.

"I'm not sure I can run but I can sure as hell walk," Sara replied.

"Come on, then."

Karen and I supported Sara on opposite sides and the three of us hustled over to an unlit side street. The sounds of the police sirens grew louder and more insistent. I did not want them catching us, me most of all.

"Which way?" Karen asked, looking anxiously up and down the empty street. Cars sat parked in narrow drives and in the street. Lights glowed inside tiny houses.

A vehicle roared around the corner behind us, tires

squealing, headlights blaring, stereo thumping Megadeath's thrash metal masterpiece *Holy Wars... The Punishment Due*. How was it that I was familiar with the tune? Karen's a metal head—and I mean that in the nicest possible way.

Brakes slammed on and the SUV shuddered to a sudden stop beside us.

Beep! Beep!

"Amil!" Karen glanced in the window. "Amil!" She abruptly let go of Sara and grabbed onto me for support. "Ohmygod! Ed, look, it's Amil!"

"So I see," I replied, struggling to hold poor Sara upright. I feared she'd been hurt worse than she was letting on.

"Ed! Karen!" Amil waved. The radio cut off and he shouted, "Quick, hop in!"

I sniffed the air. "Right, let's get in. Karen, help me with Sara."

Blood oozed from her side and she slipped into unconsciousness. Karen and I lifted Sara into the backseat of the Toyota. Karen slipped in beside her. I decided to ride shotgun and claimed the front passenger seat.

Karen rested Sara's limp body against her own. The sounds of nearby sirens told us that the police had arrived at the cemetery. We'd missed them by mere seconds.

Karen leaned towards the front and squeezed the back of Amil's seat. "We are so happy to see you! Aren't we, Ed?" she said, breathlessly. "You're a life saver, a real life saver! You can't imagine what we've been going through!"

"Oh, I think he knows..." I said from the front passenger seat. "Right, Ofeez?" Lake Pontchartrain had washed the scent of his cologne off. All that remained was the stink that was Fleek.

...And the next thing we knew, time and space were bending and twisting in pale shades of blue, green and white. In an instant, we were in the catacombs again. The Fleek's personal museum of the macabre and monument to himself. The sprawling underground series of tunnels and chambers housing the dead he'd accumulated over his centuries on Earth.

Hands on the wheel and driving madly down a nondescript narrow tunnel lit only by the vehicles' headlights, Ofeez chuckled. "So good to have you both back. You see? No one escapes me once I claim them as mine." The Fleek eyed me with the eyes of a rabid prehistoric porcupine. "No one... And you've been generous enough to include a new soul for my collection," he added, hungrily eying Sara. "How very, very kind."

I leapt across the center console and wrapped my hands around the Fleek's neck. I was a Pazu now. No longer hiding behind my human costume. I was me, a full-blooded Pazu. A full-bodied Pazu. A full-powered Pazu.

A Pazu encountering my eternal enemy... This was a life or death battle. I squeezed Ofeez's neck tighter and tighter, felt bone and sinew crushing beneath my fingers.

The steering wheel jerked, the SUV bucked. The van crashed into a wall of solid rock The windscreen shattered in a million pieces. Dust and debris filled the air. I smelled gasoline. And I smelled Fleek. Could've kicked myself for not smelling him sooner. A Fleek is a Fleek is a Fleek. A Fleek may be able to mask his odious odor—hell, he'd tricked me more than once—but he couldn't hide the stink completely. Not forever.

Flames licked out from under the hood of the Toyota. Ofeez leapt from the burning vehicle. I tried to do the same on my side but my door was bent and jammed up against a rock wall with a small chamber carved into its face.

From within the stone chamber, Lola Davies and Ursula Broussard's hovering, translucent, impassioned faces looked out at me. "You know what to do, Ed," they said as one. Their floating faces shimmered and disappeared as their words died away.

And I did know what I had to do.

I spun around. "Karen, quick, throw me your purse!" She didn't move a muscle. Yet she appeared unhurt. Sara was lying comatose with her head on Karen's lap.

"Karen! Karen?" She seemed to be in a trance or something. I climbed into the backseat. No sign of Karen's purse anywhere. I shook her, not violently but enough to get her attention, if she wasn't dead and I was sure she wasn't. "Where the hell's your purse?"

"Ed?" She blinked at me, not quite seeing me.

"Good, you're awake. Quick, your purse!" I held out my hand. "Give it to me. Where is it?" Ofeez was getting away. I heard the sounds of his retreating steps. However, I knew we hadn't seen the last of him. He was up to something. He'd be back. And he'd be dangerous.

"M-My purse?"

"Yes, your purse!"

Karen looked wildly around the backseat, all the while blinking in confusion. "Oh!" She shifted and raised herself. "Here it is. I was sitting on it."

She handed me the purse.

I hoped I was right.

All I had was a hunch. I remembered Ursula's words, how she told me not to let it out of my sight. Maybe she'd had some second sight of her own.

35

I yanked open Karen's purse and quickly turned it over, spilling its contents all over the interior of the SUV. "Aha! My voodoo box!"

Everything necessary to perform an old-fashioned hex removal conveniently included in a neat little package. Ursula had told me to keep it close. Now I understood why.

Sara groaned and stirred. "Wh—"

"Quick, I need you to get Sara to the surface! As fast as you can!"

"What about you?"

"I'll be there as soon as I can. Trust me."

Karen jumped out the door and pulled Sara along. "Which way do we go?"

I shot a look in both directions and made a guess. "That way," I told her, pointing to the left. It was as good a guess as anything. The only other direction available to us at the moment was right and the ground sloped upward to the left. Upward, hopefully meant outward. Not to mention, Ofeez had darted down the right branch of the tunnel. I couldn't have them meeting up with him.

"It's dark," Karen complained. She wasn't wrong. The headlights had blinked out and only the fire spouting from the Toyota provided us with light. And the burning vehicle could blow at any moment, leaving us smeared against the rocks.

"Use your phone flashlight!"

"Right. Duh." She flicked on the light. "You gonna make it?" she asked Sara.

Sara's eyelids fluttered. "Whaa…?"

"Never mind. I've got you." Karen wrestled with Sara and managed to get her moving in the right direction, which was left.

I gathered up my voodoo box and ran in the opposite direction. I hadn't gone 50 feet when I heard the explosion. Bits of metal, plastic and fabric flew around me. The SUV had met its end.

I prayed that Sara and Karen had not.

I caught sight of a glow ahead, illuminating the 10-foot tall entrance leading to a low chamber. I slowed. I heard nothing except my breathing. I opened the voodoo box. Everything was there and every item was intact: the small milky-glass vial containing unhexing potion, a candle half as big as my little finger, one wooden match, a stick of lavender incense, and the miniature cloth gris-gris bag.

"Come to me, Pazu," Ofeez's voice rumbled from deep within the chamber.

So he knew I was there, that I was coming… For him. I quietly untied the gris-gris bag and peered inside. As I opened the bag, I felt a strange power fly out, as if I'd let a genie out of a proverbial bottle. The unseen power washed over me as I studied the bag's contents. This included sage, rosemary, and cedar among others I couldn't recognize. There were also two small crystals and an amethyst.

Then there was the glass vial in the box. I held it to my eyes. What was inside?

What the hell was I supposed to do with any of this?

And why hadn't the damn voodoo kit come with better instructions?

Time was ticking. The longer we stayed down here in Ofeez's crypt, the greater the odds we'd be trapped here… And that meant for Eternity. And I had other things to do than spend Eternity in this hell-hole. And I meant that quite literally.

It was time to wing it, play it by ear. I'd survived this long, this far, following that principle, surely I could last another day continuing the tradition.

Clutching the voodoo box in my left hand, I stepped into the trap.

Flames danced the Watusi on torches fastened to the walls with iron brackets. Another room of bones, skulls, ribs, femurs, tibias, ulnas, occiputs, tarsals and more—everything the hobbyist body builder needed to puzzle together a human skeleton. All the bones were yellowed with age. Some looked like they'd been gnawed on. Had that been the Fleek's doing? Or did the catacombs have a rat problem?

I stepped toward the center of the chamber.

Ofeez dropped from the ceiling onto my back. But this time, I'd been ready for him. I was familiar with his tricks. I twisted to my left and threw him off.

I reached into my voodoo kit, plucked the crystals and amethyst from within and fisted them in my hand. Before he could consider his next move, I launched myself at him.

Ofeez bellowed.

Which was exactly what I was hoping for. I shoved my hand down his throat and opened my fist. The two crystals and amethyst went down his throat, forcing him to swallow them. I withdrew my arm before he could even begin to think about biting it off at the elbow.

While he coughed and sputtered, I rubbed the herbs in his face. Ofeez went apoplectic. I'd never seen a Fleek so mad—and mad was pretty much the only way I'd ever seen one.

Ofeez's long leg lashed out, tripping me. I fell heavily to the floor, dropping the open voodoo kit. The remainder of its contents spilled out on the hard-packed earth. I scrambled to recover. Ofeez pounced on my back once more and I ate dirt—literally.

I spat and stretched my fingers, hoping to reach the glass vial, although I had no idea what it contained or what power, if any, it might bring forth.

Ofeez pressed his knee into my spine. If I'd been human, I'd have been dead already—my spine fragmented like a turkey bone in a game of make-a-wish. But I wasn't human, remember? Not that I wasn't a bit inconvenienced at the moment…

I felt his arm wrap around my neck.

"Let's put an end to this, Pazu." Ofeez tightened his grip.

My neck groaned. Using all my remaining strength, I pushed myself up onto my hands and knees, all the while fighting the strain of his knee on my spine and his arm doing its best to snap my neck like a gorilla would snap a twig.

My eyes strained. I sensed myself dimming. The room appeared to be rotating… How much longer could I last?

Have I mentioned I fucking hate Fleeks?

36

Then I had an idea. And it was a brilliant idea, if I do say so myself.

Brilliant idea: Why struggle?

Why keep trying to push against Ofeez? Why fight him? That's what he was expecting. Hell, he was counting on it.

So, I let go.

Stopped pushing against the ground with my hands and knees.

Stopped trying to keep myself alive.

And I did...

My face and chest took the brunt of the impact as I hit the ground hard. But so did Ofeez. Because he hadn't been expecting me to act as ambivalent to my death as I had. In his confusion, I managed to scramble out and away from him.

I grabbed the glass vial filled with who-knew-what magic inside and lunged at the fallen Fleek. I forced my hand inside Ofeez's gaping mouth—hell, it had worked one time, why not a second?

Hand halfway down his gullet, I squeezed the vial in my fingers. I felt the glass break and an oddly hot liquid spill out. I quickly withdrew my hand and stepped back out of Ofeez's reach.

Ofeez fell to his knees and screeched. Fire and black smoke flew from his mouth. He clawed wildly at his face. He locked his eyes on me. A finger twitched.

Then, POOF! Ofeez disappeared in a cloud of foul black smoke.

I gave myself a second to breathe, then ran from the

chamber. I raced in the direction that I'd ordered Karen and Sara to go. As I popped my head up from the wooden hatch and climbed out, I reverted back to my human form and felt relief. I don't love human flesh but I've been wearing it so long it's become a proverbial second skin.

Simultaneously, the wooden hatch in the ground dissolved, morphed into a steel manhole cover. The interior of the rustic ancient Italian farmhouse became a nondescript New Orleans residential street. Stars gazed down at me, unconcerned and uncaring.

Karen seated at the curb, with a semiconscious Sara beside her, shot to her feet. "Ed!"

She rushed to my side and we hugged.

"You made it!" Karen kissed me fiercely.

"Yeah, of course. Piece of cake."

"And the Nikker?"

"Dead."

"Thank god." She let out a heartfelt sigh of relief. "You're sure? I mean, you've told me it was dead before and it wasn't."

"The Fleek, the Nikker, call it what you will, is dead."

Karen wasn't giving up. "You promise?"

"I swear," I said, taking her hand. Technically, that was a lie. But technically, I do fucking swear a lot. See what I mean?

What can I say in my defense? I'd learned my lesson after killing the Fleek the first time. As much as I wanted to believe, I didn't believe, not 100 percent believe, Ofeez was dead—because Fleek are as hard to exterminate as cockroaches—but I didn't think we'd be seeing him for a long, long time.

"Is she okay?" I turned to look at Sara.

"Yeah, she's coming around. She doesn't seem to remember much of what happened."

"That's for the best," I replied. We joined Sara. "Can you walk?"

"Yeah, yeah, I think so." Sara winced as she explored her ribs with her fingers. "I might need a trip to the ER, though. What happened? That thing... That thing that came out of the water..." Sara looked down the street in the direction of the cemetery.

"Probably a hoax," I said. "Hooligans in cheap costumes."

"But it hit me...threw a tombstone at me like it was nothing but a plastic flying saucer."

"Did it?" I said, boldly lying—hey, I was on a streak. "Or did you bang into that tombstone?"

"Well...I...Karen?" Sara looked to my partner for clarification.

Karen threw up her hands. "I dunno. Everything happened so fast."

"We need to get you looked at but would you mind if we stop at ARC's office on Derbigny Street first? Think you can make it?"

"I'll make it," Sara promised. "But I'd like to go back to the cemetery first, assuming the cops are gone. I can't find my weapon. Must've dropped it back there."

"Good idea," I quickly agreed. I was hoping to discover what had become of Fu Chun. Had he drowned? Become fish food? Rather, gator chow?

We slow-marched in the direction of the house on Derbigny. Along the way, we stopped at the cemetery, as agreed. The grounds stood empty. Except for its eternal residents, that is. No cops, no wounded or dead ARC members.

Sara managed to find her gun in some bushes and slid it inside her waistband. "Thank god. The Agency would've had a shit fit if the local police had found this with my prints on it."

I walked to the edge of Lake Pontchartrain and peered outward. Whatever secrets the lake held, it kept beneath its flat dark surface.

"What do you think happened to Fu?" Karen asked me. "Do you think he's dead?"

"I don't see any fresh corpses floating around. So let's hope not because I wouldn't want to be the one to break the news to Mister Ha or Anna Ping."

"Yeah..." Karen clasped her hands behind her back and

stared silently at the water.

"Let's go to the house to see if he left anything behind," I said.

Before long, we arrived at the little residential house serving as ARC HQ. The lights were extinguished. No vehicles remained outside and no sign of life appeared to exist inside.

"ARC's members seemed to have had enough for one night," Sara said.

"Good riddance," I replied.

The front door was locked but a little gentle persuasion from me and it opened itself up. Darkness said hello.

"Hello?" I said back. "Anybody here?"

Karen and Sara hovered over my shoulders. Sara pulled her weapon. I hoped she didn't have to use it. I wasn't sure she even had the strength to use it.

I focused all my senses and felt a presence within the house. "There's someone," I whispered to the others.

"Someone or some *thing*?" Karen whispered in my ear.

"Stay here. I'll find out."

"No way," Karen hissed. "Where you go, I go."

"Ditto," vowed Sara.

"Fine." I tiptoed through the living room, looking behind the furniture. No one. No one in the kitchen either. I checked the small bathroom, even looked behind the shower curtain. No one hiding there either, just a lot of disgusting black mold clinging to cracked yellow subway tiles.

"There are two bedrooms on the other side," Sara whispered.

We moved towards them.

Bedroom one faced the front. The room was approximately a 10 ft by 10 ft square with a tiny built-in closet. I slowly slid the closet door along its track. Inside, I discovered a broken window screen leaning against the back wall. Joining it were a couple of fossilized cockroaches and a dead black spider whose legs curled in around themselves.

The floor creaked below our feet as we tiptoed across the

short hall to the final bedroom. Plywood covered the window, held on with rusty nails in the corners. Karen shined her phone's flashlight across the bedroom floor, covered in a stained and worn-out carpet smelling of dog piss.

"Empty," Karen mouthed.

I pointed to the closet, the twin of the one in the room next door. In two steps, I crossed the carpet in silence and slowly began to inch open the closet door. As I did so, I heard the sounds of whimpering and shuffling inside.

Sara heard it, too. She pushed Karen aside and aimed her weapon at the growing gap in the closet. Her gun hand was shaking. Was it fear of the unknown—after what she'd seen and been through out at Lake Pontchartrain—or the result of the physical abuse she'd suffered there?

Maybe it was a little of both. Maybe it was a lot of both.

I slammed the door into the opposite wall.

"Don't kill me! Don't kill me!"

Fu Chun sat on the floor, knees squeezed tightly to his chest, hands flailing. "Please! Please!"

"Relax," I told the cowering youth, as calmly as I could.

"Fu Chun!" Karen cried.

Sara lowered her weapon. "Geezus."

Fu dropped his hands. "Sara? And you two!" He squirmed, his back pressed to the rear wall of the closet.

"Yes, you can come out now. Nobody is going to harm you. Everything's okay." I bent down to his level. "Karen, would you hand me your phone, please?"

"Huh?"

"Your phone."

"Sure, but why?" She handed it over.

I took her phone and snapped a photograph of Fu Chun's scared and confused mug. Then I handed Karen back her phone. "Send that pic to Mister Ha. Let him know we've completed our assignment."

Karen smiled and obliged me.

"Assignment?" Fu appeared baffled. "What's going on?"

His clothes were damp and he smelled a bit...fishy. I guess he'd managed to survive being thrown in the lake and further managed to swim to shore. As for the gators, maybe they'd been snoozing and had missed a golden opportunity for a late-night snack.

Oh, well, their loss was Fu Chun's gain.

"Why don't you come out now?" I suggested. "And I'll explain everything." Well, not *everything*, but everything he needed to know.

Fu frowned and looked into the bedroom. "What about the alien?"

Poor Fu Chun. Terry the Terror was gone—replaced by a scared little boy.

"We're not aliens. Don't worry, nobody's going to hurt you," Karen assured him.

"Besides, aliens are not real. They're nothing but a figment of your overactive imagination," I explained.

"But-But I saw it. More than once," Fu said, taking my hand and allowing me to help him to his feet.

"Kids see Santa Claus and the Easter Bunny," I told him. "It doesn't make them real." Now, the Tooth Fairy, that's another story entirely. I've heard of a species in the Cartwheel Galaxy who are avid tooth collectors. Some of those collectors shell out big bucks for an unusual bicuspid.

"But this is different. Plenty of people have seen aliens— and I'm not talking about children. These are adults! What about all those sightings?" Fu Chun persisted.

"Nothing but the result of mass hallucinations... And maybe beer."

Karen's phone pinged. "It's a text from Mister Ha. He'd like you," she said, talking to Fu Chun, "to give him a call in the morning."

Fu sighed and pressed his face into his hands. "Shit."

"After you call your aunt to let her know you are well, and to apologize for causing her such distress," Karen added.

Fu groaned. "She's gonna kill me."

"Better her than O—" I stopped myself.

"Better than what?" Fu asked.

"Better do like Karen says and call your aunt and let her know you're alright."

"Yeah, and apologize for causing the poor woman to worry so much, dummy!" Karen sucker punched Fu in the stomach.

I could've warned him that was about to happen but he was young, he could take it.

37

Fu told us he'd left his car around the corner, so we employed it to drop off Sara at the nearest 24-hour emergency care center. Karen drove. Sara's bleeding had stopped but she was sure she'd broken a rib or three and knew she'd need tending to.

"Think she'll be okay?" Karen asked as Sara limped away from the car and towards the well-lit ER entrance.

"I'm positive." That wasn't a lie. I wasn't worried about Sara Chronis. She was one tough cookie. Not as tough as one of Karen's homemade peanut butter cookies, but plenty tough enough. Besides, she told us a fellow agent would be meeting her at the ER. We promised to meet up again later.

We took Fu Chun with us to our hotel room because he had nowhere else to go. He'd sleep on the sofa.

He reeked of lake and Fleek. Karen ordered him to shower. She'd gone all Mother Hen. I loaned him some pajamas and some bourbon that I knew I'd never get back again. But what the hell, Mr. Ha's good credit would reimburse me for both.

Half-sloshed and half-asleep, we, and/or his near death experience, had convinced Fu to stop alien hunting. He'd explained that he'd always been fascinated by the idea that aliens might be visiting Earth. He'd wanted to prove himself by capturing or slaying one.

Who says kids today have no ambition?

Fu explained that he'd met Amil, who we now all knew was the Nikker who was the Fleek who was Ofeez—well, I knew that, Karen understood a little and Fu, hopefully, next to nothing. Fu had met Amil the first day he landed at the airport in New Orleans to attend school. Amil had offered him a lift to his dorm.

Gratis.

Unfortunately, there'd been nothing gratis about the Fleek's offer of a free ride. Which just proves the old saw: there's no such thing as a free lunch… Unless you're a Fleek looking for one.

I could also add: Beware of Fleeks bearing gifts.

And, of course, that famous old Pazu adage: The only good Fleek is a dead Fleek.

Fu also told us that he was certain that Lola had not written the suicide note. He claimed it was nothing but a forgery, a good one, but a forgery nonetheless, written by Amil the Fleek. He also vehemently denied killing her or anybody else. There'd been no lovers' quarrel. He and Lola hadn't even been lovers, that was just some crazy idea Alexandra had gotten into her head. He explained that the truth was that he'd been working with Lola to try to destroy the alien he thought he was hot on the trail of.

He'd found Lola Davies dead in the kitchen only minutes before Karen and I walked in on him. Fearing for his life and not knowing who we were or what our intentions might be, he'd hidden and then fled at his first opportunity.

Fu was convinced now that Amil must've killed both Lola and Ursula. He couldn't make out quite why, and I wasn't about to enlighten him. Fu came to see that Amil preyed on college kids he picked up, just as he had himself and his roommate, Daniel Hernandez. Most of the missing or brainwashed victims had no local families to miss them and ask the awkward questions.

As the situation reached its boiling point after the second murder, and next learning that Daniel had been shot too, Fu had raced to Alexandra's apartment and warned her that she might be in danger because of her association with him. She'd packed quickly and retreated to her parents' house in South Carolina.

Fu yawned and his head drooped to his chest. I slid his feet up on the sofa. Karen pulled the spare blanket up to his laryngeal prominence—that's Adam's apple for those who prefer to identify their body parts using fruits and vegetables as references.

I laid my palm on his hot forehead and said, "Free your head."

Karen turned out the lights and I fell into a dreamy sleep filled with images of Zyxltl—a planet that, although it may have lacked vowels in its name, held a special place in my heart. If you've ever been stranded on another planet than your own, you'll understand how I was feeling.

The next morning, well rested and our future assured—at least in the near term—Fu faced his aunt and Mr. Ha via telephone. He'd also decided that a change of scenery was in order and that he would be joining us on our journey westward. He wanted no more of New Orleans and looked forward to returning to LA and resuming his studies locally.

I dressed quickly and pulled open the nightstand drawer. I didn't find what I was looking for. "Hey, my money's gone!"

"Oh? You mean that money you took from under Daniel's mattress?" Karen looked at me all innocent like.

"I told you, that was repayment for the harm and emotional distress he caused you." I held out my hand, palm up. "Where is it?"

"I'm glad you feel that way," Karen said.

"Huh?"

"About harm and emotional distress. I feel the same way."

"Good. Glad to hear it."

"Great. That's why I gave the money to Sergeant Lecourt with instructions to give it to the families of Lola and Ursula."

Fu Chun's laugh was throttled by my evil glare his way.

"Carry the bags!" I ordered him and we headed for the elevator.

Karen tipped the doormen for the last time as our scheduled ride appeared. Fu and the driver tossed our bags in the back, and in we climbed and off we went.

"Hey, this doesn't look right," Karen said, sandwiched between me and Fu in the back seat of the moving taxi. We'd hired a cab. None of us was in the mood for a rideshare. "The airport's the other way."

"I know. I talked Mister Ha into letting us ride the Amtrak home. Traded in the plane tickets."

"The train? Why on earth did you do that?" Karen groused.

"You know how much I hate flying. Besides, I've always wanted to see the Alamo. And it's on the way." Well, sorta, kinda, *ish*...

Should I mention the Alamo has its share of ghosts?

"The car rental place?"

"Yes," I said. It was so much easier than explaining.

"That's a joke, Ed. I may not be the only poet in this outfit, but you are not the only historian." Karen gently punched me on the chin.

I smiled.

"You two always like this?" Fu asked, his forehead crinkling like a hot, oily french fry.

"Yes," I said.

"Weird," he commented.

"You're young. You have a lot to learn about being *human*," I squeezed my partner's hand.

Karen snorted.

OTHER BOOKS BY THIS AUTHOR

Welcome To My World - Ed Turner, P.I. Novel #1
Hold That Ghost - Ed Turner, P.I. Novel #2

Five Minutes - Todd Jones Comic Thriller #1
Five More Minutes - Todd Jones Comic Thriller #2
Nailed It - Todd Jones Comic Thriller #3

After The Fall

Engine Of My Dreams

It's A Young, Young World

To The Stars Forever

George And The Angels

Murder In St. Barts - A Gendarme Trenet Novel #1
Death Of A Cheat - A Gendarme Trenet Novel #2